A Rogue to Remember

The Hellion Club, Book One

by Chasity Bowlin

DRAGONBLADE
PUBLISHING, INC.

Additional Dragonblade books by Author, Chasity Bowlin

The Hellion Club Series
A Rogue to Remember
Barefoot in Hyde Park
What Happens in Piccadilly
Sleepless in Southhampton
When an Earl Loves a Governess
The Duke's Magnificent Obsession
The Governess Diaries

The Lost Lords Series
The Lost Lord of Castle Black
The Vanishing of Lord Vale
The Missing Marquess of Althorn
The Resurrection of Lady Ramsleigh
The Mystery of Miss Mason
The Awakening of Lord Ambrose
A Midnight Clear (A Novella)

*** Please visit Dragonblade's website for a full list of books and authors. Sign up for Dragonblade's blog for sneak peeks, interviews, and more: ***
www.dragonbladepublishing.com

Dedication

I want to dedicate this book to my wonderful husband.

Jonathan, you never fail to tell me, daily, that you love me, that you're proud of me, that I'm beautiful and then you go one better, and show me those things, as well. Thank you for being better than any hero I could create.

Prologue

THE STUDY WAS in chaos. His father had been buried that morning, the will read that afternoon, and as night was about to fall, he was searching every scrap of paper for some hint or clue as to where he might find Alice. Head in hand, Devil sat on the floor that was littered with correspondence, bills of sale, and ledgers. Cravat missing, waistcoat long since discarded, and his shirt half-untucked from his breeches from his recent exertions, Devil reached for a decanter of brandy from the nearby table and drank directly from it.

It was the finest brandy he'd ever sipped and had likely cost his father a fortune. But then, things and luxuries had always been more important to the man than his own children had. Temper swept through him, fueled by decades of neglect and hurt. Devil threw the decanter with all his might, and it smashed against the marble that surrounded the hearth. As the shards glittered and glistened, something caught his eye. A scrap of a letter was buried in the ash, having fallen beyond the reach of the blaze.

Rising quickly, he used the poker to retrieve it. It was a letter written in Alice's hand, but the contents of it were a mystery to him. All that remained was perhaps the most important part of all—her direction. The address of a boarding house in Spitalfields was far beneath his sister, and yet that is where their father's coldness had relegated her to.

Devil didn't bother with his cravat or frock coat. He simply grabbed his discarded redingote and fled the house as if the hounds of hell were at his heels. Hailing a hackney, he tossed the driver a coin when they reached that ignoble address.

It was worse than he'd feared. The building was old, listing terribly to one side. There was no glass in the windows, only shutters that let in more air than they'd ever block out. Banging on the door, a woman who could only be a prostitute opened it.

"What do you want?"

"I'm looking for Alice," Devil said.

The woman cackled. "If they told you she'd give your money's worth, Gov, they lied. Now, if it's a nice ride you be looking for, old Meg here will do you right."

"Alice is my sister. I need to find her. If you show me to her room, I will give you whatever coin you require," he said.

The woman's cackling stopped. "Her brother, are you? Well, you might be in time... but like as not, she won't even know you're here. Come on, then."

Devil followed the woman up the stairs, uncertain of what her strange proclamation meant. But the moment the door to that hovel of a room opened, he knew. The smell of sickness assailed him, something he was all too familiar with following his years in India. Entering the chamber, he found his sister lying on a thin mattress on the floor. He could hear a rat chewing on something in the corner. Her face was pale, her hair slicked to her body with sweat, and her eyes stared sightlessly up at the ceiling. A small girl sat beside her, the fabric of Alice's thin nightrail clutched in her tiny fists.

"Alice... Alice, it's Devil. I've come to bring you home."

A soft groan escaped the cracked lips of the gaunt figure of a woman that had once been lauded as a great beauty. "Too late," she croaked. "Save her. Save my baby."

Devil looked to the small girl clinging to her. It was impossible to miss that she was Alice's child. The dark curls, the wide blue eyes—she was almost a replica of Alice as a child. "I'll take care of you both."

Alice shook her head. "It hurts, Devil. To breathe. To move. I'm done in by it all."

"I'll get you a doctor," he insisted.

"There's no time," she said. "Promise me you'll care for Marina."

"I promise. I will take care of her... I will take care of you, Alice, if only you'll let me," he said, and his voice broke as tears welled in his eyes.

His sister reached out, her pale hand falling on his, holding him there with a strength that surprised them both. Her breath rasped from her lungs, and she gave one sorrowful shake of her head. Then her eyes drifted closed.

"Alice?" Her name escaped his lips on a panicked cry. But there was no response. He'd entered that room in time for her to breathe her last.

The little girl laid down, pressed her face to the pillow beside her mother, and wept with a kind of agony that was almost animalistic. She might not understand death, she might not understand the permanency of it, but she understood that her mother was gone.

Devil reached for her, lifting her to him. She screamed and kicked, fighting him with a fierceness that belied her slightness. He simply pulled her closer. And held her to him as tightly as he could. "I'll take care of her. I'll take care of you," he vowed. "Whatever the cost. I promise."

Chapter One

WILHELMINA MARKS WAS seated in the drawing room of a posh townhouse on Park Lane that faced the lush greenery of Hyde Park. The clock on the mantel ticked, marking the hour as half-past one. Late. Very late, she decided. It was not a good sign.

Her gaze traveled about the room as she waited. She had studied enough art during her rather remarkable education at the Darrow School for Girls to know that she was in the presence of very fine pieces, indeed. One appeared to be an actual Titian. If it wasn't, it was certainly a very good copy. She might well have been wasting her time, but at least she had impressive things to look at. Cutting her gaze to the side, she attempted to study it surreptitiously. So intent upon her task was she that when the door opened and her prospective employer walked in, she didn't even notice.

"It's the genuine article. Or so I was told. If not, well... it wasn't my mistake to purchase it. It was my great grandfather's and we don't seem to be missing the coin overmuch."

He wasn't very punctual but the Devil Lord was in possession of rather catlike grace, Wilhelmina thought as she rose to her feet. She allowed her eyes to drift from the Titian to the man who had just entered the room. Not for the first time, she thought she might have made a terrible mistake in coming there.

His dark hair was mussed. In fact, all of him was mussed. Yet he still rather took her breath away. Her gaze was drawn to the dusky hue of his skin, sun-bronzed despite the fashion of the day for a paler complexion. It was a testament, she supposed, to his longstanding exile to more exotic locales. His clothing, despite his untidy appearance, was excellently tailored and fit his frame with precision. Rather too much precision, given the manner in which it highlighted the breadth of his shoulders and the wide expanse of his chest as it tapered down to a lean waist and hips. His muscular thighs, no doubt a direct benefit of his acclaimed equestrian skills, strained the fabric of his scandalously well-fitting breeches.

Finding her voice after realizing she had been silent for too long, Willa said, "Forgive me, my lord. I was admiring the artwork rather intently and didn't hear you come in. It's a lovely piece."

He looked at it for a moment, then looked back at her, his amusement apparent. "I've never given it notice before. I will endeavor to do better."

His tone was flirtatious. Far too flirtatious for an employer and a prospective governess. Between that, his appearance, and his tardiness, it was not going well at all. First impressions were remarkably important and he seemed bent on confirming every dark thing whispered about him.

"Tell me, Miss Marks," he continued, "are you prepared to work in a scandalous house?"

Willa didn't bother to pretend she didn't know what he meant. Douglas Ashton, Lord Deveril, more commonly known as Devil by the scandal sheets, was a topic of intense conversation and even greater speculation by such publications. It seemed that no matter what he did, be it bad, good, or indifferent, people (and society matrons in particular) were rabid to discuss it at length.

"Scandal is of little concern to me, my lord," she said. Her own father was rather notorious himself, after all, but she felt no need to bring that up just yet, if ever. He certainly wouldn't, she thought. Her father had never made any overture to acknowledge her presence in any way. Even her enrollment at the Darrow School had been initiated by Effie and not by him. He'd simply permitted it so he could cease discussing her. Pushing distressing thoughts of her father aside, she said, "I care not at all for the opinions of others, only my own. I do, however, care for morality."

His dark eyebrows lifted imperiously and a cool smirk played about his handsome lips. If there was ever a reason not to take the position offered, that was it. He was too handsome and too certain of his own handsomeness for her peace of mind.

"That's a bold statement, Miss Marks. And what is your opinion of me? Am I the devil they say I am... or perhaps I'm something even worse?" His tone was taunting, and yet there was a note in it that seemed to suggest her opinion mattered in some way.

Willa kept her tone neutral and her expression even. It was part of her training, after all, to remain unflappable in the face of even that sort of outrageousness. "You are a man, my lord. Not a devil. Regardless of whatever moniker the gossipmongers have saddled you with. But I will tell you that I have misgivings about this position. I had them before I came here and they exist still... in ever increasing increments."

He stepped deeper into the room, his broad shoulders seeming to fill up the space. "I see, Miss Marks. Do go on. I find myself utterly fascinated. I would even hazard to say I am quite enthralled."

If he thought she would not give her honest opinion, despite the nature of their acquaintance, he was sadly mistaken. Willa was nothing if not honest. "Your reputation is not based entirely upon unfounded gossip, my lord. You are a womanizer, renowned not only for the extent of your debauchery but the frequency and intensity with which it is pursued. And your drinking. And your gaming. And your fighting and dueling and racing horses and phaetons up and down busy pedestrian-laden thoroughfares... all of these things have been taken to with, *I would even hazard to say*, unprecedented enthusiasm." The last was uttered in a mocking tone that was laden with reproach.

His once-amused expression had shuttered, becoming unreadable. "You are unexpectedly candid, Miss Marks... especially for one seeking employment."

He was quite mistaken on that score. She was not there to be interviewed by him for employment but to interview him to see if she would consent to work for him. She was a graduate of the Darrow School, after all. "I came here today hoping to see something from you that would make me question the veracity of all that I have heard. But I did not. I waited here for twenty-five minutes past our appointed time. And when you arrived..." She held out her hand, gesturing from his head to his feet, as if words were not even necessary.

"Oh, no, Miss Marks. Do not stop now. Your honesty is... well, refreshing isn't the word precisely. But it's at least unique, and I find myself anything but bored in your presence."

Her own eyebrows shot skyward at his scathing tone, so she did continue. "Fine. Your breeches are rumpled, your boots are muddy. Your waistcoat is the same one I saw you in yesterday when I walked past this house to determine exactly which address I was looking for so as not to be late. In short, you are ill-prepared to receive me, and that speaks volumes to your character."

"There are perfectly reasonable explanations for all of that, Miss Marks," he said in a droll tone. "Surely you would not be so quick to judge?"

Wilhelmina smiled coolly, but as she spoke, there was a definite bite to her tone. "There is also rouge on your hastily-tied cravat and I can smell the brandy—and rather cloying perfume—from here. Some things are quite self-explanatory, my lord. I thank you for the offer of employment, but I must respectfully decline. Good day, my lord."

DEVIL BLINKED AT the woman before him in confusion. Had she actually turned him down? No, she hadn't. Because he hadn't offered her the bloody position yet! Who the hell did she think she was?

"That's a bit premature, Miss Marks. You do not yet know if I want to hire you," he sneered.

She laughed then, the musical and tinkling sound grating on his nerves as it intensified his brandy-fueled headache. When she stopped, her lips still quivered with mirth and there was a light, far too wicked for a governess, that gleamed in her pretty green eyes. "Of course you want to hire me, Lord Deveril. I am a graduate of the Darrow School. There are no better governesses in all of England. Not only that, but we are renowned for taking on difficult cases, children who might otherwise be considered untrainable. You honestly thought that you were interviewing me, instead of the other way around? Oh, dear. You have been out of England for some time!"

Devil watched as she gathered her small reticule and the simple shawl she had worn over her rather drab gown. She was going to walk out and leave him with exactly what he'd started with—a terrified toddler who cried and wailed if any man dared enter the room she was in and who shrieked and hurled things at the maids. Only cook, with her plump cheeks, silver curls and lemon cakes could get near the child.

Despite his reputation, he hadn't been carousing and gaming as most would think. He'd been devoting himself for the last several weeks to finding the man responsible for his sister's death, the man who'd left her sick and alone in that hovel with no one to care for their child and not even a single coin to buy bread. It had, by necessity, taken him to some dissolute places. But it appeared Miss Marks had already made up her mind about that and about him.

"My niece is a particularly challenging case, Miss Marks. I would think before you leave so hastily that you would at least want to meet the child who might have been your charge," he called out in challenge.

She turned toward him then. "Your *niece*, Lord Deveril, is three years old, I believe. How challenging can she be?"

She was intrigued, he realized. There was a light in her eyes that hadn't been there before and a tension radiating from her that told the truth, regardless of what she said. The idea of Marina being a challenge piqued her curiosity. "Very, it would seem. But if you feel you aren't up to it—"

"I am more than up to the challenge, Lord Deveril," she said sharply. "Make no mistake when I tell you that my reasons for not taking the position have nothing whatsoever to do with my capabilities or the particular challenges of your young charge."

"Well, then there's no harm in meeting her, is there?" Devil reached for the bell pull and a footman entered immediately. "Have cook bring Marina down here."

"Yes, my lord," the footman said, bowed hastily and fled.

Miss Marks was gaping at him in a most fishlike and rather unattractive manner. "Your cook is watching the child?"

Taking umbrage at her tone, he replied, "My cook is the only one Marina is not utterly terrified of, Miss Marks. Are you so judgmental with all your charges?"

At that rather provoking query, her lips snapped shut and while her expression wasn't necessarily what could be called glaring, it was withering. Regardless, she remained there, shawl and reticule in hand, dutifully waiting to meet the child.

The awkward and utterly miserable silence stretched between them as she strolled past him to once more study a painting that he was growing to despise more by the minute. After a moment, as she stared at the Titian and he stared at her, there was a soft knock upon the door.

"Forgive me, your lordship," came the high-pitched, jovial voice of his plump cook who'd been spoiling him since boyhood. "I've brought the wee one in to meet her new governess!"

"Come in, Mrs. Farrelly," he said. "Though Miss Marks' appointment as governess is hardly a forgone conclusion just yet."

The cook stepped deeper inside the sitting room, Marina on her hip, the girl's dark hair cascading over her shoulders in wild curls with her face tucked firmly into the older woman's ample bosom. At three years of age, Marina had never spoken a word to Devil other than to shriek if he attempted to touch her. Mrs. Farrelly insisted the child could speak but did so very infrequently.

"Marina, this is Miss Marks," he said, as if the child didn't wish him to the devil. "She may be your new governess... if she thinks she's up to the task." He spared a glance at Miss Marks and saw that, for the moment at least, his needling was entirely worthless. Her attention was focused solely on Marina, and the little girl was staring back at her from the haven of Mrs. Farrelly's embrace. They were rather like two tigers sizing one another up.

"Hello, Marina," Miss Marks said.

Marina, in typical fashion, let out an ear-shattering shriek that almost laid him low. Much to his horror, as he clutched his head and prayed for death to take him swiftly, Miss Marks joined in. For as long as Marina shrieked, Miss Marks shrieked with her. After several long moments of torment, Marina abruptly stopped. She stared at Miss Marks, not with the terror she usually reserved for adults, but with curiosity and a little bit of confusion.

"I can scream, too," Miss Marks said to the child, her voice slightly roughened from her vocal exertions. "But it's terribly loud, and it only makes my throat hurt when it is done. I'd much prefer to just say what I want. What do you want, Marina?"

"Mama," the little girl said and then collapsed against Mrs. Farrelly's bosom once more. She wailed again, but it wasn't the terrible screaming. It was so much worse. She sobbed as if her heart was broken. And it must have been. Her mother was gone, and death was an impossible concept to explain to a child so young.

"There you have it, Lord Deveril. She is not impossible at all. She is grieving. Now, if you'll excuse me, I am set to meet friends for tea. Have a good day," Miss Marks said. "Goodbye, Marina."

And then the termagant was gone.

Chapter Two

WILLA WALKED SWIFTLY, ignoring the slight sting of tears, as she made her way back to the Darrow School. The child was hurting and not a single person in that house knew how to help her. But for the sake of her own reputation, her own sanity, and her own virtue, she could not. Lord Deveril was not a man to be trusted, and willingly going into his house, to live under his roof, even if it was for the sake of that child, would only see her ruined. She had told him she cared nothing for the opinions of others, and while that was certainly true to a degree, she did care about her reputation and her employability. She had to, after all. And heaven knew, he was a threat to both!

Even filthy, rumpled, possibly still drunk and utterly full of himself, the man was more handsome than Lucifer himself. It wasn't just his family's title that earned him the nickname Devil. He could easily have been a fallen angel with his thick, coal black hair and sinfully long eyelashes. She tried to recall what she knew of the family. There was some scandal about the grandfather marrying a gypsy girl. Her contribution to the current generation could clearly be seen in their exotic beauty.

Marina was the image of her uncle if, in fact, he was her uncle. Rumors abounded that she was one of the many bastard children society gossip insisted he had fathered. Though Willa supposed that if the child was actually the Devil Lord's, he'd just have said so. He was infamous for always telling the truth, no matter how damning it might be.

"Stop thinking about it. Not about him. Not about her. You can't save every child, and you certainly can't save one living under the roof of a notorious rogue who would seduce you on a whim!" The words were muttered low and under her breath, but apparently talking to one's self outside Hyde Park was still somewhat of a faux pas, as evidenced by the askance stares of other pedestrians.

Taking a deep breath to calm herself, Willa elected to put Lord Deveril and his beautiful but very troubled young niece from her mind. She would return to the Darrow School, have tea with Effie, and write a letter to Lillian in the wilds of Scotland and not give it another thought.

Marching through the street, her stride purposeful and perhaps a bit too enthusiastic for a proper lady, she reached the Darrow School at Cavendish Place in record time. It was a posh address for an all girls' school, and certainly one that catered to girls such as herself. *Bastards.*

It was an ugly word, but one she'd heard often enough growing up. When she'd been at the Millstead Abbey School, she'd certainly had it hurled at her by other pupils, teachers, and the headmistress. Marina's face came to mind again. She'd likely hear it, too, Willa thought bitterly. Children could be ever so cruel and spiteful. For a little girl that had already lost so much, it seemed horribly unfair that she'd have to be teased and tormented for it. That was assuming, of course, that the child was ever well enough to be around other children at a school or to have friends. If her behavior continued to consist of only shrieking at others, there might well come a time when she'd be locked away in an asylum. It was a terrible, gut wrenching thought.

You cannot save them all. It had been only a week earlier when she'd uttered those same words to Effie after word reached them that a former student, cast off by her lover, had taken her own life.

Willa didn't knock. The school was her home, after all. Instead, she opened the heavy door herself and breezed in past the few maids who were present. There was no butler. There were also no footmen. It was a household of women only, and Effie was quite strict about it. Men were permitted to enter the premises if they were there to enroll their daughters or other wards. Then and only then could they step inside the hallowed halls.

Passing the drawing room where several young girls were taking tea and practicing their manners, Willa made her way to the small study that Effie used to manage her little empire. Knocking softly, she waited for her former headmistress and dearest friend to bid her enter.

"You look positively terrible," Effie said the very moment Willa stepped inside.

"I feel terrible. I refused the appointment." *Though technically it had never been offered.* As much as she'd been immediately off put by Lord Deveril, he'd been equally off put by her. That much had been glaringly apparent in their verbal sparring.

"You knew that you would before ever going there, my dear. His reputation is quite terrible," Effie replied easily. "Why is it distressing you so?"

"Because I think the child needs me. She's terrorized by whatever has happened in her life to this point, Effie. She's afraid of everyone in the house save for an elderly cook whom she clings to," Willa admitted. Saying it out loud, admitting the truth that had filled her with guilt from the moment she walked out of his exquisitely appointed home, was both freeing and damning.

Effie's expression was one of empathy as she said, "You cannot save them all. Those were words of wisdom, Wilhelmina. That is the sort of wisdom you should adhere to rather than simply mete out."

Willa seated herself in one of the chairs that faced the delicate writing desk. "I'm aware of that. But she's such a young child. If I were to reconsider and take the appointment, I could help provide considerable change in her behavior in a very short amount of time. Then perhaps, we could transition to a different governess. One of the ladies who taught here and isn't quite ready to be pensioned off but no longer wishes to shepherd a dozen girls at once, perhaps?" *And one who would be old enough to have no fear of what Lord Deveril might do to either her reputation or her honor.*

Effie rose and closed the door, turning the key in the lock. "It's a bit early in the day for this but, under the circumstances, I think that hardly matters." She returned to the desk and from the adjacent secretary retrieved a bottle of sherry and two glasses. She filled each liberally, far more so than was appropriate, and passed one to Willa.

"I just took Lord Deveril to task for being a drunkard. Perhaps I am no better," Willa said as she sipped the liquid.

"You do not make a habit of this, and one generous sherry hardly makes you a drunkard. I understand what it feels like to want to save a child. But we have a responsibility to choose wisely, Wilhelmina, to choose to save the right ones so that we might save as many as possible. If you go into his home, knowing who and what he is, it could destroy you. All of us, after all, know the seductive power of men and the destruction such power can wreak in the lives of women who cannot resist them. Lord Deveril's reputation is not that of a man who would ever force himself upon a woman. It is that of a man who would never have to force himself upon a woman… which may almost be worse! His ability to seduce is quite legendary. And I think I am not mistaken, given just how perturbed this meeting has left you, in assuming that legend is well founded."

Willa sipped her sherry and tried not to let the guilt of it consume her. Handsome as he was, tempting as he was with his sardonic grin and wickedly arching eyebrows, it wasn't Lord Deveril's face that haunted her. It was Marina Ashton's pale face and dark curls that were emblazoned upon her memory.

⇻⇻⇻≪≪≪

Devil was on the verge of tearing out his hair. It was nigh on the dinner hour and the entire household had been in an uproar for the entirety of the day. There was also no end to it in sight.

It had been terrible enough when Marina had shrieked and screamed at the sight of anyone but Mrs. Farrelly. Now, the child wailed. Not in a tantrum, but as if her heart were broken. The single word she'd spoken earlier that day, Mama, was the first word she'd spoken in his presence since he'd taken the child in his arms at his sister's deathbed. And speaking that word had burst the dam, it seemed. The child grieved until he feared she would make herself ill.

"You must fetch that Miss Marks, my lord," Mrs. Farrelly said. The woman's round face was red with exertion and streaked with tears as she rocked and held the little girl to her bosom. "There is only so much I can do to comfort her. Your Miss Marks broke her, and she can very well come back and fix her!"

"She refused, Mrs. Farrelly. I cannot force her to work here!"

Marina wailed louder at his shout.

"I am begging you, my lord, try. Please. And not for my sake. For the little dumpling's! She's cried until I fear she will make herself ill. Not a single crumb has she eaten today, nor will she drink a drop. Please? Won't you speak to her once more?" the cook implored desperately.

With that plea ringing in his ears, Devil let out a weary sigh and turned to go, shouting for his hat and his greatcoat. He would beard the lioness in her den. He was off to the Darrow School for Girls, and he would make Miss Wilhelmina Marks see reason whatever the cost.

The school was not far, and he elected to walk, hoping the evening air would clear his head and offer some sort of respite from the cloying headache that had been nagging at him all day in light of Marina's insurmountable grief. He refused to admit that his headache might have anything to do with abundance of brandy and a lack of sleep.

The short distance between his home and the Darrow School was not nearly enough. He was still struggling when he reached it, his emotions and his temper heightened. Denial, self or imposed by others, was not something he'd had cause to become accustomed to. The very idea of not getting what he wanted when he wanted it was rather alien to him. Even exiled in disgrace, he had been a man of influence and affluence, after all. His father had deemed the army an acceptable solution to his wild ways, had bought him a commission and sent him off to India to kill or be killed. But it wasn't the natives they'd had to fear. It was disease. All the wealth in the world hadn't been enough to spare him and his compatriots from the raging fevers and illnesses that had taken so many. It was only by the grace of God, or perhaps the fact that the devil wasn't quite ready for him yet, that he'd managed to survive.

Shaking off such bitter thoughts, he climbed the steps and rapped sharply upon the door. An aging and rather plump woman, a housekeeper by the judge of her black gown and apron, answered the door. "May I help you?" she asked, clearly nonplussed at his presence.

"I'm here to see Miss Marks," he replied, his tone just as dry as hers.

"Miss Marks does not receive gentlemen in this house, sir. None of our residents do." The disapproval in her tone was impossible to miss as was the coldness of her gaze as it trailed over him in a fashion that let him and everyone else know precisely how poorly she thought of his gender.

"My lord," he said. "Not sir. And she most certainly will see me. I demand to speak with her."

He'd begun shouting at one point, but the woman's baleful stare was unflinching.

"My lord," she finally said, and there was an inflection on the words that indicated precisely what she thought of him and his puffed up manner, "We are a household of women and, as such, we do not receive gentlemen callers unless they arrive during the hours of ten in the morning and two in the afternoon. At any other time, it would hardly be appropriate."

"It's all right, Mrs. Wheaton," called a female voice from just down the hall.

"But Miss Darrow—"

"I know it's against the rules, but I am the maker of those rules, and just this once, I think we can bend them. Miss Marks will not meet with him alone. I shall stay with them the entire time to ensure that every propriety is observed," the woman said as she drew closer.

It wasn't the first time that Devil had been surprised that day. But it certainly took him a moment to get over the shock. He was looking at a woman who could only be the daughter of the Duke of Treymore.

Chapter Three

S HAKING OFF HIS stunned stupor, Devil nodded in her direction. One of her dark brows arched upward, emphasizing the sharp peak of it which was very like her infamous father's. The milk white skin, glittering green eyes, and coal black hair was unusual enough that there was no question in his mind as to her parentage. She was beautiful, more so than Treymore's legitimate daughters who shared their mother's sallow complexion, unfortunately. Yet, despite her rather startling beauty, he had absolutely no interest in her beyond idle curiosity at the story behind her current placement. It was the air of quiet dignity about her that discouraged inappropriate interest or advances. She had the governess, or headmistress in the current case, bit down pat.

"Do come in, Lord Deveril. I rather expected we would be seeing you, although I hardly anticipated that it would be during the dinner hour," Miss Darrow said.

"The dinner hour? It isn't even six o'clock," he scoffed.

"And we are a school filled with young girls who will one day be working young women. They haven't the luxury of accustoming themselves to late nights and lying abed all morning," she said. Her words were cutting, though her tone never altered from its soft, musical quality. "Do follow me, Lord Deveril. I shall show you to my study, and then Miss Marks and I will join you there. I ask that you not leave the study without me, Miss Marks, or Mrs. Wheaton accompanying you. The girls would be rather terrified to see an unescorted male roaming our halls."

He wanted to challenge her, but it was his own mood rather than her request that prompted the urge. Wisely, he quelled it. What sort of ogre would intentionally terrify school girls, after all? Frustration and temper were getting the better of him.

Once in the study, he paced the lovely if somewhat worn carpet. How many girls had traipsed in and out of that room, he wondered? Had their infractions been enumerated in the soft and gentle voice of their headmistress as they waited for their punishments? It reminded him far too much of his own school, though he dared to hazard that Miss Darrow was infinitely more merciful than the headmaster at Eton had been.

It was only minutes later that Miss Darrow returned, Miss Marks in her wake. It took only one glance at the governess' arched eyebrow and the way her full lips were pursed to know she was displeased at his presence. *No more than he was displeased to once more find himself in hers*, he thought.

"Miss Marks, I have come to beg that you reconsider your earlier decision and come to work for me. Marina needs you." The entreaty was far more humble than he'd planned for it to be. But the words simply tumbled out.

"You are not the sort of client I would typically take on, Lord Deveril. Your reputation, and being in your employ, could very well render me unemployable in the future. No other person would believe that I could reside in your home and do so without risking my virtue and my morals. If I am to be entrusted with the care of someone's children, they will want to believe me above reproach." It was a simple statement, uttered matter of factly and without accusation.

"I would not attempt to dishonor any woman in my employ, Miss Marks," he denied emphatically. "I admit to being somewhat profligate, but I am not a monster."

"It isn't about what you would or would not do, Lord Deveril. It is about what the world would think," Miss Darrow said.

"Hang the world!"

"Lord Deveril," Miss Marks interrupted, "I would be in your employ for a short time, until Marina was settled and the worst of her grief and anxiousness had subsided. What I do as governess is to help those children who need me the most. And while I recognize that Marina's need is great, I would be shirking my duty to all the children who come after her if I do this. Working for you would render me, sullied reputation and all, unemployable after."

"I will do anything that you require, Miss Marks. I would willingly remove myself to a country estate and let you have full reign of the townhouse," he offered.

"That would not work, Lord Deveril. Marina needs to learn to put her trust in you... your absence will never evoke that sort of connection," Miss Darrow interrupted. "But I do have an idea on how this might be able to work. What if no one knows you are a governess, Wilhelmina?"

"I don't understand," Miss Marks said.

For himself, Devil didn't understand either, so he waited for an explanation.

"Lord Deveril," Miss Darrow began, "You have not been returned to London long enough to appreciate precisely what this school of mine does. We take in the daughters of gentlemen."

The by-blows, he thought. Given what he'd surmised about Miss Darrow, it didn't surprise him.

"Miss Marks is, in fact, the daughter of a gentleman you know well. It would not be unheard of for you, given your reputation, to marry outside of the conventional sort of arrangement," Miss Darrow continued.

"You cannot possibly be suggesting that I marry Miss Marks in order to have her tend to Marina," Devil stated, his voice ringing with shock. It wasn't her station or the situation of her birth that made the idea untenable but their patent dislike of one another.

"Not marry," she said, placing particular emphasis on the word. "But betrothals are broken all the time. And if it is said that Miss Marks ended your engagement due to infidelity or some other wrong you might have committed, a wrong that would seemingly be true to your known or suspected character, no one would be surprised. And if she were to reside in your home, with a proper chaperone, during your engagement and spend her days working with Marina, no one would be surprised by that either. I think it is the only way."

"Why can I not just hire a chaperone to stay with her as a governess?" he snapped. The idea of perpetrating such a ruse seemed exhausting and unnecessary.

"Because governesses, Lord Deveril, are only a step above housemaids. Obtaining a chaperone for your governess would only raise scandal, not squash it because why would you bother, really? That and no lady of quality who would be deemed an appropriate chaperone would ever consent to do so for a lowly governess," Miss Marks replied. "I would agree to this, under one condition, Lord Deveril."

"And what condition is that?"

"You must, for the time that I reside with you as your pseudo-betrothed, give up drinking, gaming, any sort of immoral women, and you must be an active participant in Marina's life. You must spend time with her and teach her that you are a man she can trust."

But he wasn't a man any woman could trust. If he'd been a trustworthy man, he wouldn't have dueled himself into an exile that left his sweet sister vulnerable to a fortune hunter. She wouldn't have been ruined, borne a child out of wedlock in a back alley hovel and died of the disease that laid claim to her there.

"That is a fool's bargain, Miss Marks. I will have to obtain a chaperone, see you properly outfitted as a lady to whom I would be betrothed, and give up all that I enjoy in life. And for what? The promise that you might make the child not scream at the sight of me?"

"For the promise of family, Lord Deveril," Miss Darrow said. "And I do not believe, despite what is said of you, that you are the sort of man to whom that means nothing. Otherwise, you would not be here now, pleading your case."

Devil swallowed convulsively. "It will take some time... I have an aunt in Sussex I could prevail upon, for a price, of course. It will take some time to get her here, however. Will you still be willing to take her on in two weeks or will you have secured another position then and my efforts will be for naught?"

"If you consent to this, I give you my word, Lord Deveril, that I will make myself available to you... to Marina," Miss Marks corrected.

The idea of her making herself available to him had merit. Despite her prickly nature and apparent dislike of him, she was a beautiful woman and he was not immune to that. In fact, their sparring seemed to have fired his blood. But under the circumstances, his own needs and desires would simply have to be ignored for the greater good. It seemed to be the order of the day.

"Then I shall consent to live like a temperance-loving and teetotaling monk, Miss Marks."

"Then I, against all sense and better judgement, will be your cleverly disguised governess, Lord Deveril... and we shall see what we may do to bring Marina back to a place of contentment and comfort," Miss Marks replied and extended her hand to shake his.

It was an odd gesture for a woman, but then he was quickly discovering that they were odd women, both Miss Marks and Miss Darrow. A snippet of conversation came to him then, something he'd overheard in a club. One gentleman had been advising another on what to do with the girl child he'd got on his mistress, as his own wife adamantly refused to see her acknowledged in any way. That long ago conversation explained so much.

"The Hellion Club," Devil said softly.

Miss Darrow's smile tightened. "Some have called us that. But we are not hellions, Lord Deveril. We are women who refuse to be gobbled up in a man's world and used with no thought to our own honor, intelligence, or abilities."

"In the eyes of most men, Miss Darrow, that would qualify you as a hellion," he replied.

"And in your eyes?" Miss Marks asked.

"I wish that my sister had been a student here… perhaps then she would not have met such a dire fate," he admitted. "I will send word to you, Miss Marks, when the arrangements are made."

EFFIE DARROW WATCHED Lord Deveril as he bowed and quickly left her study. Mrs. Wheaton was on him instantly, ushering the scandalous gentleman to the door and muttering under her breath about the whole house going to the devil because they'd let such a vile person in. It wasn't necessarily directed at Lord Deveril. Mrs. Wheaton, though her past marital status was questionable at best, had always held the masculine sex to be utterly contemptible.

"Why on earth would you propose such a thing, Effie? Really! Now, I'm well and truly stuck," Willa huffed out.

"You didn't have to agree," Effie pointed out gently. "I offered you a way to take the position if you desired. Clearly, you did."

"And clearly, that will be nothing but folly. I fear we have crafted my ruin between us. Or do you have a different sense of things?" Willa asked.

Effie couldn't explain it, but she did. Sometimes, she felt as if a guiding force prompted her to do things. She had felt compelled to make that outlandish proposal to Lord Deveril just as she'd been compelled all those years ago to take on Willa and Lillian as her first pupils. They had been her students before she'd ever had a school to usher them into.

"I cannot help but feel there is more to this Lord Deveril than meets the eye. He is not the villain he has been painted to be, Willa. And that child needs us too much to simply allow a worthless thing like propriety for its own sake to inhibit our efforts." It was true. But it was also dangerous. Effie hadn't just taught the girls who'd graced her halls. She'd raised them. Each and every one of them. The number of girls who attended the school was terribly small, but by design, so that each got the attention she needed and deserved. Some stayed for the entirety of their childhood and on into adulthood. Others still graced their halls temporarily until their erstwhile fathers could make other, more suitable arrangements for them. Willa and Lillian, half-sisters who had been, if not abandoned then certainly never acknowledged by their scandalous father, had been the former. She'd taken them on when Willa was only eight years and Lillian had been seven. She had been a girl of only eighteen herself at the time, but she'd never hesitated. And there had been no regrets.

"It's the right thing to do, Wilhelmina."

"He may not be a villain as some say, but he's hardly an innocent," Willa protested.

"And who amongst us is?" Effie asked pointedly. "We all have our sins to answer for, Willa. But he is trying to do what is right for the child. Perhaps it is guilt at the fate that befell his sister, but he does seem to genuinely care. Isn't that enough to prompt us to do the same?"

"It is enough to prompt our actions," Willa admitted. "Let us pray it does not prompt regret, as well."

Effie said nothing as Willa turned and walked from the room. On that point, they were in complete agreement.

Chapter Four

Two weeks later

WILLA STOOD ON the steps outside of Lord Deveril's townhouse. He'd sent a carriage for her early that morning as arranged by their exchange of brief and perfunctory letters. Of course, it wouldn't be appropriate for his betrothed to arrive on foot with her bags in tow. It was a ruse of epic proportions in an effort to maintain any semblance of respectability that she possessed and allow her to help a poor child that was clearly suffering from intense grief and melancholy expressed in the way only a child can—tantrums.

Reminding herself of the very important reason she had consented to such a thing helped Willa to steel herself. Like a man to the gallows, she climbed the same steps she had two weeks earlier and lifted the heavy lion's head door knocker.

The heavy door swung inward and the butler bowed. "Miss Marks, we've been expecting you. Lord Deveril is in the library along with his aunt, Lady Carringden. I will have your bags taken up."

"Thank you," she said stiffly. As a governess, servants didn't typically kowtow to her the way the butler currently was. But if their ruse was to be successful, not even the servants could know what her true purpose was. After all, servants gossiped.

Down the hall, a footman waited outside one of the many doors. She could only assume it was the aforementioned library. As she neared, he opened the door and allowed her entry. Immediately, Lord Deveril rose from his seated position behind the desk, and a woman who had been staring out the window at the garden beyond whirled toward her.

Without warning, the woman rushed at her, and it was all Willa could do not to throw her arms up in self-defense. But the woman didn't strike her. Instead, she wrapped Willa in a fierce hug.

"Oh, my dear! I'm so glad to meet you. I cannot tell you how I have worried for my poor, dear nephew! I couldn't do anything to help poor Alice. Her father forbade it and I have mourned the fact since! But just look at you! You're lovelier than words can express, and now my dear, sweet nephew will settle into a happy and peaceful union instead of carousing and drowning his sorrows!" The barrage of words and the complete lack of sincerity in them were too much to take in.

"Aunt Jeannette," Lord Deveril said, uttering the woman's name in a warning tone. "While Miss Marks hardly thinks I am a saint, can we leave off with extolling all of my sins?"

Lady Carringden smiled tightly and stepped back. "Of course, of course! Forgive me, my dear. I'm just so terribly excited. We haven't had a wedding in the family for ages. We will see to your trousseau immediately! And there's no time to waste as Devil has already announced the engagement in the papers. A bit prematurely, I believe."

"Perhaps in a day or so we can see to my wardrobe, if that suits you, Lady Carringden?" Willa suggested. She'd taken note of the avaricious gleam in the other woman's eyes. No doubt she would benefit from the shopping excursion as well. "For now, I'd like to explore the house and make the better acquaintance of Marina, Lord Deveril's ward."

Lady Carringden's smile faded altogether. Her expression appeared to be resentful and perhaps even offended.

"That child!" Lady Carringden huffed. "Children love me, Miss Marks. Children have always loved me. I don't understand why she wails so whenever I go near her. I do hope you have better time of it than the rest of us."

Willa smiled in what she hoped was a reassuring manner. "I'm certain I will, Lady Carringden. I'm very good with children, especially those whom others find difficult."

"Really? Why is that?" Lady Carringden asked. Her meticulously groomed brows arched upward in an expression of challenge and disbelief.

Willa smiled, trying with all her might to will the other woman to simply be cordial. The last thing she wanted was to be locked in bloodless battle with a member of Lord Deveril's family. "I suppose I was a somewhat difficult child myself. We are kindred spirits, I think."

"Oh, you must tell me more! Who are your people, Miss Marks? I know everyone who is anyone!"

"No one of consequence, Lady Carringden," Willa replied smooth-ly. "Shall we go and visit Marina?"

Lady Carringden's speculative gaze moved over her for a moment longer. Finally, the woman nodded. "Come along, my dear, and I shall introduce you to the sad-eyed little beauty."

"You'll excuse us, Lord Deveril?" Willa asked.

"Naturally, Wilhelmina," he said. "Will you join me later for a walk in the garden? We have much to discuss."

Willa nodded. "Yes, I will be happy to join you. We do have much to discuss, after all."

Following Lady Carringden out of the room and up the stairs to the third floor, she could hear Mrs. Farrelly singing softly to the little girl. Easing the door open, they simply stood there and watched. Marina played with a doll, bouncing it along the edge of the table as if it were dancing a jig to the jaunty tune Mrs. Farrelly sang for her. Her head turned with the doll, following its progress, until at last her gaze landed upon the door and the people who stood there watching her. Immediately, the child's slight smile faded into nothing and her expression grew dark, her lips parting to emit that terrible screaming. But then it seemed that the memory of their previous encounter returned. Rather than scream at Willa and risk being screamed at in return, the child's lips clamped shut and she glared at them.

"Hello, Marina," Willa said softly. "That's a very pretty doll you have."

The child remained stonily silent. But she did pull the doll in tightly to her chest and cling to it as if Willa had threatened to take it away.

"I've no wish to take your doll from you. Only to tell you how pretty it is. It has lovely dark hair just like you," Willa continued. "I've always thought dark hair was so much prettier than my own color. Not quite blonde and not quite brown." She wasn't talking to be understood but simply to allow the child to become accustomed to the sound of her voice.

"I had a doll very similar when I was young," Willa said in the same neutral tone. "Older than you, of course, but still young enough and happy enough to play with such things. My sister and I played together often. Do you ever get to play with other children?"

There was no response, but Marina did clutch the doll slightly less tightly. She even twirled one of the doll's dark curls between her fingers.

Emboldened, Willa stepped deeper into the room and crouched on the floor near a small table set with various other toys. In truth, there was every kind of toy imaginable in that nursery, and most of them looked quite new. Was it an attempt by Lord Deveril to appease the child? To buy her affections perhaps? To offer her some comfort?

"What an interesting set of figures," Willa exclaimed as she picked up an intricately carved horse. There was a tiger, as well, with the same elaborate markings. But they were not wood. "What are these made of? It isn't wood."

"Ivory, Miss," Mrs. Farrelly said. "His lordship carved those himself while he was in India. Said he saw such a creature himself, right up close, he did!"

Willa looked back at the tiger that Mrs. Farrelly had gestured to. "Dear heavens, I might have been scared to death to have encountered such a beast! Would it not scare you, Marina? Though I daresay you are a very brave girl. Much braver than I would have been."

As Willa watched, Marina reached out with her small hand and touched the tiger's tail etched so carefully that it appeared as if it would swish in agitation at any moment. Such carvings were something that many soldiers did to pass the time, but what he had done with those was quite simply art.

"Have you ever seen such a beast, Marina?" Willa asked, widening her eyes for effect.

The little girl looked at Willa as if she'd taken leave of her senses. But it was a response, and Willa would take what she would get. Hoping to continue the progress, Willa made a silly face at the little girl. Marina's eyes lit up and a slight smile cracked her lips but it was immediately squashed and hidden beneath a manufactured frown. But it was the chink in Marina's armor, so to speak. The child was afraid, grief-stricken, and angry. She'd been taken from a poor life, but it had been a life she knew and was comfortable with. Being removed from all that was familiar to her had likely only increased her discomfiture.

"Perhaps we could go to visit the Royal Menagerie and see one together. Would you hold my hand, Marina, if I were to become very afraid?" Willa asked.

The child said nothing for the longest time. But then she gave the very slightest of nods. It was a victory. Wilhelmina smiled. "Then we shall plan such an excursion very soon, I think."

Willa rose and walked toward the door and the waiting Lady Carringden who was looking at her as if she'd grown two heads.

"Why, you spoke to her as if she were fully grown!" Lady Carringden protested. The woman appeared to be utterly scandalized by the thought of it.

Willa was aware that her methods were unconventional, but they were hardly that shocking. "Indeed, I did, Lady Carringden. Marina is not a typical child. She is intelligent and perceptive. Her life has been beset with tragedy, and that will have altered her in ways we cannot fathom."

"And how is it that you've come to know so much about her history?" Lady Carringden demanded to know.

"Lord Deveril has confided in me about the circumstances of Marina's birth and the loss of her mother," Willa replied.

Lady Carringden's eyes narrowed. "How terribly forthright of him. I don't suppose I need to tell you just how terrible it would be for such gossip to get out? Devil's reputation is already sullied enough... but mine is not. And sharing an abode with the bastard daughter of my niece who likely died from the pox is pushing the limits of what I'm willing to respect."

The woman was as cold as ice, Willa thought. "I can assure you that discretion will be maintained at all times."

"Good. As for your 'technique' in dealing with difficult children, I find it utterly preposterous. Why, the rational world doesn't even acknowledge a child's existence until they are at least twice Marina's age! Speaking to her as an adult, indeed!"

"To speak to her in any other way would be completely disrespectful of her past," Willa protested.

Lady Carringden still appeared to be dismayed by the prospect of treating Marina with anything akin to respect. "Where, for heaven's sake, did you get such a notion, my girl? Children of her age are not deserving of respect! They need discipline, my dear. Spare the rod and spoil the child! If you spank her when she begins that shrieking, it'll stop soon enough!"

"I would hardly consider Marina spoiled, Lady Carringden! The child and her mother were living in abject poverty and barely eking out the most meager of existences! And that's to say nothing of the grief she must feel at the loss of her mother!"

Lady Carringden's expression darkened to something that resembled fury. "Loss! What would a child of her age even begin to understand of loss? Children, Miss Marks, are little better than animals! So long as they are fed when they are hungry and can sleep when they are tired, they are content!"

Willa was stunned by the vehemence and the complete lack of empathy that Lady Carringden had for the child. "I assure you, Lady Carringden, that children even younger that Marina are capable of experiencing grief."

Lady Carringden laughed scoffingly. "And you are such an expert then? What sort of upbringing have you had, Miss Marks, that you are so familiar with grieving, impoverished urchins?"

"There were many younger girls at the school I attended, whom I became very close to, that have had difficult starts in life. Suffice it to say, my experience is sufficient to understand that the child is in pain," Willa replied, keeping her temper in check by sheer dent of will. "I find it difficult to fathom, Lady Carringden, that you are so firm in your belief that Marina's behavior is a choice and not a product of the trauma she has suffered!"

"My dear, if you believe that child is doing anything more than vying for attention and sweets, then you are as mad as my dear nephew!" Lady Carringden laughed again, this time with genuine if mean-spirited mirth. "All these strange ideas! Perhaps the two of you truly are a perfect match!"

Chapter Five

DEVIL SIGHED AS he stared broodingly into the fire that blazed in the hearth. He'd had second, third and fourth thoughts about the scheme they had concocted. There were a dozen ways in which it could go wrong and a dozen more in which it could fail. He'd had to consider the fact that it was quite possible Miss Marks would not be able to effect any change in Marina at all. And if that were the case, he was without recourse. What could he possibly do with a child who did nothing but shriek at anyone who attempted to speak with her? And it wasn't simply that it made his head ache or that it was endlessly frustrating. But he was not without sympathy for the girl. It was clear to him that she was in misery. There was no happiness or peace for the child, and what could he do for her? Nothing.

It was in his nature to be a man of action, whether it was drinking, gaming, fighting, dueling, wenching, or soldiering. What he was not accustomed to was being powerless. In this instance, held hostage by the emotional outbursts of a small child, there could be no other way to describe his situation. She was a sad, little tyrant. And every time he looked at her, he saw his sister. She had Alice's eyes, the soft curve of her cheek so like the woman who had given birth to her, who had used her last breath to beg him to care for the daughter she was leaving behind. Did the child sense his own grief? Was that why she wailed so in his presence? Or was it something more sinister?

She feared men. All of them. Every footman, groom, and even the aging butler sent her into shrieking fits. She'd tolerate the maids so long as they didn't touch her or come too close to her. Only the kindly and plump Mrs. Farrelly could comfort her. And yet, Miss Marks, with her mirrored shrieking and her calm, adult way of speaking to the girl, had managed to coax something from her during their first brief meeting that no one else had. Curiosity.

Perhaps that was a family trait, as well. *Being curious about Miss Marks.*

As if his thoughts had summoned her, there was a soft knock upon the library door.

"Come," he called out, and the door swung inward. Miss Marks stepped inside. She'd changed from her traveling clothes into a simple frock of blue sprigged muslin. It was a modest gown, the neckline cut far higher than fashion dictated and shielding any hint of her bosom from his gaze. It was just as well. It would be a distraction he could ill afford. "Yes, Wilhelmina?"

Her eyebrow shot upward in an expression of disapproval. "I did not give you leave to use my given name, Lord Deveril."

"And you are my betrothed, Wilhelmina. I daresay the world would believe you have given me leave to do that and quite a bit more," he remarked. It was scandalous. And inflammatory. "Perhaps there is some derivative of your name that you prefer? Something that only your intimates call you? Surely it would not be inappropriate for me to do so under the circumstances."

Her cheeks flamed, but not with embarrassment. It was anger. He could see that clearly enough in the flashing of her eyes and the way her shoulders inched back slightly. Such posture would have been the envy of any soldier.

"Lord Deveril, I might remind you that this betrothal is a sham. Any pretense otherwise while we are free from prying eyes is nothing more than a foolish waste of time. As my placement here is temporary and I do not mean to remain in your employ for more than a month, it would be quite foolish to indulge in such."

He smiled and eased back in his chair, propping his booted feet on the desk. "Foolish indulgences are amongst my favorite pursuits... and a particular skill of mine. Shall I show you?"

"Have you been in to the brandy?" she demanded.

"Not a drop, a dollop, or a dram," he denied evenly. "Perhaps that is why I'm being churlish. Would you care to have a drink with me and see if, perhaps, you can discern a difference in my behavior?"

"You said we had matters to discuss and should walk in the garden. I'm amenable to that so long as we have a maid or footman present," she said.

"A maid or footman? Do I inspire that much fear in you, Miss Marks?"

"You inspire nothing in me, my lord. I would request the same walking with any man I do not know well," she replied.

"Well, now that I've effectively been put in my place, I'll point out that the garden is small with no hidden corners where I can utilize all of my nefarious skills. You're safer in the garden than in this room, Miss Marks, and certainly better observed."

She crossed the room to the terrace doors and looked out at the small garden. He knew what she saw. A square patch of grass with some shrubs and trees around the perimeter and a gate that led to the mews. It was a disgrace, really, that so fine a house would have such a sad little garden, but his father had refused to spend money to maintain something so few would ever see. It was just another example of his skinflint ways.

"Very well," she said. "It will be a short walk, clearly."

"Clearly," he agreed, following her onto the terrace. "What is it you wished to say to me, Miss Marks?"

"I wished to speak with you about an outing for Marina. Not immediately, of course. But perhaps in a few days, when she is more accustomed to my presence here, I would like to take her to the Royal Menagerie. She has expressed an interest in the animals you carved. Perhaps foolish indulgences are not your greatest talent after all!"

"A simple way to pass the time while I was on watch at our many camps in India," he said. It was a useless hobby, something he'd done when there had been naught else to do.

"Do you miss it?" she asked.

"Miss what?"

"India," she replied. "Many men seem to fall in love with it. Others still to revile it. I wondered which camp you might fall in."

"I fall into the camp of those who were there without choice. It was the army or being disinherited entirely. India is simply a place, but it does hold magic and mystery, to be sure." He paused then, looking her over from head to toe, taking in the conservatively arranged blonde curls and the flashing green eyes, porcelain perfect skin and lips so ripe and plump he longed to nip at them with his teeth and see if they tasted as sweet as they appeared. "But England holds its own magic and mystery, if one knows where to look for it."

"Stop it."

"Stop what?" He uttered the rejoinder with as much innocence as a man of his long debauched state could muster. There was a small bench near the gate, so he seated himself on it, leaving room for her to join him if she felt inclined. She did not.

"Stop flirting. Stop being outrageous for the sake of it!"

"We are supposed to be engaged, Miss Marks." He was unable to conceal his exasperation. "How on earth are we supposed to act as a betrothed couple if there is no flirting?"

"We will hardly be in society enough for it to matter. In truth, the fewer people who see us to cast doubt on our elaborate tale, the better! Who would believe that I might ever be betrothed a man such as you?"

He cocked one eyebrow at that. In truth, he was more than a little offended by her tone. "And why would you never be engaged to a man such as me? Is it really so unbelievable that I would free myself from my scandalous past by entering into the bonds of holy matrimony?"

She blinked in surprise. "You mistake me, my lord. I am a governess. Not only am I a lowly governess, I am also the illegitimate daughter of the younger son of an earl with more scandals attached to his name than even you possess. No one would ever believe that you would stoop to such depths, and we're better off not putting it to the test."

She turned and crossed the patchy expanse of grass, over the terrace, and disappeared into the library once more, leaving him sitting in the sad little garden alone.

⟫⟫⟩⟨⟨⟨

ALARIC BANGED ON the door of the small room that had been Alice's abode for the last few years. She'd always managed to scrape together just enough to keep the roof over her head, though not much more than that. He never bothered to ask how. There were few enough options. He'd long since ceased being tempted by her ever dwindling charms. If she could turn a coin with them, so be it. He neither knew nor cared.

"Let me in, Alice," he called out. "I want that blasted ring back. You owe me!" It had been nigh on two months since he'd been there and, in those two months, his already horrible luck had somehow taken a sharp and uglier turn. The last game of cards he'd managed to scrape together a stake for had not gone well, not in the least. He was in deep, and he needed to scrounge together enough coin to pay what he owed or get himself far enough from London that the moneylenders couldn't sic their pack of mongrels on him.

"She's not 'ere!"

The flattened vowels and harsh cockney accent of Alice's neighbor, Mrs. Blye, had him gritting his teeth. He detested the coarse creature. Every interaction with her only reminded him of how far he'd fallen and how dismally the scheme with Alice had failed. Had her father not been a skinflint with a dark and shriveled heart, he'd have been wed to an heiress and dancing through the finest ballrooms in London! "Then where is she?"

"Dead. Been that way for a month past now, she 'as. Might've known it if you'd bothered to look in on the girl," she said, her voice ringing with condemnation.

"Dead?" he asked. "Are you certain?"

"Am I certain, 'e asks. I know dead right enough, sir, and dead she was. Dead as a doornail. Lung ailment, faded right fast she did. 'Tweren't nothin' to be done for the poor thing. Not that you'd know... or care. You took off right enough, shakin' the dust of this place from your coattails without even a by your leave!"

The blasted tea. She'd drank it too quickly, likely using it to fill her belly while she gave the small bit of food she possessed to the child. He needed to find that tin before it was discovered, and he needed that damned ring. "And her things, Mrs. Blye? Did the landlord take them for safekeeping?"

She cackled. "Safekeepin'! Aye, right enough then! Took 'em for safekeepin' to the pawnbroker if'n 'e got 'is 'ands on 'em! Worried about things and not even askin' after your own child!"

"I assume she's in the workhouse. It's a good enough place for her," he said dismissively. Heaven knew he wanted nothing to do with the brat.

Mrs. Blye sneered at him in disgust. "I'd like to see you in the work'ouse, I would! She didn't go there and 'tweren't the landlord, at all, what took 'er things. Miss Alice's brother showed up. Right 'andsome 'e was. Showed up in the nick of time and eased 'er mind as she passed from this world... and then took the sweet babe back with 'im. Not that you'd care to know what 'ad become of your own daughter. No. You'd rather ask about that worthless bit of tin you put on Alice's finger. I warned 'er about you, I did. A dozen times or more, I told 'er what a no-good, worthless sot you are! But she wouldn't 'ear it. That's what love got for poor Alice! Dyin' while 'er child watched and the man she gave 'er 'eart to is out with a doxy!"

Alaric didn't bother taking offense. There was nothing in what the old bawd said that wasn't the absolute truth, except for the fever bit. It had been poison that had taken Alice and well he knew it. That tin of tea he'd given her had been laced liberally with it. It was her only luxury and a gift from him, so he'd known she'd use it rather than risk offending him. Once he'd placed it in her hands, he'd vacated the premises rather than come up with daily excuses as to why he must decline the beverage. It was rather disappointing that the brat hadn't succumbed as well. He'd thought it would be the most expedient way to rid himself of them both. But she didn't share her mother's love of that particular potable. Of course, the appearance of Alice's older brother now changed everything. What he might have once regarded as misfortune may very well have become a stroke of luck. "Alice's brother... Lord Deveril? He has the child?"

"Aye, 'e does. And I 'ope 'e is the Devil Lord what folks say. And I 'ope 'e runs you right through if you dare to darken 'is door!" With that, Mrs. Blye slammed the door to her own little hovel, the thin and ramshackle walls rattling with the force of it. He was left standing in the narrow corridor, contemplating his recent and potential change in fortune.

Alice might have taken the ring he'd given her to the grave with her but, in the end, she'd given him so much else. If Lord Deveril had claimed the child, and intended to raise her, he might very well be willing to pay for the privilege. For the years of Devil's exile, all he'd heard from Alice had been about how devoted her brother was and how much things would change once he returned to England. But

Alaric had grown impatient waiting for just such a day, though it seemed that Alice had been correct all along. Her exalted brother had sought her out and tried to set right the wrongs perpetrated by their father. Too little and too late.

Alaric needed funds and needed them quickly. He'd run out of credit with any reputable sources and had resorted to moneylenders with decidedly murkier principles. They'd staked him for a game that he shouldn't have been able to lose. His opponents had been green boys with fat pockets and dim wits. But then *he* had turned up—Viscount Seaburn. The man was a notorious sharp and better at cheating than Alaric was. He'd been forced to lose, lest he be called out. It was a habit that Seaburn had developed, to openly challenge those who he deemed were taking advantage of those too stupid to know better. Regardless, it was attention he could ill afford. The last thing he needed was to have more questions asked about who he was or where he'd come from, or he'd have more to worry about than a duel or moneylenders. If his true origins were uncovered, it'd be the hangman he faced.

"Maybe the brat will finally be useful," he muttered under his breath as he made his way out of the sad shambles of the small rooming house in Spitalfields. Indeed, his bastard might finally manage to earn a small sliver of his affection.

"Would be better what you 'ad died stead of sweet Alice!" Mrs. Blye called out from behind her closed door.

A grin split Alaric's mouth, showing slightly crooked teeth. It was the only flaw in his too handsome face but it had never hindered his ability to seduce and sway women to his cause. Alice had been proof of that. Beautiful, wealthy, innocent, and his for the taking with nothing more than a smile and a few flirtatious whispers. He hadn't counted on her father disowning his only daughter, especially after the son had been exiled to India in disgrace. Alice had been his way out, his way *up*. And it had ended in disaster thanks to her blowhard of a father.

Poisoning her had been his only out in the end. She'd proved stubborn in her unwillingness to set aside their sham of a marriage and give him the freedom to pursue a wealthy bride. But if the brother had cared enough to take their little bastard out of the slums, he might be willing to pay Alaric a bit to keep her there. Then there would be no need of leg-shackling himself to a horse-faced heiress just to live the life he deserved, a life that should have been his by right.

Alaric was whistling under his breath as he descended the crooked and none too sturdy stairs of the small rooming house that had been his murdered bride's only shelter.

Chapter Six

WILLA WENT DOWN to dinner in her borrowed finery. Her own wardrobe was fairly meager. As Effie had a better relationship with her father and her family, it necessitated the need for gowns that would suit the hallowed halls of Heathcote Grange, her father's home. With some hasty alterations, several of her gowns had been made over for Willa so that no one seeing her on the arm of Lord Deveril would label her an opportunist. While the gown was beautiful, it was more revealing than Willa was used to. Being of a slightly plumper figure than Effie, there was a great deal more décolletage on display. Of course, she had no intention of being seen by anyone other than Lord Deveril and his aunt. And he looked at her as if he knew what lay hidden beneath her clothes anyway.

As she neared the drawing room, she could hear Lady Carringden talking. Unless the woman was talking to herself, which was distinctly possible, it meant Lord Deveril was with her. Bracing herself to face him in a gown that, to her modest sensibilities, bordered on indecent, Willa took a steadying breath.

The footman opened the door for her and she stepped inside the very same room where she'd first encountered Lord Deveril. As if mocking her, he leaned nonchalantly against a pillar that flanked the Titian she'd so admired. A slow smile spread over his face as she entered and his gaze traveled over her, pausing strategically at the parts of her that were spilling out of her borrowed gown.

"There she is, my lovely betrothed," he said. "I was just telling my dear aunt what a lover of art you are. You're familiar with Titian, aren't you?"

"I've seen a few of his works, but I am hardly an expert," she said. "But the one you're standing next to is lovely."

"So it is," he said. "There's a lovely Rubens in the gallery upstairs. I'll show you after dinner, if you like."

Willa smiled noncommittally. "Perhaps Lady Carringden, you can join us? I'm certain you'd have delightful insights regarding the works of such a renowned artist!"

Lady Carringden laughed. It was a hard and brittle sound, typical of society women. A bit too loud, without any hint of real feeling or emotion in it, like tinkling shards of glass. "Oh, my! I do believe that she is wary of your intentions, Douglas! How delightfully wise you are, my dear! But alas, as an engaged couple, I think it behooves you to have a bit of time to get to know one another without me hanging on your every words. You should go with him after dinner to the gallery. And you should stay precisely ten minutes. I will be timing you. And alas, as fond as I am of Rubens, I'd have to walk past the glowering and dour likenesses of my ancestors. Frankly, it's not worth it. But you enjoy yourselves."

That had not gone as planned. In maneuvering to avoid him, she now found herself stuck firmly in a trap of her own making. She was saved from commenting by the ringing of the dinner gong.

"Let Douglas escort you in, my dear. We're dining informally tonight, and so I've placed you to his right and myself to his left. I know it's a slight bending of the rules but, well, if ever there was a man who understands the bending of rules, it's your betrothed!" Lady Carringden offered with false cheer. "Tell me, dear, how precisely did the two of you meet?"

"We were introduced by a mutual friend, Aunt, and I was taken with Miss Marks instantaneously," Lord Deveril said as he appeared at her side, offering his arm for her.

Reluctantly, Willa accepted it. As she placed her hand on his arm, she could feel the heat of his skin through the fabric of his coat. Standing next to him, she felt dwarfed by his height, by the breadth of his shoulders. He smelled faintly of sandalwood with a hint of brandy and something else that was just him. It was an enticing scent, one that reminded her of all the many reasons why it was a terrible idea for her to be there, in such dangerously close proximity to him. He represented temptation and, with it, all the fear of consequences. He wouldn't have to ruin her. She might very well ruin herself for him, and then where would she be?

"I do not bite," he whispered close to her ear. "Not over much at any rate."

"You do not behave either. Not over much at any rate," she retorted.

"Aunt Jeannette," he said, "Go on ahead and we'll join you shortly."

She looked at them with slightly raised eyebrows, but nodded. "Of course. I'll await you in the drawing room."

When Lady Carringden had gone, Willa stood there at his side. "What is it that you wish to say, Lord Deveril?"

He looked at her for a long moment and then, with a seriousness she had not expected from him, said, "I've no designs on your virtue, Miss Marks. I'm not a ravening beast or a monster. I've never resorted to forcing myself on women, and I have no intention of doing so now. Regardless of the rumors you've heard, I'm not without honor, and you've no reason to fear me," he said.

It was, perhaps, the first time in their short acquaintance that he'd not been flippant or sarcastic. He spoke that vow, for it could be nothing less, with complete sincerity. It disarmed her, and Willa wasn't certain what to say. "I did not mean to give you offense on that score, my lord. I certainly would never presume—"

"But you have presumed, Miss Marks. And given my reputation, I cannot even say that I blame you for such presumptions. But the truth is, all you know is my reputation, and my reputation is not based entirely in truth. Right now, I need you here. I need your help so that Marina might have a chance at... I won't even say a normal life. But so that she might be able to have some happiness, some peace in life. That is my wish above all things," he said firmly.

"Why?" The word slipped out before she could stop herself.

"What do you mean *why?*" Deveril demanded. "Why wouldn't I wish for those things?"

Willa shook her head. "It isn't that you wouldn't wish it, my lord. It's simply that in my experience most men, especially gentlemen, cannot be bothered to expend effort on their own children, much less the children of others."

"Then Marina is not the only one who is burdened by the ugliness she has witnessed of the world thus far. I am saddened for you, Miss Marks."

Uncomfortable with both his scrutiny and his pity, Willa turned to face the dining room doors. "We should go in. Your aunt will be wondering what is keeping us," she said softly.

"Hardly. She's probably managed to nab some of the silver and tuck it into her reticule, Miss Marks. About my aunt... she is as respectable a woman as ever lived, in the eyes of society. But my family is not close, or even remotely caring. She is here for payment and not for duty or any familial obligation. To that end, be careful of her, Miss Marks."

While she hadn't known the truth in its entirety, she'd certainly gleaned that Lady Carringden appeared to be somewhat self-serving. "Certainly, Lord Deveril. I shall exercise caution in all things."

"Let us go then."

⟫⟫⟩⟨⟨⟨

DEVIL ESCORTED MISS Marks to her chair and then moved to take his own seat at the head of the table. Had she really known so few decent men in her life that even the idea that he could have a child's best interest at heart was alien to her? Not that he would have ever considered himself to be a decent man. But he wasn't a monster. Marina was his niece, his blood. She was the only daughter of his beloved sister who had pleaded, with her dying breath no less, for him to care for the child. Could any man refuse?

Sadly, the answer was yes. Many could and many did. His own father had. The man had turned him out for his scandalous antics and sent him off to India where he might have been killed in battle or died of some wretched disease. For poor Alice, it had been worse. She'd been cast out into the streets, abandoned by everyone she had ever known. Banished to the slums, forced to do heaven knew what to survive, and all because she'd loved unwisely. Because she'd had the misfortune to love unwisely, she'd lost everything, even the love she'd made such a sacrifice for. Indeed, her lover had been nowhere to be found while she lay dying of a terrible fever. Of course, he supposed that it hadn't really been love at all.

He glanced at Miss Marks once more. Where would she have been if not for the Darrow School? Would she have met a similar fate to Alice? It was impossible to say. A part of him thought not, thought that she was stronger than that. But then, who was he to judge anyone's strength when they were starving in the streets and had to use any resource at their disposal to survive?

Shaking his head slightly to clear it of such unpleasant thoughts, he waited for the first course to be served. He blamed his rather uncomfortable thoughts on his recent foray into sobriety. But that had been his bargain with Miss Marks, and he would keep to it, even if it did give him a very bleak outlook on life.

The butler appeared with a bottle of wine, but Devil shook his head. "I'm refraining, Carlton. By all means, serve Miss Marks and Lady Carringden."

Devil felt Miss Marks' gaze on him and glanced up, meeting those sharp green eyes and allowing his own to lock with them for a moment. It wasn't condemnation or even curiosity he saw there. It was grudging respect. It was something he'd had very few occasions in his life to experience. Somehow, from her, it was even more significant.

It was that thought, more than anything else, that made him realize just how dangerous Miss Marks was. There was something about her that was altering him. Or perhaps, her presence was prompting him to alter himself. *Dangerous.*

Chapter Seven

T HE PARK WAS crowded in the early hours of the morning. Ladies were strolling on the arms of their suitors under the sharp-eyed gazes of their chaperones. It would have been a gross exaggeration to say that she'd taken Marina on an outing. The simple fact was that she'd invited herself along on an outing that Marina was having with Mrs. Farrelly. The cook had made it a point to bring the child to the park daily for fresh air whenever the weather permitted. It was an escape from the house, an escape from the tension that always seemed to develop whenever she was in Lord Deveril's presence. His teasing and flirting were bad enough; worse was the fact that she'd glimpsed something in him the night before—something fine and noble. There was honor in him, perhaps far more than even he realized. If he were truly just a wastrel and womanizer, she'd see past his fallen angel appearance quickly enough. But that other side of him made him truly dangerous to her.

Keeping back several paces, Willa was lost in thought as she walked behind them. Still, she was aware of the interplay between the cook and her charge. Marina didn't speak, but Mrs. Farrelly did. She pointed to flowers and named them for the child, she pointed to horses and to pretty birds, to random squirrels and even a few dogs that people had accompanying them as they took their morning walks. Occasionally, Marina would glance behind her as if to make sure that

Willa still followed. The girl was intrigued by her. It was her curiosity that would eventually force her to open up. At least, Wilhelmina hoped it would. In truth, she'd never encountered another child troubled in quite the same way that Marina was. It was all simply a guess, really.

For the first time, Willa worried that perhaps she'd overestimated her abilities. Marina was a stubborn child, willful. She actually admired that in the girl. It might have been conceit or pride since it was a trait she possessed herself in rather shocking abundance. She certainly hadn't experienced quite the same degree of trauma that Marina had at such a young age, but she could certainly empathize. Her own mother had not died, but she had deposited Wilhelmina in the arms of her very negligent and absent father and simply walked away. Painful as it had been at the time, and as disinterested in her as her father had been, it had ultimately been for the best. It was that very decision that had set her course so it might one day intersect with Euphemia Darrow's. Conceit and pride notwithstanding, she hoped one day that her charges might think of her as she did of Euphemia—with deference and respect and with no small amount of affection. Effie was her family, the only one she had ever known.

Musing on that for a moment, Willa surveyed their surroundings. A man standing near a copse of trees that nestled next to a curve in the path gave her pause. There was nothing furtive in his actions. He made no attempt to conceal himself, nor was his manner threatening. He simply stood there. But it was the intensity of his regard, the way he simply stared at them that took her aback. He looked at Marina briefly, then at Mrs. Farrelly, and then at her. It was as if he were taking their measure, though for what she could not begin to imagine.

Unnerved by his presence, Wilhelmina asked, "Mrs. Farrelly, do you know that man?"

Mrs. Farrelly glanced up from where she'd been chatting with Marina and looked about curiously. "That man over there? No, Miss! I can't say I've ever seen him before… I can say I don't much like the looks of him."

"On that point, we are in agreement." Willa uttered the words without ever taking her eyes off him. "We should go the other way."

"Aye, Miss. We should at that."

At that point, Marina turned to look back at Willa but, as she did, the child caught sight of the man in question. The girl's eyes widened. Then a blood curdling scream escaped her. It went on and on, the sound of it deafening. But Marina wasn't looking back at her or even Mrs. Farrelly. Her gaze was locked on the strange man. And Willa realized something. It wasn't a tantrum. It was fear. She could see it on the child's face.

Willa looked up and saw that the man had stepped forward, moving toward them with an expression of cold determination. Knowing that Mrs. Farrelly was the slower of the two of them, Willa didn't hesitate. She swept the little girl up into her arms and turned away, moving as quickly as possible toward the gate that would set them out of the park almost directly across the street from Lord Deveril's townhouse. She could hear Mrs. Farrelly huffing and puffing behind her, but she didn't look back. She dared not to, not until they reached the front door of Lord Deveril's townhome. Only then did Willa spare a glance behind her. The man was standing there at the entrance to the park that faced the house, watching them as intently as before. Willa grasped the knocker and let it bang against the plate with far more force than was necessary. She kept her gaze locked on their pursuer until she felt the door open behind her and quickly ducked into the house.

Perhaps it had been an overreaction. But she'd rather be safe than sorry, and she wouldn't take unnecessary risks with Marina. Sinking to her knees in the foyer, Willa struggled to catch her breath. Hauling a sizable three year old through the park, across the busy street, and up the steps, all when her stays were too tightly laced for vanity's sake, had left her breathless. Mrs. Farrelly was right on her heels, and the cook slammed the door behind them. The sound of the woman's ragged breathing filled the expansive space of the foyer.

The butler stared at them in confusion. Doors opened down the corridor. Lady Carringden appeared in one and Lord Deveril in another.

Lady Carringden drew one hand to her chest as she stared at them with concern. "Whatever has happened, my dear?"

"Yes," Lord Deveril seconded. "What has happened?"

"There was a man in the park... watching us. He made me very uncomfortable and then when Marina saw him—" Willa broke off. "I think he is known to her, and I'm also fairly certain that she's terrified of him."

»»»«««

DEVIL TOOK IN Miss Marks' ashen face as she struggled under the child's weight. The fact that poor Mrs. Farrelly seemed to be on the verge of some sort of seizure of the heart, and that Marina, screaming as she was, appeared to be just as Miss Marks' had described her. Terrified. The little girl was wild eyed and clinging to her governess. That she was clinging to Miss Marks rather than Mrs. Farrelly was the very thing that had first caught his attention.

"Marina allowed you to hold her rather than Mrs. Farrelly?" he questioned.

Miss Marks' sheepish expression gave away her answer. "I am afraid I didn't give her an alternative. When I saw him lurking in the shrubbery at the park, watching us, I simply snatched her up and ran."

Devil noted the way Miss Marks held the child—tenderly, protectively, fiercely. He had little doubt that she would have done battle for Marina had it come to it. On the one hand, he was thankful she was so ready and able to defend Marina with such ferocity. On the other hand, it terrified him. If the man had posed a genuine threat to them, what might have occurred?

"Did this man say anything to you?" Lady Carringden asked, her tone just shy of censorious. It was clear that she thought them hysterical and reactive.

"No, my lady," Mrs. Farrelly replied. "He just stood there, lurking in the trees and watching the wee one in a way that—well, suffice to say, I can't think he'd have had anything but wicked intentions."

And Marina could tell them nothing. Or if she could, she would not. He wasn't monstrous enough to attempt to interrogate her. Given that she was already terrified of him, it would hardly help his case with her. But he could go to the park and see if the man was still lingering.

"He followed us," Miss Marks said, and her gaze was locked on Lady Carringden, challenge in her eyes. "When I looked back as we reached the door, he was standing at the gate of the park facing the house and was still watching us. I've no doubt that he was there and waiting for us. Had we been less vigilant, I cannot think what might have happened."

"What did he look like?" Devil asked.

Willa sighed, "He was tall, nearly as tall as you. He had dark hair and was rather handsome… but he looks dishonest."

"How does one look dishonest?" Lady Carringden scoffed. "Really, Miss Marks! It's likely nothing more than hysterics on your part!"

"Aunt, please," Devil snapped.

Lady Carringden's eyes widened, her expression managing to appear both deeply wounded and indignant at the same time. "Very well, I shall retire to my room if my opinions and input have so little value!" She did just that, her skirts whirling as she turned and swishing behind her as she marched away.

"I can't say really how a person looks dishonest," Miss Marks said softly. "It's just a feeling when you look at certain people. I'm certain you understand that, Lord Deveril."

He'd give her that. He did. "Wait here."

Devil moved past Miss Marks, sparing a glance for Marina who continued to cling to her in apparent terror and hysteria. He moved quickly, though it was unlikely the man would still be present. But as Devil crossed the street and stepped through the gate to the park, he realized very quickly that he'd been wrong. The gentleman, if he could, in fact, be called that, was still there. He'd changed positions, likely in pursuit of Miss Marks, and was now leaning nonchalantly against a lamp post, but with a perfect view of their front door to observe any comings and goings. When he saw Devil, his nonchalance fled. The man rose and turned, walking quickly until he disappeared into a throng of pedestrians.

Devil forced his way through the crowd as a bevy of nannies attempted to return their charges home for nap time. But it was no use. The man had the perfect camouflage—dressed as a gentleman. He had vanished into the ranks of others with similar attire and bearing. The mysterious man was simply gone and, with him, any hope of uncovering his motives.

Devil let out a muffled curse, and one of the ladies walking past him squawked in dismay. He offered her what he hoped was an apologetic smile, but she did not appear to be the forgiving sort. She glared at him and whirled away, presenting her back to him as she huffed out a breath.

Reluctantly, Devil turned and headed back to the townhouse. He crossed the street and entered the chaos that was his home. Marina was still crying, though not quite as intensely. Mrs. Farrelly was fanning herself more furiously than a debutante trying to draw attention to herself.

It seemed that curiosity had won out over pique and his aunt had returned to the drawing room. She was glaring daggers at everyone else present as she paced stridently back and forth.

Miss Marks stood in the midst of it all, perfectly still as she held

Marina, a bastion of calm in the midst of insanity.

"It was a waste of time, wasn't it? Wild goose chases for a dishonest-looking person! It's London, for heaven's sake. You'd be hard pressed to find anyone who doesn't look dishonest!" his aunt snapped, her eyes lighting with victory.

Devil eyed her with reproach. "Perhaps you could retire to your room again. I find your presence more tolerable when it's at least one room removed."

"Did you find him?" Miss Marks asked, ignoring the barbed exchange entirely as her malcontent of a chaperone stormed past her.

"I saw him. But he also saw me. He fled and I lost sight of him in the crowd."

Miss Marks' brows drew together, a tiny furrow forming there as she asked a troubling question. "Then it couldn't have been a random occurrence or an overreaction on our part! He was watching us and ran from you… that means he knows who you are and, consequently, knows who we are."

"So it does, Miss Marks," he agreed. "So it does. From this point forward, any outings will be accompanied by at least two footmen, and I will see about obtaining more suitable protection. Until we even the odds and at least know who he is and what his intentions are, it's a risk I'm unwilling to take."

She didn't argue. That, in and of itself, was a surprise. But her frown only deepened and then she nodded. "I think that's for the best."

"Let's get the wee one upstairs, Miss Marks. Perhaps she'll calm down away from all of these prying eyes," Mrs. Farrelly suggested.

"Once she's calmed down, meet me in the library, Miss Marks," Devil said. "We clearly have far more to discuss than either of us realized."

"I'll return shortly," she said and turned to climb the stairs with the little girl still clinging to her.

Devil followed behind them until they reached the landing that would lead them to the upper floor and the nursery. He stood there, watching their figures until they disappeared from sight.

"Well, whatever else may have come of this mess today," his aunt said softly as she approached from behind him, "at least Marina appears to have bonded with Miss Marks. We may never manage to separate them. Now you'll have two chaperones."

Devil didn't respond to his aunt's comment or the speculation he heard in her voice. He'd never been overly fond of his aunt, but he'd never thought her a viperous person. It was clear that she had little regard for Miss Marks and that she had her own agenda. What it was, he could not say. Rather than continue to spar with her verbally, Devil retreated down the stairs once more, lost in his own thoughts.

Miss Marks had been remarkable. Fierce, protective, maternal. She'd been like an avenging angel or a warrior queen ready to defend Marina. He couldn't think of another woman of his acquaintance who would have gone to such lengths. But she was a product of The Hellion Club that was so often whispered of amongst gentlemen, not because it produced remarkable women but because it was a place for them to put their more embarrassing or difficult female offspring. And yet, he had witnessed precisely the kind of honor and courage such an education and upbringing would engender in its recipient. Such qualities had been readily apparent in Miss Darrow herself, as well.

For his part, Devil had never given much thought to marriage beyond that it was something he would have to do one day. But a man could do much worse than a woman with such character. Birth and connections be damned.

Chapter Eight

IT TOOK LONGER than she'd expected to lull Marina to sleep. The little girl had clung to her, her cries slowly fading into silence as exhaustion claimed her. Once she was deeply asleep, Wilhelmina laid her on her small bed and covered her gently, careful not to disturb the child. She rose to her feet, spared one last look at the sleeping toddler, and wondered what it was that she'd witnessed in her short life that made her so terrified.

Mrs. Farrelly was seated in a small chair in the corner. "Bless the wee little one's heart," the cook said. "What on earth could he have been about?"

Willa shook her head. "I can't say… but, Mrs. Farrelly, how closely did you look at him?"

"A bit, Miss, but perhaps not so much as you did."

There was something about the man's appearance, his dark hair and something about the shape of his face that she realized reminded her very much of the child who now slept so peacefully before her. "There are things I must discuss with his lordship, Mrs. Farrelly, about the events of this afternoon. I'll check in on her again shortly."

"Aye, you had better, Miss. I think I've been replaced. I haven't seen the little thing take to anyone else quite like she did with you today."

"It's only because she was afraid and I pose no threat to her," Willa protested. "I've certainly not replaced you in the girl's affections."

"'Tisn't affection she has for me, Miss. The poor wee one is terri-fied of everyone and everything. Perhaps I remind her of someone from her old life... before her mother was taken too soon from this world. I remember her mother, you know? I worked here as a housemaid when she was born. Dear, sweet Miss Alice! No one was kinder. It fair broke all our hearts when old Lord Deveril tossed her out. It wouldn't have happened if he hadn't already sent his lordship away. They were thick as thieves as children, you know? Always together. But I suppose they had no one else, not with their mother dead and their father colder than ice to everyone!" As if realizing that she'd said far too much about the family who employed her, Mrs. Farrelly suddenly clammed up. She closed her mouth with a snap and sat stonily for a moment before adding, "I'll sit with her a while, Miss."

"Thank you, Mrs. Farrelly. And you needn't worry. I've no inten-tion of saying anything about our conversations to anyone, including Lord Deveril."

The cook nodded. Despite her silence, the woman's expression softened and she seemed to be put at ease.

Leaving the nursery, Willa headed downstairs to the study where Lord Deveril awaited her. She could easily bring to mind the fierce expression he'd worn when he'd flown at the doors and through the heavy throng of traffic to the park. He'd been ready to defend Marina to any extent necessary. *And her.* He'd been just as willing to defend her.

Firmly, Willa put that thought from her mind. The last thing she needed was for his already considerable appeal to increase. Besides, he was a fighter, a dueler, a brawler, if gossip was to be believed. He'd fight anyone just for the sake of it. It had naught to do with her. With that thought uppermost in her mind, she took a steadying breath at the library's entrance before knocking softly upon the door. From inside the room, she could hear a muffled reply as he bade her enter.

Opening the door cautiously, uncertain what she would see, Willa stepped into his study. His back was to her, and the sound of his voice had been muffled by the heavy curtains that draped the windows. He was peering out at the park across the street through a spyglass.

"Has he returned?" she asked. "Or did he ever leave?"

"He fled on foot earlier. He has not returned. Not that I've been able to discern, at any rate," Lord Deveril answered, turning to face her. "Do you recall ever having seen him before, Miss Marks?"

"No. I've never seen him before. But at the risk of sounding contradictory, there was something terribly familiar about him," Willa said softly. "I think we must face the rather terrifying fact that he may, perhaps, be a relation of Marina's."

His expression darkened alarmingly. The fearsome temper that had resulted in duels and brawls was there suddenly. Uncertain, Willa stepped back.

"A relation to her? If he is a relation, pray tell, Miss Marks, where was he when my sister lay dying? Where was he when she'd struggled for months to keep even the most meager roof over their heads? She died because her body was weakened and malnourished because she'd been abandoned in that hellhole by those who should have been there to care for her... and I include myself in that number," he snapped.

"I'm not suggesting that he has a right to be part of Marina's life, to importune this household in any way, my lord," she offered as soothingly as possible. "But the question isn't what I think or even what you think. At this moment, we must concern ourselves with the business of what he is thinking and why he took it upon himself to seek her out. What does he want?"

"He likely wants money," Lord Deveril said. "Men like that always want money."

Willa frowned. "And isn't her peace of mind worth paying him?"

Lord Deveril sighed and looked at her as if, perhaps, she'd taken leave of her senses. "If I pay him, I'll be paying for the rest of my life and possibly the rest of hers. Not that it matters on that front, but it sets a dangerous precedent, and it gives him a kind of power in the situation that I find intolerable. The more I give him, the more he will ask… and that increases the likelihood of Marina having to see him or encounter him throughout her life when it's obvious that he terrifies her."

Willa clenched her hands in front of her. She knew that he was right, of course. Payment would only provide a short term solution to the issue. He would return and demand more and more. That was true of anyone who resorted to blackmail or extortion. Of course, they were making a leap there. What if he simply wanted to be certain of the child's safety? While she'd only seen him for a brief time, she felt certain that wasn't the case. He'd been cold, and there had been a cruelty that she sensed in him that belied such a motive.

A shiver raced through her as she recalled the calculating expression he'd worn as he watched them. No. Her welfare was not his motivation. Of that, she was certain. The man had been evil, and whether Marina knew him or simply sensed that in him, she couldn't say.

"I know that you're right, but I simply want her to feel safe. Even if he only goes away for a short time, perhaps it would be enough to bring her round, to make her feel safe enough here to tell us what has occurred with him," Willa admitted. "A child isn't intended to be solitary and silent."

"She's hardly silent," he said on a bitter laugh. "She screams the house down on a daily basis."

"But that isn't communication, Lord Deveril. That doesn't allow her to express what she needs or ask for the help she requires… and the further she retreats into her pain, into her own mind, the more difficult it will be to reach her." Willa's voice had risen, her tone impassioned. She was terrified of what would happen to the girl if things continued on as they were. They might lose her forever.

"Are you certain you can help her, Miss Marks? Truthfully? She has spoken to no one else. She doesn't even speak to Mrs. Farrelly!"

"Because others speak to her as they would speak to a child," Willa protested.

"She is a child!"

"Yes, but she isn't like other children, is she? She's seen and experienced something horrific. As terrible as it was for you to see your sister in such a state, think what it must have been like for her! The person she depended on for her care, the person she loved and who loved her beyond anything in this world, and now she's gone in a way that such a young child cannot possibly understand," Willa replied, her voice rising once more. "To speak to her as one would any other child is to trivialize her experience."

"The maids she will tolerate. Mrs. Farrelly she adores. Myself, the butler, the footmen... she shrieks in terror," he said, and there was a kind of desperation in his voice. "Men terrify her the most, Miss Marks, either because of what they did to her or what she has seen done to her mother. And that thought haunts me every minute of the day. When I think what might have happened to her in that vicious place to make her fear men so much—do you understand the implications of that, Miss Marks?"

"I was not always at the Darrow School, Lord Deveril. I was placed at another school prior to it—one where the headmaster was so cruel and vicious to those girls whom no one cared for that I cannot even bear to repeat what it was he did. And before that, I lived with my mother in a place that I imagine is not so different from the very place where you found your niece. Yes, I understand the implications very well," Willa replied. Her mother, despite the nature of her profession, had tried very hard to protect Willa. And yet it had been impossible to shield her from all the seedier aspects of daily life in their neighborhood. "I'm very thankful that you found her and that you've brought her someplace where she might grow to feel safe and be nurtured into a happy and healthy life. But it will take time."

"Time we may not have if the identity of the man I saw today is who I suspect," he mused.

"You think he's her father." It wasn't a question. She'd suspected as much herself, but it cemented it further to hear him imply just as much.

"I think he was my sister's lover. I think he abandoned my sister while she was with child or perhaps later. I don't know. Regardless of when he left her, I would hesitate to ever call such a man a father."

"And your own father?" It was an impertinent question, and no sooner had she uttered it than Willa regretted it. Regardless, she couldn't call it back. She felt the heaviness of his gaze on her but, regardless, she wouldn't shift her feet and hang her head like some misbehaving child caught in mischief.

His head came up, his gaze locking on her in a way that was beyond intimate. "You asked for very specific boundaries between us and you violate them. That is a very personal question, Miss Marks."

"It is. But as you often invoke our betrothal as license to be impertinent, I thought I might as well," she said.

"That's fair enough, I suppose. My father did not deserve the moniker either. Cold, cruel, unfeeling, and without even a shred of mercy in his heart even for his own children. I will do whatever is necessary to ensure that Marina is never forced to endure the less than tender mercies of such a person. I vowed to my sister that I would protect her and that, Miss Marks, is a promise I mean to keep."

His resolve was completely firm. It was apparent from the intractable expression on his face, the stubborn jut of his chin, and the tension in his shoulders. She'd thought he was the most attractive man she'd ever seen the first day she'd met him there. Dirty and disheveled from his carousing, he'd been ridiculously appealing. But what she was witnessing from him in those quiet moments in his study only intensified that attraction.

"I will do whatever I can to help you to help her," she said softly. She wanted to look away, to turn from him. And yet, in that moment, she found herself unable to do so. Something happened in that moment, an awareness that stretched between them, taut and filled with tension. *With attraction. Awareness. Desire.* All those things were there, and try as she might to ignore them, she could not. It had been problematic from the moment she encountered him, and the longer she was in his presence, the worse it would get.

As if sensing her thoughts, he approached her then, pausing long enough to deposit the spyglass on the edge of his desk. He kept walking, closing the distance between them until he stood near enough that her skirts brushed his thighs when he stopped. Willa's breath caught. Uncertain, she looked away, casting her eyes down at the floor rather than upon him lest she do something reckless and stupid.

"I have a personal question for you now," he said softly.

She couldn't refuse. She had been the one to initiate such an exchange, after all. "Very well, my lord."

"Have you ever known a man's kiss?"

"Not by choice," she said and glanced at him from beneath lowered lashes. Her view was clear enough to show the clenching of his jaw and the quiet fury that sparked in his eyes.

"And did this happen at your school? The one you attended before Miss Darrow took you in?"

Shame nearly swallowed her whole. "Yes, it did."

"You've been with her for how long?"

"I was eight and my half-sister, Lillian, was seven," she answered, still unable to look at him directly.

"Then it wasn't a man's kiss, Miss Marks. It was a monster's, and I promise you that the two could not be more different. One day, with your permission, I will show you that," he murmured and then stepped back, widening the distance between them. It did nothing to dissipate the sense of intimacy, however.

Willa looked up at him then, stunned that he had not taken liberties; that he had not judged her for the ugliness that had occurred in her life. He was forever doing and being the unexpected. "You befuddle me, my lord," she said in reply.

He shrugged as if it were something he heard frequently. "Thank you, Miss Marks. For all that you have done thus far and all that you will do for her... and for your selflessness and your willingness to put yourself in harm's way for her sake. I will do whatever is necessary to be certain you are never forced to make such a choice again," he vowed softly.

"We cannot even be certain that he meant her harm. I have questioned and doubted my interpretation of it since I arrived back here with her."

"A man doesn't skulk if his intentions are pure," he said.

"And are your intentions pure, Lord Deveril?" she asked. Again, it was an impertinent question and one, given their recent exchange, that was too dangerous to ask.

"As pure as my intentions can be, Miss Marks," he said with a slight smile. "You can rest assured that I have no nefarious plans for you."

"You never have nefarious plans for anyone, my lord. You rarely plan anything as we both know. I'm rather more concerned about what might happen spontaneously," she admitted.

"You mean in moments like this? Where we're alone... where, for a brief moment, you forget your disdain of me?"

"I don't disdain you, my lord. I simply do not trust you. I do not say such to be an insult or a personal affront," Willa replied. "Merely to acknowledge it as a precaution that a woman in my position cannot afford to neglect."

"A woman in your position? Do you mean as a governess or as my betrothed?"

Willa stepped back abruptly, widening the distance between them. "As a woman who has no one in the world to care for me should I fail to take proper care of myself. It isn't about my station, my lord. It's about the fact there is no one to hold you accountable for your actions if they are not honorable."

JUST LIKE ALICE.

The implication was there even if it wasn't spoken aloud. Perhaps it only rang so loudly in his own mind and wasn't at all in hers. Neglected and ignored by their father, Alice had been easy pickings for the man who now stalked Marina. Just as Wilhelmina Marks had been easy prey for the headmaster at her school when she was too young to protect herself from him. It was an ugly story and one that occurred all too frequently. It wasn't only young girls who suffered such advances. Such things had gone on enough in his own school as a boy. It was there that he'd learned to fight and determined that he would, no matter the cost. Perhaps his admiration of Miss Marks was a result of his own vanity because, in many ways, she reminded him of the better qualities of himself, few as they were.

He was drawn to Miss Wilhelmina Marks. Her spirit, her character, and certainly her beauty. She did not attempt to hide it, but nor did she let it shine. Her hair was dressed in a manner that would draw little attention to her, and her gowns were modest enough for her to have nearly passed as a Quaker, the exception being her borrowed finery for evenings. And yet, she tempted him. And tormented him, as well. For all the temptation she offered, she was entirely forbidden to him. He'd never seduced an innocent. As debauched as he was, he did have his own brand of morals and honor.

"Touché, Miss Marks. Your point is well taken," he said. "You've nothing to fear from me. I will remain aware of my place and of yours in the grand scheme of things."

"I'll be going now. I want to check in on Marina again. She was sleeping soundly, but after the fright she received today, I'm uncertain how long that will last. I'd prefer to be there when she wakes up," Miss Marks said softly.

"I will see you at dinner, Miss Marks. In the meantime, I plan to pay a few calls and discover what I can about this man who convinced my sister to run away with him. Perhaps if I can ascertain his name, I can determine where to find him. I'd rather beard the lion in his den if I can."

She frowned, her brow furrowing with concern. "Be careful. I truly did not like the looks of this man. We know he lacks scruples. It's very likely that he is dangerous."

"So am I, Miss Marks," he answered. "So am I."

Chapter Nine

ALARIC HAD CIRCLED back around to the park. Leaning nonchalantly against a tree, he looked like any other gentleman who'd taken a rest while out for a stroll or, perhaps, someone waiting for a companion. But through the trees and the intricate iron bars of the nearest gate, he had a perfect view of the front door of Deveril's townhouse while he himself was well concealed. He'd been too brazen before because he'd underestimated the pretty chit.

Dressed too fine to be simply a governess and yet too prudish for one of Deveril's high-flyers, he was unsure what to make of her. Then, of course, the brat had seen him and begun to wail as if the very hounds of hell were after her. Of course, that wasn't uncommon. The girl hated him, and he liked her no better. He'd warned Alice that if she didn't get rid of her little problem, it would ruin everything between them. And it had. *She had.* Every fight they'd had, every time he'd been forced to knock Alice to the floor had been because of that worthless little bastard.

Alice hadn't even loved him at the end. She'd been clinging to the hope that he'd pull himself together and live the honorable life of a happily married man. But her father had put the nail in the coffin by cutting her off. He needed an heiress, after all—a woman who would be able to support him in the manner to which he'd like to become accustomed, the manner which his credit would no longer afford him.

He'd wasted valuable time on Alice Ashton, time that would have been better spent coaxing a wealthy and aging widow to the altar.

The door to the townhouse opened and Lord Deveril emerged. Dressed to the nines, Alaric could easily recognize that Deveril's coat was Schweitzer's. No other tailor could fit a man quite so well. The well turned out lord wore boots that were shined to a mirrored gloss, and his doeskin breeches fit the man like a glove. It was easy to be fashionable when money was no object, Alaric thought bitterly. He was making do in his old clothes. In truth, he hadn't been able to purchase a new suit for himself in nearly a year.

Resentment burned hot in his belly. Who the hell was Deveril to have such when he was without? But while he was out, Alaric had an opportunity.

Crossing the street, he knocked softly on the door. Almost immediately, a butler answered. The sticklike man stared down his nose at him. Alaric was down to the man, after all.

"May I help you, sir?"

"I'm here for my daughter. The Devil Lord has abducted my sweet Marina," he said.

"His lordship has abducted no one," the butler said. "He has brought his niece into this home as his ward upon the death of her dear mother."

"And I am her dear father," Alaric insisted. "And I am here to ascertain her safety and welfare. Surely even you cannot question that I would want to be certain of her care?"

Before the butler could say anything else, the woman from the park appeared at the foot of the stairs, just behind the servant. He was getting a far better look at her now than before in the park. She was lovelier than he'd first thought, with fine and delicate bone structure and a perfect, bow-shaped mouth. Her skin glowed with health and vitality, and her pretty blonde hair was arranged in a severe fashion that, while not flattering, could not conceal the thickness and luster of the mass.

"Is there a problem, sir?" she asked softly. She might have looked brave, but there was a slight quaver in her voice that belied her fear.

The cultured tone of her voice marked her a lady, but Alaric had his doubts. There was something about her that suggested working class. Governess, it was. "There most assuredly is, Madame. May I inquire as to your identity and why you feel it is within your right to keep me from my daughter?"

"Your daughter?"

"Yes, my daughter. Marina."

Her eyes narrowed and she gazed at him with steely determination. "Marina is the daughter of Lord Deveril's late sister."

"And she is mine as well," he protested.

She cocked her head in a manner that he recognized. All women had that look just before the dressing down came.

"If you wished to exert your parental rights, then perhaps you should have married her mother and legitimized her birth, *sir*," she said. "You have no legal rights to the child based on your unsubstantiated claims. You could be anyone hoping to exploit a vulnerable child for your own financial gain."

"I am her father!" he persisted. "And her mother and I were wed by common license."

"You are not married in the eyes of the law unless you can provide proof. Until then, in the eyes of the law, she has no father. But she does have a guardian. She has her uncle, Lord Deveril, in whose care her mother entrusted her to on her deathbed. Despite his rather colorful reputation, I doubt there is a judge in the land who would question such an arrangement. You should leave now," the woman insisted. "Before Lord Deveril returns."

He'd take her down a peg or two before it was over. No woman had ever spoken to him thusly, and he'd not allow her to get away with it. "Your name, Madame? As you speak so freely on Lord

Deveril's behalf, I feel it only appropriate that I know your identity."

"Despite the impropriety inherent in your insistence that a lady introduce herself to you," she said with censure, "I am Lord Deveril's betrothed, Miss Wilhelmina Marks."

"Well, Miss Marks, please be advised that I will not simply accept this terrible situation. She is my daughter, and I will have her back."

Miss Marks smiled at him coolly. "That will not happen, sir. Not today and not ever... but in the interest of reciprocity, I'd have your name so that I can give it to Lord Deveril and advise him of your stance on the matter."

"Alaric West," he said, offering the false name with ease. He'd used it often enough that he no longer had to search for it in his mind. "It's a name he'll know, I imagine."

There was a gasp from the landing. Alaric looked up and saw a very familiar figure. Jeannette. The orchestrator of it all. He glared at her, furious to see her there, to see her still meddling in his business when she was the cause of his current situation.

"I will be certain to let him know, sir. I bid you good day," the younger woman said, her voice sharp with dismissal.

Alaric spared another glance at her, ignoring the still beautiful but avaricious woman on the stairs behind her. Then he turned and walked away, hearing the snick of the door closing behind him. A smile tugged at his lips. He'd laid the groundwork for his claim to the child. It was enough for the time being. And much as he despised Jeannette, he'd seen in that last look at her that she still pined for him. He had an ally.

DEVIL STOOD IN the foyer of another Mayfair townhouse that was as equally well-appointed as his own. But it was dark. The brocade drapes were closed, no lamps or candles burned, and the servants that were present were particularly close-mouthed. No one in Highcliff's household would dare to gossip.

"His lordship will see you," the butler offered in a low-pitched tone as he stepped back into the marble and gilt entryway.

"I know the way," Devil insisted as the man started to show him to Highcliff's lair.

The butler drew back as if mightily affronted but offered a curt nod.

Devil walked past the man and down the corridor, but he didn't enter the extravagant library or the morning room or any other room where a person would routinely see callers. Instead, he moved beyond all of them and toward the conservatory. It would be devoid of plants but would contain several braziers placed strategically about the room to offer some comfort from the chill air. It was a concession to his sparring partners for if Highcliff had a weakness, even the cold, Devil was unaware of it.

Entering the large open space, he saw his friend immediately. Highcliff was shirtless, dressed only in breeches, and even his feet were bare on the cold stones. He was wielding a heavy scimitar in the Eastern fashion, something he'd learned during one of his many times in India, no doubt. Highcliff had disappeared for days and sometimes weeks on end while he'd been there during Devil's own tour. There was little doubt he'd been doing business that they were all better off not to know about. It had been the same while he'd been on the Continent, but it was not something they'd ever spoken of.

"Is there some reason you've darkened my door, Devil?" Highcliff asked, never breaking stride as he swung the scimitar in a wide arc that set the air whistling about him.

Devil walked over to one of the braziers. As expected, not a single coal burned within it. "Are you so completely averse to the idea of comfort that you won't even have a bit of warmth for yourself?"

"I don't need it," Highcliff replied. "As long as I'm moving, I'm warm enough."

Devil looked back at him. He was sweating profusely so Devil supposed that was true. "How long have you been out here?"

"What time is it?"

"It's half-past two," Devil answered.

"Then I've been out here for three hours," Highcliff said.

Three hard, grueling hours no doubt. "I need a favor," Devil said abruptly. He despised asking for help. But if there was anyone he'd go to in a time of need, it was Highcliff.

"I assumed you would or you would not be here." Highcliff gave one more flick of his wrist, the blade moving through the air with a loud whoosh. When he was done, he walked over to a carved wooden box that sat along the far wall and placed the blade in it. "It was a gift... from Rajah Amkir."

"He never sends me gifts," Devil replied.

"Because he detests you... you very nearly slept with his wife," Highcliff pointed out.

"I did not. And I didn't know she was his wife," Devil snapped. "It was just harmless flirtation."

"There is no such thing as harmless flirtation when a woman is draped in Burmese emeralds and living in a palace. There is sanctioned flirtation and there is you nearly being executed." Highcliff shook his head, a smile tugging at his lips as he was clearly more amused by the memory than he wished to let on. "I saved your hide that day. I suppose I can do it once more. Whose wife have you diddled this time?"

"No one's. It isn't that kind of help." Devil took a deep breath. "Alice had a child... a daughter. And the bounder who seduced her and lured her to some cesspool of a rookery in Spitalfields is the father, and he seems to want to lay claim to Marina."

Highcliff nodded. "And what is it you want from me? He is the girl's father, after all. Poor doesn't automatically disqualify him from the role."

"I need to find out who this man is. He goes by the name Alaric though I have no family name. I heard the name upon my return from India. His poverty isn't the issue. His character is."

"And what do you mean to do with this man when you find him? The last time you shot someone, you wound up banished to India and nearly died for it yourself."

Devil sighed. "I don't need to find him, Highcliff. He's already found me. He was spying on the gover—my betrothed as she walked with Marina in the park. He terrified them both. Marina screamed for an hour at least after they returned. She fears him."

"He's her father. We both know how capable they are of inspiring terror in their offspring."

"He's a bounder," Devil responded. "If he were any kind of father, he'd have been there as her mother lay dying. Instead, that small child was thrust into my arms when she had no notion of who I was or what was happening to her mother. I cannot believe that his interests are paternal in nature. I'm assuming he wants money."

"And you don't want to give it to him."

Devil paced the width of the room looking out onto the gardens beyond. "If that would be the end of it, I would. But we both know that isn't how people like that work. If he gets paid once, he'll come begging again and again. If he wants money, Highcliff, it's likely he owes money. Find out to whom. I beg of you."

"Fine. This betrothed governess of yours. What's that about?"

"She's from the Darrow School. The Hellion Club. A feigned engagement and staying under my roof with a chaperone was the only way she could tend to Marina and not have her reputation destroyed."

Highcliff laughed at that. "Then the old bats don't even listen to their own gossip. Everyone knows the only women who interest you are those who already have husbands."

Devil wanted to protest, but there was some truth to it. It wasn't that he only liked married women. It was that he didn't have to worry about being forced to the altar if someone else had already stood there before him. "Let me know what you find... I promised Alice that I would care for her child. That isn't a promise I'll have broken no matter what I have to do."

Highcliff studied him for a moment. "I'm sorry. I know you loved your sister and it's terrible what your father did to her... to you both. I wish you'd found her sooner."

"So do I, Highcliff. Every damned day. I didn't save her, but I will save her daughter. At all costs."

"I'll let you know something tomorrow, whether I find anything or not."

Devil nodded. "Thank you, my friend. We'll add it to the account of all the many things I owe you."

Highcliff laughed again, but it was a bitter sound. "If I ever collect on all the favors owed me amongst my compatriots—it hardly signifies. We both know I won't. And this is for a child... and for Alice. You owe me nothing."

Devil said nothing further, just gave another quick, jerky nod and left the conservatory to make his way back through the darkened house and into the street beyond. Highcliff was a man haunted by his past and burdened by the prospect of his future. But he was a damned good friend to have.

Chapter Ten

WILLA'S HANDS WERE clenched into fists at her sides. It was less from anger and more to control their trembling. The man was no less terrifying at a close distance. His lurking aside, there was something cold and calculating about him. She had little doubt that he was plotting something. His desire to lay claim to Marina as his child had nothing to do with any paternal inclinations he might have. He wanted something and Marina was a means to an end for him. Of that, she was certain.

"Where is Lord Deveril?" she asked of the butler.

"He has stepped out, Miss Marks," the butler replied. "He had a matter of business to attend to but is expected to return shortly."

"Does the matter of business pertain to Mr. West?" she asked.

"I cannot say, Miss," the butler replied.

Cannot say. It was a far cry from he did not know. She was fairly certain that given how difficult the afternoon had been that Lord Deveril would not have left unless it was to deal with the problem at hand.

"When he returns, please inform him that I'm awaiting him in his study." Her manner was as stiff and formal as the butler's. She was well aware that he disapproved of her, that he remembered her well enough from her previous visit to the house and likely saw through their sham of a betrothal as if peering through a pane of glass.

"I see no reason why that man should not have access to his child," Lady Carringden proclaimed from her position on the landing. "It isn't our place to prevent a father and his daughter from reuniting."

"Other than the fact that the child is terrified of him?" Willa demanded. "I cannot understand the hardness of your heart toward an innocent child."

Lady Carringden laughed. "My dear, are any of us ever really innocent?"

"Yes," Willa said, beyond infuriated by the woman's cavalier answer. "I aim to wait for Lord Deveril in his study. Alone."

Breezing past the butler and his disapproving glower, and ignoring Lady Carringden's indignant harrumph, she made her way down the corridor and into the study that was his sanctuary. It was the first time she'd been in that room alone, without his overwhelming presence to fill it. It was a strange feeling—almost as intimate as those charged moments that had passed between them earlier. It was a room filled with his letters and personal items. It was where he conducted his business, where he greeted his intimates, and where he spent the better part of his time. And every piece of furniture, every book, every letter, all seemed to be infused with the intoxicating scent that was simply him.

Free to explore without his knowing and watchful gaze upon her, Willa did so. Walking around the perimeter of the room first, she studied the art work on the walls, the figurines that graced the shelves and mantel. The bookshelves behind the desk held a treasure trove of delights, many of them forbidden. There were books she'd read, devouring page after page until she could recite them. There were others that she'd never heard of and still more that she had, but only in hushed whispers. Erotic poetry. Novels that booksellers refused to let unmarried women purchase. She could have spent hours upon hours just drinking it all in, but the risk of discovery and the embarrassment she would feel if he were to see her reading one of those salacious books was enough to stay her. Still, she trailed her fingertips lovingly over the spines. The temptation was almost as great as her trepidation.

"I fear that particular volume would make you blush so profusely you might actually burst into flames."

Willa gasped, her hand flying to her throat in an instinctually protective gesture as she turned toward him. He'd slipped in, opening the door silently and entering the room while she'd been engrossed with his wicked library. "You startled me."

"Caught you more like," Lord Deveril replied. "If you really want to read those books, I won't stop you. And what's more, I won't tell anyone either. They are quite… enlightening."

"I was simply curious about your collection, my lord. I didn't realize you were such an avid reader," she replied dryly. "Though I imagine a great many of these books consist primarily of illustrations."

He laughed, throwing his head back and doing so freely without any fear of censure. "Are you suggesting that I am only capable of reading picture books like a child?"

"These are hardly children's books."

"Indeed, they are not," he agreed. "Though I daresay they have contributed greatly to the production of children the world over. They are quite inspirational in that regard."

Deciding to change the subject for the sake of her own comfort as well as propriety, Willa asked, "Where were you?"

A raised eyebrow accompanied his sardonic response. "Am I to answer to you, then? Perhaps submit my schedule to you for approval?"

She wouldn't tolerate highhandedness from him. He might be a gentleman of a rank, but bastard or not, she was the daughter of one. "He came here. Alaric West is the name he gave. Whether it's genuine or not is not for me to say. He came to this house and demanded to see Marina."

"I'll see him dead first." The words were uttered quietly, but there was a ferocity in them that was unmistakable.

He was known for fighting and for dueling. By all accounts that she'd managed to uncover, he'd acquitted himself well while serving in India. But until that moment, she'd not understood what he'd meant when he referred to himself as a dangerous man. It had all been laconic charm, teasing smiles and flirtation that bordered on the inappropriate simply because of its source. *Him.* In rare moments, she'd glimpsed the serious side of him, that deeper part where all his pain and guilt resided. But what she saw in that moment was something else altogether. He had the appearance of a warrior, of an avenging angel.

"That may be a bit extreme," she replied.

"He left my sister to die. He seduced her. And when it became known she carried his child, she was cast out. Where was he then, Miss Marks? As soon as he realized that she would not be his path to a life of ease and luxury, he left her and her child to fend for themselves in a squalid hovel. I cannot bear to think of what my sister was forced to do there, to endure there, in order to survive."

He'd bitten out the words, his tone harsh and a far cry from his usual dry, sardonic delivery. They were fueled by fury and suppressed grief. And by guilt, Willa realized. He blamed himself for his sister's fate as much as he blamed West. *His behavior had resulted in his exile and his exile had left his sister vulnerable to fortune hunters and opportunists.* It wasn't the truth. Willa knew that. How many girls at the school had slipped away and met with unsuitable men, running off with them, despite all the safeguards in place to protect them? If Alice had wanted to be with West, she would have found a way.

"It wasn't your fault," Willa said softly. "She hid her relationship with him from everyone. Not even her maid knew... until it was too late. She would have hidden it from you as well."

He strode across the room and reached for the decanter of brandy on the table. At the last moment, as if remembering their bargain, he removed his hand from it and let out a weary sigh. "How do you know that?"

"Women have been loving unwisely and secretly for as long as they have existed, my lord. Not even you can prevent such a thing." Willa moved toward the door, but paused before exiting, "If you feel the need to partake of a bit of brandy, my lord, I won't protest. Under the circumstances, I'd say it's well deserved."

That arched eyebrow and droll tone returned. "Thank you, Miss Marks, for granting me permission to partake of my own spirits."

"You're quite welcome, my lord," she murmured. "He claims they were married and that he has proof. If so, the law will be on his side. What shall we do?"

"It's best you do not ask," he replied darkly.

Willa shivered at the implied threat. She didn't want to know, she realized. And whatever it was that he would do, she'd not have any censure for him because of it. It was warranted, after all. "In the meantime, we'll need guards. Not just footmen, as you suggested earlier, and the sooner the better. Marina cannot be kept as a prisoner in this house. She needs sunlight. Air. She needs to learn what it's like to be a child again. That will not happen if she is trapped inside constantly."

"I'll see to it," he said. "I know some retired soldiers who'd be happy enough for the work."

Willa nodded her thanks and exited the room.

WHEN SHE'D GONE, Devil took advantage of the reprieve she'd offered him and poured himself a glass of brandy. He didn't simply throw it back as he might have before. He wasn't drinking to numb his pain or bury his guilt, but rather to savor the taste of it and to ease the tensions of the day.

But he didn't want to think about Alice. Nor did he want to allow Alaric West to occupy any more of his thoughts on that evening. Instead, he allowed his thoughts to drift to something far more dangerous. What would Wilhelmina Marks have done had she opened that volume she'd been caressing so lovingly? She would have been shocked to be sure. But would she have found it titillating as well? Or, heaven help him, arousing?

Moving back to the bookshelf, he picked up the very volume Miss Marks had been looking at. He placed it on the desk and opened it to a familiar engraving. It depicted a woman sprawled across her lover's lap as he brought her to release with his hand. It was an exquisite piece of erotic art. But he wasn't looking at it as a connoisseur of art, but as a man bedeviled by lust. He wanted Wilhelmina Marks sprawled across his lap in just such a manner, his breath hot on her neck as she strained against him and her cries echoing softly in his ears.

It was a complicated thing. He needed her to provide a service, to care for Marina and help him reach the child he feared was beyond him. And he needed her because she could reach a part of him, something inside him that he had thought long dead. Wilhelmina Marks had somehow reached the romantic heart of him buried beneath years of cynicism and debauchery. It was a hell of a thing to feel; he'd need to choose between what he desired most and what was best for his niece.

Cursing softly, he closed the book and left the library. Carrying his glass of brandy, he made for the stairs and the safety of his own chambers. He needed to be alone with his thoughts in a place where he knew he would not be disturbed, in the one place in the house her scent had not invaded. It was not in his nature to deny himself the things he wanted but, for once, he would have to.

Chapter Eleven

ALARIC ENTERED THE tavern and made his way to darkened corner at the back. It was a place to do business, and he was a man with business to attend to. He meant to get them both, and if he was going to do so, he'd need the assistance of some fellows who couldn't be bothered with scruples.

Easing onto one of the hard benches, he signaled for a tankard of ale. One of the serving wenches came over shortly and placed it before him. "You've got no credit here," she said.

Alaric smiled and tossed her one of his few remaining coins. "I've no need of credit," he said. "Soon, I'll be as flush as Golden Ball himself."

"Aye," she said, clearly skeptical. "And until you are, you'll pay for every tankard as it's delivered."

"You'll get your money," he said. "I'm looking for a couple fellows to do a bit of work for me. Big. Strong. Not missish if it gets a bit messy."

She surveyed him for a moment. "I might know of one or two. I reckon they'll be in tonight. They usually are."

"There'll be another coin in it for you if you send them my way."

"You're all flush now, aren't you? Where you getting this money from?" she demanded.

"I can spend what I have because there is a promise of more… so much more," Alaric said. "And maybe, when it's all said and done, I can buy you a new frock and help you out of that old rag you're wearing right now."

She threw her head back and cackled, her generous bosom jiggling from her mirth. "I'd like to see the day you'd spend a groat on anyone other than yourself... and new frock or not, you'll not be warming yourself beneath my skirts. I knew Alice, you see. Knew her to be kind and sweet... and too bloody good for the likes of you. So I'll take your money, I'll send the miscreants and criminals that you want to hire to your table, but only because you're a paying customer. And you'll only ever get a drink in this establishment, no matter what you pay!"

Alaric watched the serving girl stomp off, her skirts and her ample backside swishing. She'd come around. They always did. Loyalty was a commodity few could afford in the rookeries. Her rent would be due and she'd be tossing her skirts up for him soon enough. It wasn't even that he wanted her, but he'd be damned if she wouldn't want him.

It didn't take long for two younger men to enter the tavern. They spoke with the barmaid for a moment or two and then ambled in his direction. The larger of the two spoke first.

"I hear you're looking for fellows to do some work."

"I am," Alaric replied. "My daughter has been taken by her uncle. He's a toff. He means to keep her from me. Her governess walks her in the park often enough... I need you to help me get her back."

"In the park. You mean Hyde Park? Where all the gentlemen and ladies associate?" the younger one said. "We're not going to swing for the likes of you."

"She's my daughter. He cannot have us arrested for taking my own daughter. If he were not a lord, I'd be the one having him taken to the gaol," Alaric said, and he sounded so morally outraged that he almost convinced himself. "This is my daughter... now that her mother is gone, she's all I have left in the world. I need your help to get her back. Please."

"What's the pay?"

"A pound each," Alaric said.

"Not enough to even bother with," the larger of the two answered. "We won't do it for less than five each."

The other one nodded in accord.

Alaric bit back a smile. He'd have paid ten to both, so it was still a bargain. "Five pounds each it is then." He pulled some coins from the small purse he carried. "Half now and the remainder when the job is done. Fair enough?"

"Fair enough," the other man agreed as his companion nodded. "When?"

"We'll watch the house tomorrow and see what they're about," Alaric replied. "That's why I need the two of you. They know my face and they'll be watching for me. Meet me here at nine in the morning."

When the two men had gone, Alaric returned to his ale. If he could get Marina out from under Deveril's watchful eyes, he had no doubt the bastard would pay to get her back. At least a thousand pounds. Perhaps even more. He'd just have to wait and see. Perhaps he'd let Deveril make the first offer and see just what he thought the brat was worth. He certainly didn't want to cheat himself out of the largesse that Lord Deveril could clearly afford.

A tiny bit of doubt played at the edges of Alaric's mind. What would he do if Lord Deveril didn't pay? What would happen if he wound up stuck with the child? *Get rid of her.* It was what he'd asked Alice to do from the beginning, after all. Children disappeared in the city all the time, lost to the rookeries and abbesses. No reason that screaming brat should any different, he decided.

DEVIL HAD ELECTED to avoid the complications of dinner with Miss Marks and his intolerable aunt. He fled to his club. If he were to be entirely honest, it was not the women in his house who had sent him fleeing. It was his own thoughts. Temptation, especially when one was honor bound to resist it, was torment.

As he approached White's, he realized he wasn't in the mood for it either. He would keep his promise to Miss Marks and not indulge in drink. Gambling was not exactly fun without it, and given his recently "betrothed" state, other vices were forbidden to him as well.

"Going in, Devil? Fancy a game or two?"

Devil looked up to see the Earl of Sefton waggling his eyebrows at him much like an old woman. "Not tonight. Just looking in," Devil replied.

"Another time then!" Sefton said. "I'm always looking for a good partner for Whist!"

Because the man was terrible at the game himself, Devil thought. No one who had ever been partnered with Sefton for a game had done so out of choice or in admiration of his skill. More often than not it was because he had Prinny's ear. Reminding himself of that fact and that Sefton was a good ally to have, Devil nodded in agreement. "You may count on it."

Allowing Sefton to precede him into the club, Devil looked about him and noted Highcliff in rare dandy form. The man's waistcoat was blinding. Few knew better than him just what an act Highcliff's fashion obsession was. Tailors were a font of information because they were invisible to the nobility and things were discussed freely in front of them that should not have been. Highcliff visited them all and paid them well for their services. *Well and on time.* That set him apart from others of their class and inspired tradesmen's desire to remain in his favor.

Highcliff didn't smile or grin, but the man's lips did twitch with mirth. "Partnering with Sefton? If you're really so desirous of giving away money, I can recommend several excellent charities."

"Let's get a private room... I can't drink, and I haven't the patience to be around drunkards," Devil suggested.

Highcliff's brows shot up. "Then why the hell would you come to a club?"

"Because there are no women here," Devil replied. "And any place where there are no women is a vast improvement to my own home at the moment."

"So it is," Highcliff agreed. "I would like to point out that women tend to congregate where you are, my friend. All the ladies adore you."

"Not these," Devil said. "They are all impervious to my charms, and my house is positively overrun with them right now."

Highcliff grinned. "Surely you don't expect me to remain sober as a symbol of solidarity, do you? If so, you'll need to make other arrangements for a companion this evening. We share a common problem, my friend, and I intend to raise my glass to the lowering disdain of much admired women—repeatedly."

"You may drink as you wish… just don't expect me to pick you up off the floor later," Devil said drolly.

Highcliff signaled for one of the footmen. "A bottle of brandy for me… and a pot of tea for my soon to be leg-shackled friend." When the servant had gone, Highcliff looked back at him. "By the way, I have some information for you about Alaric West. It's not good."

Devil grimaced. "I never suspected that it would be." Finding one of the small alcoves that surrounded the dining room and pulling the heavy drapes to separate it further from the remainder of the room, Devil seated himself in one of the leather chairs. He didn't question Highcliff immediately, but waited until their libations had arrived.

With the footman gone and privacy assured, Highcliff began. "His name isn't West. I'm not certain from whence he hails, yet, but he's quite proud of telling everyone he knows, or simply meets, that he went to Oxford. But there are no records at Oxford of anyone attending by that name."

"So he lied about Oxford," Devil said. "I'm not saying he didn't lie about his name, but the university seems a more likely route for his dishonesty. And I can think of a dozen men right off the top of my head who have lied about what schools they attended or whether they attended them at all!"

"True, but I don't think he's lying about Oxford. I think he's lying about his identity, and Oxford may prove our surest source of information." Highcliff paused and took a long, slow sip of the amber liquid and let out a satisfied sigh. "I do love a good brandy!"

"Now you're intentionally being an ass," Devil accused as he sipped his weak and insipid tea.

Highcliff nodded. "Indeed, I am. Now, back to Mr. West... he wears a signet ring bearing the letter M. He told his tailor it was a W, but the man didn't believe it. The design doesn't work if turned upside down," Highcliff said. "So why lie? Unless there is some scandal attached to his name that would make his moving about in society impossible?"

"That's the question, my friend. That and how he managed to place himself in my sister's path. It's easy enough to know why he abandoned her. My father and his highhanded, tightfisted ways were as much to blame for her disgrace as West. Or whatever his name may be," Devil mused. "But I will not allow this man to destroy my niece, nor will I stand by while he lures some other innocent to the same ill fate that met Alice."

Highcliff's expression was somber but his tone, when he spoke, revealed how puzzled he truly was. "So now you're a crusader? A protector of the innocents? While I know you better than most and know that your sins are not so numerous as others might believe, it's still an unlikely mantle for you to don."

"I've never seduced a woman who didn't understand precisely what sort of arrangement we were entering into," Devil protested. He might have played fast and loose with the rules of society and more than a few less than happily married ladies, but he wasn't without his own brand of morality and honor.

"And to seduce women who already had husbands, thus freeing you from the burden of ever having to wed them yourself. I daresay that was a large part of their appeal, wasn't it? That you'd never find yourself leg-shackled to one of them?"

It was a truthful statement, but that didn't make it sting any less. "And your behavior is so much better?"

Highcliff shrugged. "It isn't about me, my friend. And I'm not condemning you. Just observing."

"Am I the profligate my father always believed me to be then? Beyond redemption?" Devil asked, clearly annoyed with the route the conversation had taken. "I didn't come here for lectures on morality from you, Highcliff. Our sins may be different in nature, but hardly in number."

"Touché," Highcliff replied and poured himself another measure of brandy. "None of us are beyond redemption, Devil. Not you. Not even me."

Perhaps it was the hint of melancholy that he heard in his companion's voice, but something prompted Devil in that moment to utter the very question that had plagued him so. "Have you ever met a woman who tempted you? Not with lust, not with seduction and wicked promises... but with the idea that there might be something more in this life than simply hedonistic pursuits?"

Highcliff sighed. "So that's what it is. It's a woman that's taken your mind on such unusual paths. But to answer your question, I might have. But she's got her causes, just as now you apparently do as well, and they leave no room for me. Perhaps one day, I will be lucky enough to encounter a woman who does inspire such thoughts and who is not opposed to the notion of exploring them with me... when my work is done, of course."

"Your sort of work is never done," Devil pointed out.

"Then I shall invest in a generous store of brandy… I've got ears on the ground about West. I expect to know more about his origins tomorrow."

"The labyrinth of spies—"

"That's an unfortunate term. I prefer informants," Highcliff corrected.

Devil managed to avoid rolling his eyes, but only just. "Your net of informants, then, is capable of finding the information that quickly?"

"Yes, indeed, it is. But we hardly go through traditional or even legal channels."

"And where have you started?" Devil demanded.

"Money," Highcliff replied. "He likes expensive things. He likes to gamble. He tried to ensnare an heiress. It stands to reason that if he's already in debt and using an alias, he's having to seek out alternate sources of funding. Less than reputable sources."

"And you can simply ask these people who he is and what he's about?"

"Not directly," Highcliff conceded. "But that's where my *informants* enter the picture. If money is at the root of what he's doing, then he's already exhausted any other means to lay hands on it. If that's the case, there is no place he can hide forever."

"And how do you know these sources can be trusted?"

Highcliff laughed softly. "I never trust anyone, Devil. Not even you. But that doesn't mean we can't be useful to one another. In my line of work, it pays to cultivate friendships in places low, high, and at every stage in between."

"Friendships?"

"Working friendships," Highcliff corrected.

"It's lonely, isn't it?" Devil asked. "I wasn't in that particular game as long as you, but I did my time in India. It's a hard thing to connect with anyone when the truth can never pass your lips."

Highcliff said nothing for the longest time. "My friend, I have been a professional liar for so long, I doubt I'd know the truth if it bit me on my arse."

Their conversation had taken a dark turn, and Devil wanted nothing more than to make his escape. At the same time, whether he offered any comfort to him or not, Highcliff was his friend and it seemed a terrible thing to leave the man alone to drink away his sorrows. So they sat in silence, as Devil looked enviously at the glass in his friend's hand and then poured himself another cup of tea.

Chapter Twelve

SINCE LORD DEVERIL had made himself scarce at dinner and she had no wish to perpetuate the lie of their betrothal without his assistance, Willa had elected to have her dinner served on a tray in the nursery with Marina. There was something troubling about Lady Carringden with her snide, challenging comments and the way she always seemed to be finding fault with everything and everyone. She knew that Lord Deveril had essentially bribed the woman to come there, but there had to be something else going on.

Entering the nursery, she found the little girl sitting on the edge of her small bed, sleepy eyed and clutching a doll. "Hello, Marina. Are you hungry?" she asked. Willa felt that it was imperative to make things seem as normal for the child as possible, despite the fact that her entire world had been turned upside down.

Cautiously, the little girl nodded.

"Good. Cook has made us a feast. I thought we could have a picnic right here in the nursery," Willa went on and then took the blanket she had brought with her and spread it on the floor. "One of the servants will be bringing our food shortly. Would you like to sit here with me?"

Marina said nothing, just watched her with eyes that were far too wise and far too somber for one so young.

Willa lowered herself to the floor and arranged her skirts about her. "I don't suppose sitting on the floor sounds all that appealing. Not when you have a comfortable bed to rest upon. But I'm too big for your bed. I can't imagine what would happen if I were to sit on it! Why, think how embarrassed I would be if it should break!"

The little girl didn't laugh or smile, but her lips did purse in a manner that indicated she was trying not to. Willa continued, "Imagine, falling on my rather large hindquarters, with skirts all askew, my hair falling down... I'd look ridiculous, wouldn't I?"

Marina's smile broke fully then. It was the first that Willa had seen from her, and it was quite possibly the most beautiful thing she'd ever beheld.

Willa took that as a very good sign. "Marina, can I ask you a question?"

The little girl said nothing, but her gaze became watchful and quite wary.

"Can you speak?" Willa asked. "I heard you ask for your mama. So I know that you can. But I wonder if you can say more than that."

The little girl remained steadfastly silent. Yet, Willa had little doubt that every word she said was perfectly understood. She also had no doubt that the girl was capable of saying whatever she chose to. But for some reason, Marina had elected to be silent. "Are you afraid of someone, Marina? That man in the park, perhaps?"

The little girl said nothing, but her wary gaze was telling enough.

"He frightened me, too," Willa admitted. "But your uncle, Lord Deveril, seemed very determined to keep you safe from him, don't you think? It would help if you could tell us why you're afraid of him. Did you know him before you came here?"

The little girl's eyes narrowed speculatively as she surveyed Willa. It was unnerving to be so thoroughly skewered by a child. Finally, after a long moment, Marina rose from her small bed and crossed the distance to where Willa sat on the blanket spread over the carpet. The little girl sat down beside her and simply leaned against her side.

"You don't want to talk about him, do you?" Willa asked.

Marina shook her head. It was at least a direct response to a question and thus an improvement.

"Fine," Willa agreed. "We won't talk about him... but you have to talk. What is your doll's name?"

There was silence for the longest time. Finally, in a small voice that was little more than a whisper, the little girl said, "She don't have one."

It nearly took her breath away to hear those softly spoken words. Closing her eyes and willing her own tears to remain at bay, Willa managed to ask, "Shouldn't you give her one, then?"

The little girl shook her head again.

"Very well, we'll just wait until she tells us what she would like to be called," Willa stated just as a knock sounded on the door. One of the maids entered, carrying a heavy tray laden with food. She placed it on a table. "You may go. Miss Marina and I will serve ourselves."

"Yes, Miss," the maid said and bobbed a hasty curtsy before exiting the room.

Willa rose and began to fill one of the provided plates with bits of food. She completed one for herself and one for Marina and carried them to the blanket where she sat them before the child. Turning back to the tray, she poured a glass of milk from the provided carafe and a glass of wine for herself. Carrying both back to their small picnic, she seated herself in front of the child so that they were facing one another as they'd eat their meal.

"Do you know that my father never married my mother? Do you know what that makes me, Marina?"

"Bastard," the little girl whispered softly.

"Illegitimate," Willa said. "Some people might use that other word, but it isn't a very nice word. Is it?"

Marina shook her head as she took a small bite of the ham on her plate.

"I don't like to be called that, and I imagine you don't either," Willa offered as she slathered butter on a piece of bread and placed it before the child. "Are you afraid of your uncle, Marina?"

Marina looked up at her then, cocked her head as if considering her answer very carefully, and then shrugged.

"Then you're just not certain about him?"

To that, Marina nodded.

Willa smiled. "You know, I don't think that you need to be afraid of him. He cares about you very much. Do you know what a brother is?"

The little girl nodded once more, her dark curls bobbing.

"He is your mama's brother, and he loved her very much. He was very sad that she was ill."

"Why didn't he save her?"

The question was uttered so softly that, at first, Willa wasn't quite sure she heard it. But the expectant gaze of the child confirmed that Marina had, in fact, spoken aloud. But it wasn't the child who held her interest in that moment. It was the man who stood in the threshold of the open door, Lord Deveril. He was stricken. His face had lost all color and was etched with pain and guilt. Before Willa could say or do anything, he simply stepped back, allowed the door to close softly, and he was gone.

Forcing her gaze back to Marina, Willa explained, "He didn't know where to find her, and he didn't know she was sick until it was too late to save her. He'd been away in the army, you see. But he came for her as soon as he could... and for you. He promised her that he would take care of you and he means to do that if you'll let him."

DEVIL COULDN'T BREATHE. The first words he'd heard his sister's child speak and they damned him completely. Uttered quietly and in that small, thin voice; she was orphaned because he had failed. His wild and erratic behavior had resulted in his exile and that same exile had left his sister vulnerable to fortune hunters and the less than tender parenting of their father, a man who could have given lessons in the art of cruelty.

Retreating, he felt hollow, as if those softly spoken words had gutted him. Entering the solitude of his own chamber, Devil jerked at the knot of his neckcloth. It felt too tight, as did his coat. He managed to strip the offending garments off without shredding them. His waistcoat followed. Finally, in only his breeches and shirtsleeves, he sank down into the chair that faced the fireplace. Leaning against the chair back, he pinched the bridge of his nose to ward off the headache that threatened. He had no notion of how long he sat there that way, lost in his own thoughts and mired so deeply in guilt he might never break free of it.

At the soft knock at his bedchamber door, he barked, "Go away!"

The sound of the door creaking open had him rising to his feet. Fists clenched at his sides, he was prepared to give his valet the dressing down of his life. But it wasn't Whittinger who stood there. It was Miss Marks.

"You cannot take it to heart," she murmured softly. "What she said... she's a child and has no understanding of the kinds of obligations that kept you from her mother's side. Nor does she understand that there were others who, had their hearts been more inclined toward mercy, should have stepped in and offered assistance to her."

"You should not be here," he said. In his present state, his emotions raw and his mood even more unpredictable, having Miss Marks in his chamber, without any prying eyes about them, was a disaster waiting to happen. "You need to leave. Now."

"Lord Deveril—"

He strode toward her until only a scant inch separated them. "If we are familiar enough with one another for you to make free with my bedchamber then the very least you can do, Wilhelmina, is call me by my given name."

"Devil?"

"Douglas," he replied. "But you may call me Devil if you wish… and I will endeavor to give you reason to."

Perhaps it was temper, perhaps it was her impudence in coming into his own bedchamber, or perhaps it was just that the desire to do something that had been tormenting him incessantly from their very first meeting when she had looked down her lovely nose at him. Regardless of the reason, he kissed her. Hauling her close to him, pressing her firmly to his chest, he slanted his lips over hers and tasted the sweetness of her mouth like a man starved for it. But the reason for it was swept away along with every other thought he had. Instead, he could only feel. Heat, softness, the yielding of her body against his, and then the sweetest movement of her lips as she, against her better judgement no doubt, kissed him back.

He let himself simply drink it in, to savor the sweetness of the moment. As much as it stoked the flames of desire in him, it offered something else. There was comfort in having the touch of another. There was something in that kiss that had been lacking in all the debauched and lascivious encounters of his past. Intimacy. He felt close to her, connected to her, as he'd never felt connected to another person in all of his life. And whatever her past, whatever pain and sorrow she'd known, she kissed him back fervently. Her arms came about him and held him to her in a way that was a balm to his soul and to his battered heart and conscience.

That kiss transformed him. It was a revelation for him. He'd bedded some of the most skilled and decadent women in all of London. From those who plied it as a trade to those who were simply unrepentant and extravagant sinners, none had affected him so singularly as the painfully innocent governess in his arms. She kissed like the virgin she was, timid and hesitant. Yet there was passion in her, passion that would likely mortify her to the depths of her prim little soul.

Unable to resist the lure of her incendiary response, he guided her. He nipped at the gentle curve of her lips with his teeth. When she parted her lips in surprise, he swept inside, tasting the sweetness of her mouth in an ancient dance. When she shivered against him, her hands that had rested on his shoulders moved further about him to lock behind his neck, he reveled in it. Whatever else occurred between them, her first taste of true passion would be his.

He spun her around, walking her backward until her back was pressed against the wall next to the hearth and his hands were free to roam over the generous curves of her form. He was mindful of her innocence and mindful of his own honor, unorthodox as it was. While he skimmed the curves of her breasts, the indentation of her waist and the flare of her hips, he didn't linger there. Those touches were simply a method of creating a map in his mind, of memorizing the shape of her so that when he revisited that moment again and again, he might do so with a clear picture of her.

They kissed for what could have been mere seconds or could have been hours. Every tentative touch of her lips and stroke of her tongue against his was both victory and defeat for him. But there was only so far they could go, and he knew beyond question that they were reaching the limit of what a simple kiss could be. And so he eased back and, with a kind of willpower he'd never before had to call upon, gradually lessened the intensity of the encounter until finally the kiss simply ended. Neither of them broke away from the other. They remained there, locked in one another's embrace for the moment as their lips drifted apart and the reality of what had transpired settled around them.

"I told you that you shouldn't be in here," he said as she finally came to her senses and pulled away from him completely.

"I didn't realize my entering the room gave you license to take such liberties!" she snapped as she placed her hands against his chest and shoved with all the might she could muster.

Devil stepped back, allowing her the space she needed in that moment, though it was the last thing he wanted. "Did I take that liberty, Wilhelmina? Or was it given?"

"Of course it was taken. I never gave you permission to kiss me," she insisted hotly as she moved past him. She'd clenched her hands into fists to halt their trembling, but he saw it regardless.

"And yet, you didn't resist. You didn't pull away. And I'm not some young, inexperienced boy who's incapable of recognizing when a kiss is returned," he retorted. "I may have initiated the kiss, but it was completed with cooperation and no small amount of enthusiasm from you."

She faced him then, her eyes blazing with temper and her chin jutting forward with a stubborn tilt that was unmistakable. But even as she glowered and glared, she was silent. There was nothing she could say to that. Any denial that sprang to her lips might be swift, but they both knew it wouldn't be truthful. It was obvious from the mutinous expression on her face as she simply whirled on her heels and marched from the room.

Watching her go, Devil braced himself for what was to come. He had the sinking sensation that Miss Wilhelmina Marks was about to turn his far from well-ordered and quite debauched world entirely on its head.

Chapter Thirteen

WILLA ENTERED THE breakfast room and immediately stopped in her tracks. Lord Deveril was there, seated at the head of the table and reading the morning news sheets as if he hadn't a care in the world. Meanwhile, she looked utterly ragged. She had dark hollows beneath her eyes, and her hair was resistant to any attempts at taming it that morning, likely from the ridiculous amount of tossing and turning she'd done the previous night.

He had kissed her. And despite her wish to deny it, she had kissed him back rather fervently. She had kissed him and, perhaps even worse, she had enjoyed it. And despite the foolishness of such a desire, she wished to do it again. When she'd finally managed to sleep, she'd dreamed of it, but he hadn't stopped at a kiss.

She knew that the encounter, by his standards, had been tame. He could have touched her far more intimately had he wished to do so and, in that moment, she would not have had the sense to stop him. In a strange way, his own way she supposed, he'd been a gentleman. Any other man would have taken her walking, uninvited, into his bedchamber as an invitation to do far more than simply kiss her.

A sigh escaped her as she surveyed him looking, if not smug, at the very least, quite pleased with himself. There was no point in berating herself for it or even being angry at him for it. Douglas Ashton, Lord Deveril, drew women like bees to honey. It was innate, and he couldn't help it any more than he could help drawing his next breath. It was his nature to lure and, heaven help her, she was not so impervious to lust and infatuation as she had once believed. As much as she was learning about Lord Deveril, she was learning even more about herself.

"Good morning, Wilhelmina. I trust you slept well?" he queried.

Smug. Arrogant. Insufferable. Man. Each word was punctuated in her mind, and despite the fact that she was seething, Willa pasted a polite smile on her lips. "Quite well, Lord Deveril." The lie tasted as bitter on her lips as did the pride she was having to swallow. She placed particular emphasis on his title, a reminder to them both of the differences in their rank.

"I thought we had agreed that you would call me by my given name. Given that we are soon to be married, it could not possibly be considered bad form. And when I hear Lord Deveril, I still think of my father. I'd dearly love to avoid thinking of him as much as possible."

She wanted to protest but couldn't come up with a single argument for his perfectly reasonable points that would not damage their paper-thin masquerade even further. But she was saved from answering by the opening of the door. Lady Carringden entered, and her gaze fell like a pall over Willa, surveying her from head to toe.

"What a charming dress. A bold color choice for one with your complexion, though. I'd consider relegating it to items that should only be worn in the house," the woman said as she moved to the sideboard to fill her own plate.

"I thought you made it a habit to breakfast in bed, Aunt?" Lord Deveril asked, a warning in his tone.

"I like a change of pace from time to time, Nephew," she replied haughtily. "And your Miss Marks and I have a great deal of shopping to do if she's to be turned out satisfyingly fashionable enough to be your betrothed. Imagine if people caught sight of her in such a drab thing as she has on now?"

"She is right here," Willa interrupted. "She hears and speaks well enough on her own without being discussed like a misbehaving child who has been banished to her chamber!"

Lady Carringden turned to her then. "My, what a temper you have, Miss Marks. Mind you, it typically behooves one to control such impulses until after the wedding. No man wants to take a shrew to wife."

"If I was shrewish, it was hardly directed at Lord Deveril," Willa replied. She was finding it very difficult to like Lady Carringden and couldn't help but feel the woman had some sort of ulterior motive.

Mrs. Farrelly entered, Marina in tow, sparing any need for further conversation. The little girl was dressed in a pink frock with pretty ruffles, and her wild, dark curls had been tamed with a length of ribbon. The same doll she'd clutched yesterday was tucked beneath her arm.

"Good morning, Marina," Willa offered.

The little girl didn't say anything. She was watching Lord Deveril warily as Mrs. Farrelly assisted her into a chair and fetched her a plate from the sideboard loaded with sausages and bread. She did not acknowledge Lady Carringden at all. "Don't wipe your hands on your dress now, dearie," the cook chided in a gentle way. "Use your serviette as you were taught."

"I thought," Lord Deveril said, "we might go on an outing today, Wilhelmina, along with Marina if she'd like. But if you'd prefer to go shopping with my aunt—"

"An outing sounds lovely. But whatever for?" Willa asked. She'd have gone to look at fertilizer if it would have spared her Lady Carringden's company.

"What do you mean what for?" he replied. "For pleasure. For enjoyment. For fun, Wilhelmina. Surely you are familiar with such things?"

The way his lips had caressed the word pleasure was a sin in and of itself. "I didn't mean what for but rather what sort. What kind of outing are we going on? I'd like to be certain that Marina and I are both dressed appropriately."

He turned to Marina, and there was a shift in his expression, a softening of that impossibly and perfectly masculine face that only made him more appealing. "Would you like to see the Royal Menagerie, Marina? They have tigers and bears and all sorts of creatures. It might be a little frightening, but they're all in cages or enclosures where you'll be perfectly safe."

The little girl's eyes widened. It was clear that she was torn. She desperately wanted to see the animals, but she was still very uncertain of her uncle, that much was apparent. Still, after a moment, Marina's desire to see the menagerie clearly outweighed even her very strong reservations, and she offered him a hesitant nod.

"Wonderful," Lord Deveril said. "We shall leave after you have both broken your fast. And perhaps, this afternoon, before we return home, we can stop at Gunter's for ices. Have you ever had an ice, Marina?"

Of course, she hadn't. They'd lived in abject poverty and squalor, a fact they were both well aware of. But Willa watched the little girl give a wide-eyed shake of her head. She recognized what he was doing. He was feeding the child questions she could answer with a simple shake or nod of her head. He was lulling her into communicating with him. It was brilliant.

He clucked his tongue. "Well, that simply will not do. Everyone should get to enjoy an ice. They have many flavors. Do you like lemon?"

Marina stared at him blankly.

"Have you ever tried lemon?"

Again, the child stared blankly.

Taking pity on him and his complete failure to grasp the deprivation of poverty, Willa stepped in. "The biscuits you had last night before bed were lemon. You liked them didn't you?"

Marina's eyes widened further, and she bobbed her head excitedly. Apparently, the child could be quite motivated by food.

Lady Carringden rose. "I find I'm really not hungry after all. If you'll pardon me, I have some correspondence to attend to." Her tone was one of complete disdain.

Breakfast continued in much the same vein. Marina ate until she was full and then picked at the remaining items on her plate. Lord Deveril would periodically ask her a question that could be answered with a yes or no, and occasionally Willa would step in to save him when it became apparent that he had no notion of what a three-year-old girl might actually know.

After a time, Lord Deveril rose. "I have something I must attend to before we depart. Shall we meet in the foyer at half-past?"

"We will be ready," Willa replied coolly.

"I am looking forward to a day spent in the company of my lovely niece and my lovely betrothed," he said. "I daresay, I will be the envy of every man we meet."

"Empty flattery will not turn my head, Lord Deveril. Douglas," she corrected before he could remind her again to use his given name.

"It is not empty flattery. It is simply the truth. But if you wish to tell me precisely what will turn your head, Wilhelmina, I will endeavor to do it always."

Until he grows bored of me, until he sees another woman who turns his head, until Marina is comfortable enough in his household that I can be dismissed and forgotten. Willa knew that if she let herself lose sight of such things, it would only spell disaster for her. Watching him leave the room, Willa turned her attention to Marina, who eyed her speculatively.

"What? Do I have something on my nose?" she asked and made a face, crossing her eyes and sticking out her tongue.

The tiniest of giggles escaped the girl, and that made all her silliness worthwhile.

>>>><<<<

JEANNETTE CARRINGDEN WROTE the note quickly, scribbling out the information about where her wastrel nephew and his bastard niece would be for the day. The upstart governess—for if they thought they were fooling anyone with their phony engagement, they were sadly mistaken—was beneath her notice. Alaric West had been her niece's lover, but long before he'd been in Alice's bed, he'd been in Jeannette's. It was she who had told him about Alice, after all. Her worthless husband had left her all but penniless, and her brother, Alice's skinflint father, had only given her a pittance to live on. She'd thought if Alaric could seduce Alice into eloping with him, he'd get his hands on her marriage portion. It would have been little enough effort to get rid of her. But her brother had once more ruined her plans. Now, she was scurrying to get back into Alaric's favor as he maneuvered against Devil.

Of course, it wasn't only that. No man had ever entranced her the way Alaric did. Whatever he was accused of, whatever sins he had committed, she adored him... and the way he made her feel. She'd never known pleasure like she experienced in his arms, certainly not with her cretin of a husband. That sort of passion had been sorely missing from her life and she wanted it back. She wanted to feel young and beautiful again... desired.

Looking over the piece of parchment, she read it twice more to be certain it conveyed everything.

If you want the girl, they're taking her to the Royal Menagerie this morning. He has obtained guards, but how many and how heavily armed I do not know.

I miss you. I long for your touch. If I help you with this endeavor, please say we might once more be together.

All my love,

J.

With the missive complete, she sealed it with wax, pressing into it not her own seal but the simple ring he'd given her so long ago. She hoped it would soften his anger toward her in knowing that she had kept it close after such a long time. Rather than summon a maid, Jeannette donned a shawl and quickly slipped from the house to the park entrance across the street. She stood there in full view for several minutes, knowing that if he watched the house, he'd recognize her instantly. Walking to the gate post, she laid the letter at the base of it and placed a stone atop it to hold it there and then fled back to the house. He was her only hope to escape her life of penury and deprivation. If it meant kidnapping that squalling brat and ransoming her back to Devil, so be it. She cared not at all.

Chapter Fourteen

ALARIC RETRIEVED THE note, keeping his hat pulled low to hide his face lest he was observed. It didn't surprise him to see Jeannette there. It did surprise him that she was holding up so well. She'd been a middle-aged woman when they embarked on their affair, more than forty and widowed. But having never had her figure ravaged by child bearing, she'd been supple and had stirred his lust easily enough. But he wasn't typically the forgiving sort, and she was the very reason he found himself in his current predicament. His seduction of Alice Ashton had been her idea, after all, but if she wished to make amends and aid his efforts, he would not deny her the chance.

The missive was short, but conveyed her desperation well. Jeannette had always been a needy and clinging thing. The only thing she wanted more than she wanted him was access to her late brother's fortune. It was what had prompted her to offer up her niece as the sacrificial lamb so to speak.

Retreating into the park once more, he spoke to his hirelings. "We're off to the Tower, boys. The Royal Menagerie."

"I like that. Only been once, but I like to look at the animals," one of the men said. "Like watching 'em feed the tigers. Have you seen one when it's ripping into a side of beef?"

"I've no interest in the bloody tigers, and you're not going to look at them either," Alaric warned. "You're going to watch Deveril and the child. We'll likely not have an opportunity to take her there, but I want to stay close just in case."

"We're gonna hang for this," the wiser of the two brothers said.

"You're being paid for the risk," Alaric snapped. "Now get across the street. I want you right behind them when they head out."

As the brothers departed, Alaric turned his attention back to the posh Mayfair home and watched as the group left the luxurious townhouse. The brat was tucked close to the side of the same woman who'd run off with her the day before, and Lord Deveril was right next to them. As he watched, two men fell in step behind them. Dressed in dark trousers and coats, they had a rough look about them. Runners. The bastard had gone and hired Bow Street Runners. Not that it mattered. Eventually something would happen in the London streets that would provide the distraction he needed.

It would take seconds to snatch the girl and, in a crowded enough street, only seconds to disappear. He'd simply have to stay close and watch for his opportunity.

Glancing across the street, he caught sight of the two men he'd hired. They were standing at the corner of the street, looking for all the world as if they were simply awaiting an appropriate chance to cross. Not even the runners looked twice at them.

With his hat pulled low, Alaric remained several paces back, never getting close enough to be seen. Regardless, he knew that the pretty lady on Deveril's arm sensed something amiss. Several times, he caught her looking back over her shoulder. He smiled at that. There was something quite pleasing to him in the confirmation that she found his presence unnerving. For Alaric, women had always been a means to an end, a way to shore up his always fading fortunes. He'd learned over the years that there were women who only wanted to be hurt. They needed the challenge inherent in loving a man who needed to be saved. And he was willing enough to let them try so long as their purses were plump.

The only reason he'd hung on as long as he did with Alice Ashton had been the vain hope that her father would reconsider and welcome his daughter back into the fold. Sadly, that had never happened. But it no longer mattered. He could use the child to get what should have rightfully been his all along. It wasn't an unreasonable thing to demand what should have been Alice's marriage portion had her father not disowned her... not in exchange for the return of the child. And as much as it stroked his sense of self-importance to know that the pretty blonde was aware of him on such a primal level, as if her very survival depended on it, it was a nuisance as well. So long as she was watchful, he'd have no opportunities to snatch the brat. Not unless he made to snatch them both. It was a complication, and one that he hadn't anticipated, but eyeing her figure beneath the velvet pelisse she wore, he realized that it was an idea that had its own merits as well.

THEY'D REACHED THE Tower without incident and had entered the menagerie with a throng of others. Marina stood only two feet in front of them, her little face pressed against the bars that provided a safe barrier to the pit below where tigers paced in their enclosure. He could feel tension radiating from his faux betrothed.

Devil was not unaware of Wilhelmina's unease. He'd caught her glancing over her shoulder no less than a dozen times. It wasn't that he didn't think her fears were well founded, or even that he didn't feel they were being watched. The truth was that he knew they were. He'd anticipated it. There were half a dozen men surrounding them that he had hired to protect them all, and no one was even aware of them. So if Alaric West, or whatever his bloody name was, attempted anything, short work would be made of him.

"You must relax, Wilhelmina. If you do not give the appearance of enjoying yourself, then Marina will not enjoy herself," he admonished softly.

She looked up at him, her concern evident in her troubled gaze. "I think we've taken an unnecessary risk. I've no wish to make her feel like a prisoner in her home, but I cannot feel that this is safe. What if that man is here? What if he returns?"

Devil offered what he hoped was a reassuring smile. "I expect that he will return. I have little doubt that he is watching us even as we speak. Do you truly think I would have brought either of you here without taking every safeguard and precaution?"

"I hadn't considered it one way or the other. What sort of safeguards and precautions?" she demanded.

"I have hired guards. Not just the runners who followed behind us, but there have been others on the street, following much more discreetly, since we left the townhouse. These are men who have made it their life's work to function in the shadows and go unnoticed. In the past, they did so for king and country. Now, they do so for hire."

"Mercenaries?"

"Soldiers who no longer have a war to fight," he corrected. "We are as safe as I can make us without remaining locked inside the house."

Her eyes narrowed. "Are we bait then? A piece of meat laid in a trap to lure him in?"

"No. That is not at all what I mean... I am bribing my niece, Wilhelmina. There is no other word for it. I am offering up these outings and toys and treats as a way of getting her to spend enough time with me to no longer see me as a threat," he admitted. "You wanted me to get close to her, to be her family. And I am trying. I need her not only to feel safe with me, but to want to be there as well. My greatest fear, Wilhelmina, is that she will be so miserable in my home that she will try to run away to what is familiar. I don't need to tell you what dangers exist in this city for a child so small and so incapable of protecting herself."

It was a fear he'd never spoken aloud, but it was one that made him wake up in a cold sweat nearly every night. He could easily recall the wails and screams the poor child had emitted as he'd carried her away from the rapidly cooling body of her mother. The memory of those moments, of watching the light leave Alice's eyes and knowing the very second that her soul was gone and only the shell remained, haunted him. But the child didn't know. She couldn't know. And she likely hated him because he'd pulled her away. Why wouldn't she run?

"I think you underestimate her intelligence, my lord. Marina is a child, but she's one who has grown up in an environment that promotes a deep understanding of self-preservation. And while the concepts of life and death may not be something she can put into words, I've little doubt that she understood that her mother was no more. What else would she attempt to return to? She knows she cannot fend for herself in this world because, while it might pain you to hear it, she likely has been for some time. As ill as your poor sister was, she could not have been providing much for the child. And if this Mr. West is the bounder we both recognize him to be, then we know he was not providing for them either."

The words were offered gently—factually—and lacked any hint of reproach. He was thankful for that.

"I should have been there to take care of them. And I was not through no one's fault but my own. I can lay it on my father's head all I wish to, but the simple fact is that, had I not been so consumed with pursuing my own pleasures with no thought of the consequences, I could have protected her had I not been exiled."

"And perhaps if your father had been a kinder and more loving man, you might have had something in your life beyond hedonistic pursuits. We all have our ways of dealing with pain, my lord."

"Douglas," he corrected automatically. "Or Devil, if you prefer."

She looked at him for a moment, her gaze thoughtful and surprisingly gentle. "I do not prefer. Too many people in your life have attached such an unfortunate moniker to you. You have been labeled wicked so often you believe that you can be nothing else... Douglas."

Devil said nothing, just turned his face away and watched his niece as she stared in rapt wonder at the beasts below. Moving closer to her, he knelt down. "When I was in India," he whispered, "there was a man, a prince, who became a friend of mine. He had one of them as a pet. It had been orphaned as a cub and had been raised on milk from other animals and then hand fed meats. It was gentle as a lamb. I got to pet it once."

"Soft?"

It took him a moment to realize the child had even spoken, her voice was so timid and low. But when it registered, he smiled. "It's actually very rough, but only on top. If you dig a little deeper, there's fur underneath that top layer of coarse hair that is as soft as down."

Devil watched her and saw her eyes widen, saw the smile that curved her little doll-like lips. She was the image of Alice, and he vowed in that moment she would never know the kind of pain and suffering that his sister had, no matter the cost.

⁂

WILLA WATCHED HIM and felt her heart stutter beneath her breast. He robbed her of breath in that moment and she knew, without even having to utter the words aloud, that she was doomed. In a matter of days, she'd become completely infatuated with him. Not his wickedness. Not his handsomeness. No. She'd fallen completely and utterly under his spell as she bore witness to the hidden gentleness in him that he showed so rarely but that seemed to influence every decision he made. It was a terrible balancing act, providing opportunities for Marina to discover happiness in his household and also keep her safe.

As much to provide a reprieve for her overstimulated emotional state as to monitor their safety, Willa glanced around them looking for the guards he'd indicated would be nearby. If they were, then they were clearly the experts at clandestine engagement he'd labeled them for she couldn't spot them at all. But even as she thought it and turned back to Lord Deveril and his ward, she caught sight of a familiar face.

"He's here," she said, but there was a loud shriek from a woman nearby as one of the tigers in the enclosure leapt at another one. It masked the sound of her voice. Fearful of losing sight of him, she kept her gaze locked on Alaric West. But he simply tipped his hat to her and once more receded into the crowd.

"What did you say?" Lord Deveril asked, rising to stand at his full height beside her.

"I saw West," she replied. "He was over there, and he had two other men with him. But he saw me. I looked right at him, and he tipped his hat and then vanished into the crowd. I think he's simply toying with us."

Lord Deveril looked over the top of her head into the crowd and waved his hand in the direction she'd indicated.

Looking back, Willa saw six men in respectable but hardly note-worthy clothing suddenly separate from the crowd and move in the direction he'd indicated. She'd looked right past those men, unassuming and appearing to be simply part of the throng. She'd had no idea they had been so close to them all along. "My heavens. I had not realized they were all within shouting distance."

"I was taking no chances," he replied. "I will do whatever is necessary to keep you safe."

"To keep Marina safe," she corrected.

"To keep you both safe," he amended. "It is not just her to whom he poses a threat, Wilhelmina. And I would not have you in danger either."

Uncomfortable with his steady regard, Willa looked away hurriedly. "We should move on from here on the chance he might return."

"We should," he agreed and added in a slightly louder tone that Marina was certain to overhear, "There are elephants to be seen after all."

The little girl left the bars where she'd been peering down into the tiger cage and ran up to them, eagerly taking his hand.

What unfolded in that moment nearly broke her. Willa saw his face—the hope and the joy that filled him when the child reached out to him. But she also saw his loneliness. He'd worn it like a familiar cloak, and it was only obvious in its absence. For all his womanizing and drinking, for all his gambling and fighting, Douglas Ashton—Lord Deveril—was a very lonely man, one filled with pain and grief. It moved her in ways she knew would be disastrous.

For her own safety, for her own peace of mind, and for her ability to maintain any semblance of propriety in her thoughts, she needed to not see that in him. Being attracted to him was difficult enough. Being infatuated with him was terrible for her. But genuinely liking him was nothing short of ruinous. But feeling that common bond of loneliness placed her on the precipice of disaster. It was that which could transform reckless infatuation into love, and she could not afford to love him. The cost was too great.

"Come, Wilhelmina," he urged softly and held out his other arm to her. "Let us enjoy the remainder of our day here and not think of West and his plots and schemes."

With trepidation and a heart that beat far too quickly, Willa placed her hand on his arm and allowed him to lead her through the crowd.

Chapter Fifteen

THEIR AFTERNOON AT the menagerie had been a success. He wouldn't say that Marina was completely trusting of him just yet. The child was still speaking very little, and when she did, it wasn't more than a whisper. But she no longer cowed or shrieked if he was near. Somehow, Wilhelmina's presence had created enough of a buffer that she could at least begin to open up to him. He longed for the day when Marina lost that cautiousness and her slightly haunted gaze.

A carriage had been hired to take them home as the weather had turned and the threat of imminent rain had materialized. Marina was asleep on the carriage seat, exhausted from her adventure. She rested serenely against Wilhelmina's side. They looked like a Renaissance painting. In the dimly-lit interior of their hired conveyance, Wilhelmina's blonde locks could pass for the same red-gold hue that her much beloved Titian had favored.

"It's impolite to stare, Lord Deveril" she murmured softly.

Despite the presence of the sleeping child, there was something incredibly intimate about sitting in that small, enclosed space with her. With the sound of the rain outside dampening the sounds of the city, it felt as if they were the only people in the world. He found he rather liked the feeling and that, in and of itself, was reason enough to panic. He'd been attracted to women before, had been drawn to and infatuated with them. And yet with Miss Wilhelmina Marks, it was more than that. He felt an ease and a comfort with her, a sense of peacefulness in her presence that made him all too aware of what had previously been missing from his life. In short, she made him want things that he'd never imagined he would or even could.

What if they were truly betrothed? What if the two of them were to build a life together and bring up Marina in a real family? What if they were to have children of their own?

"I thought we agreed you'd call me Douglas? And you'll have to forgive my impudence," he replied. "I have seldom seen something so worthy of being stared at."

The light was too poor for him to see her rolling her eyes at such flattery, but he was aware of it nonetheless. And while it might have sounded like empty flattery, it was one of the most truthful statements he had ever made. Somehow, every time he looked at her, she seemed to grow more lovely. "It is quite true, Wilhelmina." She looked away, and while he couldn't see her blush, he was sure it was present.

"I despise that name, if you must know," she said quietly.

He had suspected. "Why?"

"My father's name is William. My mother couldn't give me his surname, so she did her best to give me his given one. It's a reminder of things I'd rather not be reminded of," she admitted.

The answer was given in an almost flippant tone, as if it were something that she had no emotion about whatsoever. Yet, he knew that was not the case. He could sense the tension in her, could feel the anger and, yes, the hurt. Her father's rejection of her, for it could not be considered anything less, still pained her. But one didn't have to be a bastard to feel that.

"William. And his last name?"

"Does it matter?" she asked.

"Oddly enough, yes."

"Why?" she demanded, mirroring his earlier query to her.

"Because I find it distasteful to know that I might have sat across from him at a card table or at a dinner. I might have laughed and joked with him at a club. I'd like to be certain I do not do so again," he offered.

"William Satterly, he's the youngest son of Lord Heatherton. And yes, you've likely done all those things."

He had, in fact. He neither liked nor disliked Satterly. The man was a bit of a rake but nothing untoward. His reputation was innocuous enough that he was permitted by even the most fastidious of hostesses.

"Have you ever actually met the man?"

Wilhelmina nodded slightly, a faint movement that he sensed more than saw in the dim interior of the carriage. "A time or two. Most often, he could not be bothered."

"Perhaps that is a blessing," he suggested. "If the man is so lacking in character and morals, then being subjected to him more frequently might have done you greater harm."

"Or he could simply have been a better man. Would that have been so difficult?" Wilhelmina asked.

"My father sent me to India hoping I would die there. He meant to get himself a young wife and have another son to inherit because he despised me so," Devil said softly. "And he discarded Alice just as quickly, because when she fell from grace, she was no longer an asset to him. That's what we were. Property. Assets. Things to be bought, bartered, sold, and used to further whatever agenda he possessed at any given time. So to answer your question, some men are better, some men can be better... and some are simply broken inside, like sharp bits of glass."

She was silent for the longest time. Marina stirred in her sleep, mumbled softly, and then settled again. "I'm sorry that your father failed you as well, Lord Deveril."

"Douglas," he corrected again. "And you still haven't told me what you'd prefer to be called."

"I would have you call me Miss Marks, but as you are insistent upon taking liberties and maintaining this farce of an intimate acquaintance, you may call me Willa. It is what my friends call me."

Devil smiled. "And are we friends, Willa?"

Her head tilted to one side, not coquettishly though it might have given that appearance had he not had a better understanding of her character. She answered thoughtfully, "We are not enemies. But we must, specifically in private, recall that our stations in life and the paths we must take are quite divergent."

"Our stations? Are you not the daughter of a gentleman?" he challenged. Did she really think the matter of her birth was such an obstacle?

"I am the illegitimate daughter of a gentleman and your governess in secret," she replied sharply. "A bastard."

Marina mumbled in her sleep once more. A single word escaped her. "Bastard."

Devil couldn't help but grin. "Well, at least we know she can speak."

"It isn't funny. And it's not a word she should know much less utter. But my status is not something either of us can afford to forget. I'll be no man's mistress, and if you were prepared to be someone's husband, it would not be to a woman of my standing. That, my lord, is what we should endeavor to remember. Whatever you think, whatever you may desire of me, it is not something I can afford to give you."

"I have not asked you to." *Yet.* They both knew he would. It was a feeling between them, inevitable and irrefutable. Every moment in her presence cemented for him that there was something special about her, something different. She was not swayed by his looks, by his fortune, by his reputation. In fact, all of those things seemed to prompt contempt in her. Yet when he revealed anything of his pain, of his guilt and misery, she was sympathetic and compassionate. In short, she was unlike any woman he'd ever known.

"No, you have not. And yet I'm aware of your interest," she said pragmatically.

He didn't insult her intelligence by denying it. She spoke nothing less than the truth, so he simply let it be.

After a long pause where she looked out the window into the rain, she added, "The things that passed between us yesterday, in your chamber and in your study... they cannot be repeated. And moments such as this one, we should seek to avoid them. While Marina's presence does provide us with a reason to be together, we both know that it alone is not adequate to prevent temptation. Any future outings should include Lady Carringden, much to my dismay, not only for the sake of propriety, but because—"

She'd broken off abruptly, uncomfortable at finishing the thought.

"Because?" he prompted.

"Because it isn't merely your intentions that are the cause of concern. I am not immune to your charm, whatever you may believe. I am drawn to you, as it appears you are to me, and failing to acknowledge that could be disastrous for us both. It's best to be open and take precautions against any inadvisable action."

A soft laugh escaped him. "I've never heard it termed such... inadvisable action. How can you be certain that my intentions aren't honorable?"

"Even if your intentions are honorable, we both know I would have to reject any offers from you. To do less would be dishonor on my own part."

"Because you are illegitimate? Many men marry women whose birth is questionable and vice versa!"

"The illegitimate offspring of titled lords and ladies, or the exalted mistresses of men who have wealth, power, and social cache! My mother was the daughter of a baker, and she was selling far more than bread when she met my father! It's hardly the same thing!"

"What a terrible snob you are, Willa. If your birth and station are not obstacles for me, why on earth should they be for you?"

It was her turn to laugh. "Are you proposing then?"

"Not as such," he said. "Merely pointing out that if I should choose to do so, your station would be neither an impediment nor an inducement. It is inconsequential, in fact."

"Inconsequential?" she asked with a snap to her voice.

"Rest easy. I do not say so to dismiss what you have surely endured in your life as a result of your father's dishonorable behavior toward your mother... I only say that I care not for the opinions of others. They do not dictate my choices."

She scoffed at that. "Nor do they dictate your behavior given how freely you have courted scandal. I'd be nothing more than another one to add to your very long list. I wonder, in fact, if that is not a source of my appeal to you. What better way to thumb your nose at society, after all?"

"You do yourself a disservice, Wilhelmina—Willa—if you think that your appeal is sourced from anything but your own person and the numerous charms you possess. But we shall call Pax for now, and I can attest that my intentions are pure, even if my thoughts are not," he vowed firmly.

There was no further opportunity to speak as the carriage rolled to a halt before the townhouse. The guards were not present, but then it was a short enough distance from the carriage to the door that he felt perfectly able to defend them from any threat in that space. "Wait inside the carriage until I tell you it is clear," he said.

"We will, my lord."

"Douglas." It was an absentminded correction, because his mind was already occupied outside the carriage, scanning the street for potential dangers prior to disembarking.

"DOUGLAS." THE NAME was but a whisper upon her lips, but he was already gone, out into the street to survey their surroundings. Next to her, Marina stirred but did not awaken. The conversation in the coach had left her shaken, uncertain and as terrified of her own intentions and her own potential wickedness as she was of his.

He was too handsome, too witty, too much of everything, in truth. He left her feeling unsettled—*wanting*. She wasn't so foolish as to not understand attraction and even desire. Had she not borne witness to her mother's disgraces, after all? While she'd had no experience herself with carnal matters, she was not ignorant of them. It took little imagination to suspect that Douglas Ashton, Lord Deveril, would be an expert in such matters and that if she chose to travel that dangerous path, no one else could lead her down with such abandon and undeniable pleasure. But such thoughts were not conducive to her maintaining the propriety that she demanded from him.

"Come along, Marina. Wake up, child," she muttered softly. "We must go into the house, dear."

The little girl did not rouse but simply snuggled more deeply into her side. Clearly contenting herself with the notion that she'd be forced to simply carry the tot inside, Willa smiled. "I know you're awake and that you are simply pretending, but it's all right. You needn't walk if you do not wish to. I shall carry you."

She felt the girl's smile though it was far too dark in the carriage for her to see it. Still, it prompted one of her own. Tugging the child closer, Willa lifted her and rose to disembark from the coach. Opening the door, she peered out. "Is it clear?"

Lord Deveril didn't immediately respond, remaining quiet. After a moment, he gave a jerky nod. When he spoke, he said, "Stay alert. I see nothing, but I cannot help but feel there is something that is not quite right." He'd no more than uttered the words than two dark figures emerged from the shadows.

"Douglas?" Willa whispered, her voice tremulous with fear.

"Run. Get her inside," he commanded sharply.

Chapter Sixteen

S PURRED BY THE urgency in his voice and by the fear she felt for Marina, Willa did as he commanded. She leapt down from the carriage, ignoring the pain in her feet as the thin soles of her walking boots connected with the paving stones. She made for the door with Marina clutched closely to her. She had not even raised her hand to knock when the door opened and the butler stared askance at her. Willa ignored his scandalized expression. "Send footmen out at once to aid Lord Deveril. He's been set upon by footpads!"

The butler sprang into action immediately, and several strong and able-bodied footmen rushed through the door from whence she had just entered. It was fear more than anything else that prompted her to sink onto the stairs with Marina still clinging to her. She glanced down at the child and saw that the girl's face was white and her eyes were closed so tightly.

"It's all right, love. You're safe here. I've got you. And Lord Deveril will be just fine."

"He sent them to get me," the little girl whispered. It was apparent from her tone and the look of terror on her tiny face that she feared the man she spoke of and that she had good reason to.

Willa stroked the little girl's hair and murmured softly, "No one's going to get you, my darling girl. You uncle will send them away and all will be well."

"No. No. No."

"Who do you think sent them, Marina?"

The little girl sobbed again. "Man in the park."

"Did you know him before you came here, Marina? Perhaps when you were with your mother?" Willa asked.

The little girl nodded but closed her lips together in a way that indicated she'd say nothing further. It was an expression Willa was becoming accustomed to.

"Is he your father?"

The little girl nodded again, still clinging to her fiercely.

"Did he strike you, Marina?"

This was answered with a shake of the little girl's head.

"Did he strike your mother then?" Willa asked.

To that, the child nodded and sobbed harder.

"He'll never hurt her again. She's far beyond his reach, my dearest, and your uncle will never let him harm you. I promise," Willa offered as soothingly as she could. It was difficult to keep her tone calm when she was terrified of what was occurring just beyond the door. She'd seen the two men emerging from the shadows though she hadn't gotten a good look at them. Nonetheless, she feared for Lord Deveril. He had been a soldier, and she had little doubt that he would be able to handle himself adeptly in such an altercation, but those men were criminals and armed.

DEVIL STARED AT the two large men, sizing them up and measuring his own ability to emerge unscathed. It didn't look good. They looked enough alike that they could be twins. If not, they were brothers at the least of it. That was unfortunate. Fighting a pair of siblings was always difficult. They seemed able to read one another's minds almost, to predict what the other would do. It made them formidable opponents even more so than the size of their bodies. But there were certain points in his favor. The larger of the two was a bit more lumbering in his movements. He lacked the grace of a natural fighter, and if he fell, he'd fall hard. That was the goal then, get him on the ground and out of commission right out of the gate.

As they circled one another, the slightly smaller and significantly more nimble of the two chuckled. "A toff like you... think you can take us, do you?"

He didn't need to take them. Only delay them. At least some of the guards he'd hired were en route via a hired hack while others made the trek on foot. Some of them would no doubt arrive within minutes. "I think I'll give you more trouble than you're expecting," Devil said. It was a modest statement. He'd been trained in hand to hand combat, in Eastern styles of fighting that those men would likely have never seen before. It was to his benefit if they underestimated him.

The larger of the two lunged at him then. Devil sidestepped easily and, as the man passed him, grasped the man's coat and tugged it upward, binding his arms and putting him off balance. The hired ruffian careened into the side of the building, his head bouncing off the stone steps as he tumbled.

"Lummox," the other henchman murmured as he withdrew a wicked-looking blade from inside his coat. "You'll find me a bit harder to knock senseless."

"Duly noted," Devil said, fully aware of the blade and the fact that the man handled it with a degree of skill that warranted wariness. "I suppose the question is what motivates you? If it's money, I can offer you as much to go away as West paid you to come here."

The man shrugged. "Toffs ain't the only ones what keep their word."

"West won't. He's promised you funds he doesn't have," Devil said.

"That's between me and him, ain't it?"

There was no reasoning with the man, Devil realized. He'd made his choices and he meant to stick by them. The only thing he could do was prepare to defend himself. With that in mind, Devil watched him closely. He ignored the blade. It would never tell the story. To know what the villain would do, he'd need to watch the man's eyes. His every intent would play out there for the world to see, if one had the ability to read it. And Devil did. His time in the army had seen to it.

They circled one another slowly. But, just as he'd suspected, Devil could tell. The other man's nostrils flared, his eyes narrowed, and then he lunged. Devil was ready for him. He stepped to the side once more, but his opponent was far more skilled than he'd allowed for, and ambidextrous. As he moved past him, the blade switched from one hand to the next and sliced through the sleeve of Devil's coat.

His flesh burned from the cut, but Devil ignored it. He whirled away swiftly, preventing further damage, just as he brought a booted foot up and caught the other man on his knee, sending him to the ground just as his brother roused.

At that moment, a bevy of footmen erupted from the house. They eyed the melee with trepidation. They were ill-suited to intervene, all of them young and green as grass. They didn't know how to fight, much less face an assailant armed with a blade. But it was the commotion at the end of the street that caused them all to glance up. It was the remainder of Devil's hired guards making their way toward them in the nick of time.

"Get up!" the knife-wielding assailant hissed at his companion. Together, the two men stumbled toward the nearest alley. Only seconds later, a cart emerged, the two of them on the back of it and made off down the street.

Gripping his upper arm to stanch the flow of blood, Devil watched their escape. Perhaps it was unwise to let them go. Of course, West likely didn't have money to replace them as assailants. Knowing their faces would give him an edge as they could no longer blend into the crowd. At least, if they were to come after them again, Devil would spot them a mile away.

Cursing, he climbed the steps and made his way inside. He wanted a drink, but had given up all of his vices, not to mention his endless suffering from somewhat unrequited lust. Almost from the first moment he'd set eyes on Miss Wilhelmina Marks, he'd been exercising self-denial. The physical altercation outside had provided at least some kind of release. Resolving to go more frequently to Gentleman Jackson's, Devil surveyed his niece and her secret governess with concern.

"How badly are you injured?" Willa demanded. "We need to send for the doctor."

"There's no need," he said. "It's but a scratch."

Her eyes widened even as her jaw firmed with indignation he knew he would pay for later. "A scratch? And was this scratch made with a knife or a sword?"

Devil noted the high color in Willa's cheeks, the firm jut of her chin, and the tightness of her features. She had gone from terrified to angry, and it was safe to say that her anger was, in that moment, directed at him. "My valet can tend the wound with skill that is at least equal and likely surpasses what most physicians might provide. Why don't you get Marina settled with Mrs. Farrelly and then we may discuss it further." He made the offer in a conciliatory tone though it was apparent to him that she was in no mood to accept it accordingly.

Willa rose with Marina still in her arms and began to climb the stairs, Devil right behind her. He was enjoying the sway of her hips beneath her skirts far more than was advisable. That was the problem with a good row; it got the blood up, and there was no relief in sight. Mrs. Farrelly met them on the landing, clucking sympathetically as she plucked Marina from Willa's arms and fussed over the girl. He wondered if perhaps the housekeeper's cosseting of the child was the best approach but, at the same time, Marina would let so few people near her there was really no other option.

At the top of the stairs, their paths diverged. Willa followed Mrs. Farrelly toward the nursery while he turned toward his own chambers. The door had not even closed behind him as he began stripping off his ruined coat and waistcoat. He was pulling his shirt over his head and tossing the stained garment on the floor when a soft but rapid series of knocks sounded on the door. It opened, and Wilhelmina stepped inside. She closed the door behind her and turned toward him. Only then did she note his state of undress. Her eyes widened, her cheeks pinkened even further, and then she simply averted her gaze.

"I did not realize you were not dressed," she said, clearly discomfited. "I will return later."

"Are you certain you don't wish to inspect the wound yourself?" he asked. It was as much about goading her as it was about the fact that he didn't want to see her go. Being so close to her was a temptation he could ill afford, but it held its own unique pleasures.

While she was not looking directly at him, her perfect profile was presented, and it was evident when her eyebrows rose upward. Her expression revealed her suspicions. "And deprive your very capable valet of the chance to utilize his medical skills? I think not."

Nothing more was said as the valet did, indeed, come rushing in at that moment, his medical supplies in hand. A maid was right behind him, carrying a ewer of clean water.

"My lord," the valet said, his tone concerned.

Devil looked down at his chest which was liberally coated with blood and conceded that the wound might be more than a scratch, but it was hardly cause for such worry and fuss.

"Don't be a mother hen, Whittinger. Just dress the wound and be done with it. My betrothed and I have much to discuss, particularly the fact that there will not be any further outings of any sort until West is apprehended," Devil said. He looked up at Willa. "No protests from you?"

"No," she replied. "I have no reason to protest. In fact, I was going to suggest that very thing. I think, for the time being, that Marina should be restricted to the confines of the house and the small garden out back. The risks are too great and Mr. West too unpredictable... and too determined it would seem."

Devil nodded as Whittinger began cleaning the wound, plucking at the fibers from his clothes that were now trapped in it. Wilhelmina's face blanched and she looked away once more. Using her shock and upset at his condition to his advantage, Devil pressed on. "I'm glad you are in agreement, Miss Marks, because that edict will apply to you as well. West has seen you with Marina. He knows the girl is attached to you just as he has now seen that you are attached to her. He may not understand the nature of our relationship, but he will likely have surmised that you could be used to sway me just as Marina could. It's a risk I will not have you take."

She blinked owlishly for a moment. "I am to be confined to the house as well then? I am not a prisoner, my lord. I am a go—"

"My betrothed. And as such, I cannot risk the stain upon my conscience and, even more so, the pain it would cause me if something were to happen to you when it is in my power to prevent it," he cut her off. While he was fairly certain that most of servants suspected their betrothal was a sham, no one needed to know the true nature of their arrangement. It would create gossip that West could likely use to his advantage.

Wilhelmina drew in a deep settling breath. "For how long?"

Whittinger began stitching the knife wound. He'd applied the disgusting salve that he always used for such injuries, a repulsive but effective concoction that he'd discovered while serving as Devil's batman in India. The mixture had pain relieving properties and had also prevented putrefaction of the any wounds it had ever been applied to. The smell was indescribable and positively rank. But as the valet began dragging the needle through his flesh, Devil felt only the tug and pull of the thread rather than the agony he should have. It was unnerving but relatively painless.

"I hope it will not be for very long, Miss Marks. It is not my wish that you should feel confined or imprisoned in my home. But these are risks we cannot afford to take. Please, I would have your consent," he said.

"Why?" she asked. "We both know that if you elect to keep me within these walls, there is naught I could do to prevent it."

"I'm not a villain, Miss Marks, attempting to keep you locked away like some Drury Lane monstrosity," he said with exasperation as Whittinger tugged the thread taut and tied off the last of the stitches. "I want to keep you safe. Do I really need to list all the ways in which a man such as Alaric West could pose a threat to you?"

She glared at him. "Contrary to what you may think, Lord Deveril, I am neither stupid nor particularly naive."

It was at this point, Lady Carringden knocked upon the door and simply let herself in. "I can hear the two of you shrieking at one another down the corridor! Really, Douglas, must you behave so abominably? And as for you, Miss Marks, it is highly improper for you to be in here alone!"

"We are not alone. The servants are present," Devil snapped, unwilling to be besieged by two angry women at the same time.

"Servants are hardly adequate!" Lady Carringden insisted. "If you mean to utterly destroy Miss Marks' reputation, by all means, persist. Otherwise, I have to insist, Douglas, that she leave this room with me at once!"

"I do beg your pardon, Lady Carringden, but in light of Lord Deveril's injury, it is hardly improper that we should be here to attend him," Willa stated emphatically.

His aunt harrumphed loudly. "Honestly, my dear girl! It's not as if you'd know what is proper at all! You seem to be about as well informed on that matter as you are on proper child rearing techniques—"

"Enough!" Devil shouted. "Aunt Jeannette, you are here to preserve the illusion of propriety. That is all. Remove yourself from my chamber, please."

She drew herself up, shoulders back and stiff. "And if I do not?"

"Then you will be forcibly removed from it. Miss Marks is in no danger from me at this moment, but we do require privacy. There are matters which must be discussed, and those matters are of a private nature." His response had been uttered in a more carefully modulated tone, but it was no less firm and brooked no argument.

A squeak erupted behind him. "In your bedchamber, my lord?" Whittinger queried, utterly scandalized.

"Now is hardly the time, Whittinger, unless you wish to be removed from this chamber along with my aunt!" Devil said bluntly. "And I'm more likely to throttle her than seduce her at this point, so the both of you may rest assured her virtue is safe!"

The valet drew himself up to his full but still diminutive height. "Very well, my lord. But I shall remain in the corridor for the sake of propriety."

"I shall not!" Lady Carringden snapped. "I've had about enough from you both! You, Douglas, with your snapping and your temper. And your betrothed," the word was uttered with a derisive sneer, "she reeks of the gutter, and you may pretty it up as you choose, but it's clear to me that this is an immoral household and my influence will make no matter there! As soon as I can make proper arrangements, I'll be returning to my own home. I'll not gossip about you, but I'll not support whatever lies it is that you mean to tell. If I am asked, Nephew, I will speak the truth!"

When she was done, Jeannette turned on her heel and strode from the room, leaving shocked servants in her wake. After a moment of stunned and very uncomfortable silence, the servants bustled out. "Am I really so lacking in authority in my own home?"

Wilhelmina looked at him with pure venom in her gaze. "Clearly not, as you have expressed that I am to be cloistered here!"

"Do not say cloistered," he snapped. "I may have to live like a monk for the time being, but I refuse to have my house likened to a monastery!" He rose from the small settee at the foot of the bed where he'd sat while Whittinger had tended his wound. Crossing to his wardrobe, he removed a fresh shirt and began the arduous process of putting it on while moving his right arm as little as possible.

"Stop it! You're going to open your wound again," she admonished. "You need a bandage over it anyway!"

"Well, I'm not bloody well calling my missish valet back in here to do it. My own mother did a damned poor enough job of it that I'm not inclined to let anyone else take over mothering me now!" He all but shouted his response.

She blinked at his cursing. If he'd been in a better frame of mind, he would have apologized to her for it. Or preferably, he would never have used such language to start. She was not one of the soldiers who'd served under his command in India, nor was she one of his rakehell companions. Governess, illegitimate, under his employ—whatever could be said of her, Wilhelmina Marks was still very much a lady.

"I will bandage it," she offered. "If you will sit down... you are too tall and I cannot reach."

Devil bit back a churlish reply. His shoulder was beginning to ache, the excitement of the altercation was beginning to fade, and in its place was a not so quiet fury. They'd invaded his own space, lain in wait for them outside his very own home. If he'd been less watchful, if he'd been a moment later in recognizing the danger—thinking of it made his heart race and brought a fine sheen of sweat to his skin.

"Are you feverish?" Willa asked, pressing the back of her hand to his forehead.

"I am not feverish, Willa. I am furious. I understand you do not wish to remain trapped in the house, and it isn't my wish for you be trapped either. Regardless, it is the only way I know at this time to ensure your safety and Marina's. Please, just until we can resolve the issue of West," he implored. "Do not ask me to risk having another innocent woman's life on my already burdened conscience!"

❯❯❯❯❮❮❮❮

WILLA TOOK A deep breath. As she pressed the bandage over the wound, she could feel the warm, silken smoothness of his skin, the firm and sinewy muscle beneath. Distressing was not necessarily the word, though she could not think of a better one in the moment. He left her feeling very unsettled, unsure of herself, unsure of the situation, and unable to adequately categorize her feelings.

"I will concede... for the time being," she relented. Her voice sounded breathless and thin, a clear indication of the state of her nerves.

Once the bandage was in place, Willa reached for the shirt still clutched in his hands. "Let me help you with this."

"I can manage," he said. The tone of his voice was gruff, but not angry.

Willa looked up, meeting his gaze. What she saw there took her breath away. She was a virgin, but she was not innocent. She knew precisely what his expression meant. Desire. And she had to acknowledge the spark of it within herself.

"You'll dislodge your bandage, bleed on your shirt, and we'll have to start the process over," she insisted. "Let me help you with it and we can call it done. I'll return to my room, and I will not leave this house or the immediate grounds for at least two days."

"If I agree to let you help me with the shirt, will you make it three days?" he bargained.

"Potentially... but only if you agree to share any information with me that you garner about Mr. West in the meantime," she countered.

"Fair enough," he agreed.

Willa took the shirt, her fingers brushing his as he allowed her to claim the garment. It was an impossibly intimate feeling, that brush of their naked hands while he sat before her clad only in his breeches and the bandage she'd applied. With a hitch in her breath, Willa bunched the fabric of the shirt until she could slide his injured arm into the sleeve first. As she pulled the garment over his head, her fingers brushed against the dark waves of his hair, the crisp texture both unexpected and intriguing.

The movement, stepping closer to pull the garment over his head entirely, had brought her so near him that she was cradled between his parted thighs, feeling the heat of him. So close, in fact, that the firm muscles of his inner thigh pressed against her and her breasts brushed his shoulder. The hiss of his breath across her skin told her that he had not missed the contact. Her flesh tingled everywhere they had touched, even if those touches had been unintended and entirely innocent.

Willa looked down, meeting his gaze once more, and what she saw there sealed her fate. He drew her in with that look, luring her closer and closer without uttering a word, until their lips were just inches from touching. "This is a terrible idea."

"It is," he agreed. "And I don't give a damn. I've been aching to kiss you again... to see if it was as incredible as I remember from that all too brief encounter yesterday."

"Then do it already, so we can both stop wondering." Her words were as much a challenge to herself as they were to him. In that moment, poised on the brink of doing something wild, reckless, and quite possibly disastrous, Willa didn't know whether to fall into his arms or run as fast and far as she could away from him. But temptation, the lure of the man himself, and the lure of the unknown held her in sway.

Chapter Seventeen

U NABLE TO RESIST her and, if truth were told, unwilling to do so, Devil slid his hand over the soft slope of her shoulder until it cradled the nape of her neck. His fingers speared into the mass of her blonde tresses. Hair pins scattered, pinging on the wooden floor as the lush waves fell over her shoulders like the finest gold silk. The firelight caught the various shades of it, highlighting all the subtle variations in hue. With only the slightest pressure of his hand, she moved toward him until he could feel the rush of her breath over his lips. To close that small distance between them, to claim the soft sweet curves of her lips with his own, it was as natural to him as breathing, and possibly as necessary.

By all accounts, it was a chaste kiss. His lips moved over hers, brushing, teasing, mapping every contour and committing it to memory. He was well aware that it might be the last opportunity he would have. Her response, sweet and untutored, was as tempting as the most skilled of courtesans. It evoked a reaction in him unlike anything else he'd ever known. Every part of him was focused on those points of contact between them. The silken skin of her neck beneath his palm, the sensation of her hair tangling about his fingers, the taste of her, the softness and sweetness of her lips—it was intoxicating. And then she leaned into him, and the weight of her against his chest and the crush of her breasts against the hardness of his own flesh prompted him to deepen the kiss.

Gently, he stroked the line of her jaw with his thumb, and with the slightest pressure, prompted her to part her lips. She did so, and he swept his tongue into her mouth, exploring the soft recesses and swallowing the sound of her gasp. She'd been kissed before their encounter the day before, she said, but not really—not by a man who only wished to worship her body and bring her pleasure. Anyone else who had ever touched her thusly had done so with a desire to take.

But even as he plied her soft lips with his own, even as he plundered the sweetness of her, he struggled to hold fast to his control. He had no wish to scare her, to paw at her like some green lad who didn't know how to pleasure a woman and thought only of himself. And yet her innocent response inflamed him. As debauched as he was, as much as he had thought himself forever burdened by the sense of ennui that plagued him for so long, in that instant he knew himself to be very much mistaken. There was not a part of him that was not consumed by that kiss, that was not affected by it in a profound way. If he'd thought the power of their earlier encounter was an anomaly, he was being proven very wrong. If anything, it seemed that with every kiss, the power of his attraction to her only grew.

She was like water to a man lost in the desert, land to a man lost at sea. For that second, with her in his arms, she was all that he needed and all that he desired. It was a strange thing to feel whole for the first time in his life, and yet he did. It was wondrous and terrifying all at once.

As much as he savored the kiss, and as much he had desired it, he used all of his considerable knowledge and skill to decipher what she enjoyed. Every sigh, every shudder, every stroke of his tongue against hers or caress of his lips that made her tense and shiver, he paid heed to.

Whether she sank against him fully or whether he guided her across his lap, he could not say. But she was there, her thighs draped over his and only the few layers of fabric from her skirts and petticoats separating them. He let his hand trail along the slope of her shoulder, down her arm, and then over to her rib cage. Every move was measured and careful, slow and languorous. When the pad of his thumb brushed against the underside of her breast, she shivered and pressed closer. Her back arched in invitation and he accepted greedily. Cupping the softness of her breast fully, feeling the hard peak of her nipple as it pebbled against his palm, Devil's pulse quickened. Pulling his lips from hers, he trailed kisses along her jaw line, the silken column of her throat, and then lower.

He pressed a dozen kisses to the swells of her breasts above the neckline of her gown, nipping gently with his teeth and then soothing the sting of it with his tongue. It was an easy enough thing to release the bib front of her gown, for the fabric to part and reveal the simple stays and chemise beneath it. Continuing his exploration, he made a vow. He would not take her innocence. Not like that. It was a line he had never crossed, and he did not mean to begin in that moment. But he could show her passion and, if she permitted, he could show her pleasure.

With her stays laced in front, he simply tugged the knot until it slipped free. The garment sagged, and he slipped his fingers beneath the quilted fabric. Her skin was hot to the touch and smoother than the finest silk. Tugging the fabric aside, he pressed the softest of kisses to the rosy tip of one perfect breast. When she sighed in response, pressed closer to him, and let her head fall back, he repeated the gesture more intently. Opening his mouth, he captured that peak between his lips, teasing the sensitive flesh until a soft moan escaped her lips. But that sound, in a room previously silent, broke the spell that had been woven about them. He felt her tense, felt the very moment when reality, nay sanity, intruded.

She placed her hands against his chest and pushed. Dutifully, he disengaged himself from her and looked up into her flushed face. Her expression could only be categorized as stricken.

"What have you done to me?" she whispered.

He could have lied about it. He could have dismissed it as only a kiss, a few stolen liberties. But it was not. To say so would have been to deny the power of what had just passed between them, to deny that what had occurred had changed him forever. "It is Pandora's box, Willa. And now there is no going back for either of us."

She withdrew from him completely then, all but tumbling from his lap as she rose to her feet. She stepped back from him and drew into herself. Her arms wrapped tightly about her and her disheveled clothing as she stared at him with resignation. "I knew the risks coming here. I knew what you were—who you were."

Anger hit him swiftly. What she implied was beneath him, beneath them both. "I did not force this upon you, Willa. We kissed, and it was by mutual agreement," he said. "As was everything else. All you had to do, at any second in that exchange, was tell me no or push me away."

"I was not implying that you had, Lord Deveril—"

"Douglas, dammit. Or Devil. But do not call me by father's name in a moment such as this," he demanded angrily.

"Fine, Douglas! I am not implying that I was forced nor would I even say that I was seduced by you. But men such as you, men who are devoted to pleasure, lead women astray without even making an effort to do so. You are the serpent in the garden," she said bitterly.

"I would remind you, Wilhelmina, that you came to me. One might even argue that by pursuing me into my bedchamber—"

"Pursuing you?" she demanded hotly. "I came here to speak with you, not for... not for—"

"For pleasure? For passion? For desire? To know what it is that you've been so dead set on denying yourself for all of your life? You are a woman, Willa, a passionate and sensual one. Draping yourself in dull colors and trying to disguise your beauty does not alter that. Denying your nature does not change it."

"My nature is not yours," she replied. "My life does not allow for hedonism."

"A kiss, magnificent as it was, does not constitute hedonism."

"It was more than a kiss!"

He smiled coldly. "Yes. It was. Significantly more, and I don't say that because I had you half-undressed on my lap. There is a power between us, Willa, that neither of us can deny."

"I cannot be a party to this kind of debauchery!"

He rolled his eyes. Not on purpose. It simply happened of its own accord. "Debauchery? I know debauchery, and I know it well, Willa. This was not it. One kiss and a bit of petting is hardly a downward spiral!"

"And how did you begin your descent into it, then? Was it a slow process or did you simply race headlong for it? A thing, once known, cannot be unknown. Pandora's box, just as you said," she accused.

"You are a plague on me," he said. "A beautiful, maddening plague. I didn't kiss you to lead you astray, Willa. I kissed you because I had no other option. I needed it as I need air to breathe. And now I need peace. Go, Willa. Go to your room, go back to Miss Darrow's. Go anywhere but where I am and leave me be." He uttered the last word on a heavy sigh. She exhausted him with her morality, with her guardedness, with the unshakeable idea that she would haunt him for the remainder of his days, even if she was long gone from them.

"We will never be alone again after this. Not for any reason. The risk is too great and there is too much at stake." With that final proclamation, she turned on her heel and strode toward the door. It was the most forceful and strident retreat that had ever been made.

IT WASN'T TEMPER that had Willa shaking as she entered her bedchamber, it was fear. Of course, it wasn't Lord Deveril she feared, but herself; herself and her inability to resist him. She'd known from the moment she first met him that he was dangerous to her, that he provided a temptation she was ill-equipped to resist. Devil was aptly named, indeed. Lucifer himself had no greater ability to turn a woman's head or make her forget herself so easily.

Only one thing kept her from simply packing her things and returning to Effie. Marina. The child still needed her. In the few days she'd been there, Marina had begun to open up. Where before she'd said nothing, the child had begun to utter small phrases and to answer questions, though not with any real consistency. Still, it was progress, and if she left, it would not only cease but the child could potentially regress. At that point, not only would her coming there have been a waste, she would actually have caused harm to the child. It would be an unforgivable sin.

Willa was in an untenable position. She could not stay under Lord Deveril's roof and resist him. She hadn't the strength. And her behavior, going into his chambers, had been courting disaster. She'd known it and had done so anyway, using his injury as an excuse to be close to him, to flout convention for a moment. Seeing him there, shirtless, in such an intimate setting, had weakened her already tremulous resolve and she had fallen, quite willingly, into his arms. On that score, he was absolutely correct. But what woman could resist him?

Truly, he was the most handsome man she'd ever seen with his dark, chiseled visage and sardonic wit. More than that, there was a hint of vulnerability in him. At times, he failed to hide that part of himself, and she could glimpse the pain of his father's rejection, the guilt he suffered for the terrible tragedy that had befallen his sister and his resolve to do better by his sister's child. It was those things that made him truly irresistible to her. It was also those things that made him a danger to her. Falling prey to his naturally seductive nature was bad enough, but the rest of it endangered far more than her virtue. He was not a man to whom she could ever risk giving her heart. It would be returned to her in shattered pieces no matter his intentions.

It occurred to her that she'd been very fortunate to be a student at Effie's school. It had given her an unparalleled education and an opportunity to have suitable employment without facing the pitfalls so many young governesses did. As a general rule, Effie vetted all prospective employers of her students very carefully. The rather impetuous decisions that had resulted in her now being employed in such a scandalous house was quite out of character for them both.

But her time at the Darrow School had also sheltered her significantly. She knew all about the dangers of men, at least in a very abstract sense. But she'd had no opportunity to learn about the dangers of temptation. That was something she was ill-equipped to handle. Clearly there was a wildness and a recklessness inside her that had not been accounted for.

"It cannot happen again," she murmured aloud. "Whatever is required, whatever I must do, it cannot and will not happen again. My duty is to help that child. Not to fulfill his desires or my own."

Uttering that statement offered her momentary strength. She had no idea how that self-imposed edict would be maintained but, for the moment, it helped her to remember both her purpose and her place. It was a sham engagement. Whatever her feelings for him or about him, she needed to remember that at all costs. It wasn't only her reputation at stake, after all. Her feelings for him were complicated at best and far too tender for her peace of mind.

Crossing the room to the delicately carved dressing table, one of the many fine pieces of furniture that graced the suite of rooms she'd been given, Willa seated herself there and surveyed her reflection critically. The high color in her cheeks, her swollen lips, and the wild mane of hair that fell over her shoulders made her look as wanton as she had felt in those moments in his arms.

There was no denying the truth she saw there. Things had escalated quickly and heaven knew he'd taken liberties, but none she hadn't given freely. The very instant she'd protested, he'd halted. But while she was a virgin, she was not so innocent that she hadn't understood what the firmness of his body pressed against hers signified. His passions had been aroused and, yet, at no point in time had he taken more than she'd been willing to give, nor had he encouraged her to reciprocate the pleasure he'd been lavishing upon her. With the distance of the corridor and several chambers between them, Willa could admit that she'd been perfectly safe with him. She might not have left there untouched by him, but given what she knew of his reputation, his intent had not been to relieve her of her virtue. He'd been in control the entire time. The Devil Lord himself had preserved her innocence on that occasion, for she'd have given it to him for the asking. It was a lowering thought. But honesty, even with herself, was a necessity. Lying to herself, hiding from the truth, would only leave her vulnerable to her own fallible nature.

With more force than was necessary, Willa began to brush her hair. It was as if taming the mass of wild curls and restoring some semblance of order would somehow erase the past half-hour. When the task was complete, she carefully braided the heavy mass as tightly as possible and then pinned it securely back from her face. The style would flatter no one. It was the quintessential look for a plain spinster or a governess and a stark reminder of precisely who and what she was in the grand scheme of things.

JEANNETTE KNEW TO the second when Miss Marks had left her nephew's chamber. Whatever she might have said to the contrary, she had not retreated to her chambers at all but had remained close by to monitor the situation. Lurking in a nearby room, she watched, waited, and listened. The last thing she needed was for Devil to be taken in by some gutter-born doxy who'd managed to convincingly put on airs. She was dependent on his charity, after all, and the one thing wives always managed to do was to convince their husbands to curb their generosity to relatives not their own.

If Devil married, she'd likely be cut off without so much as a tuppence, or expected to exist in a kind of penury that was worse than death to her. No servants, no new gowns, constantly dodging creditors! She was barely avoiding that existence already. Of course, it was her own fault to some degree. She'd spent too much, saved too little, and often failed to pay her debts. Invariably, Douglas had covered them for her without complaint and was much more agreeable about it than her late brother had been. But a wife would alter that, she was certain. Then there was the other matter... the parentage of the little urchin he'd foisted upon the family.

Gossip bandied about that she was his bastard would ruin the family. Not that siring a bastard was such a terrible thing. Most gentlemen did, after all. No, it was bringing her into the home and making her part of the legitimate family! They would never recover from such. They would have been far better off if the child had perished in the rookery where he found her. She was naught but a burden to everyone, both Devil and her dear, dear Alaric. It was unfortunate that Alaric had failed to retrieve her that afternoon with the information she'd provided to him. Another opportunity would have to be engineered, and that would not be easy. Devil would be on guard. More so than ever, and Miss Marks was now confined to the house because Devil was so concerned for her well-being. If there was any doubt that the phony betrothal bore a threat of becoming a legitimate one, it was the degree of her nephew's concern.

The child wasn't the only one who would need to be eliminated, Jeannette decided. Miss Marks would simply have to go.

Chapter Eighteen

H E HADN'T BEEN sleeping. Thoughts of Wilhelmina Marks had kept him from it. From the very moment she'd entered his home, he'd recognized that there was something different about her. She was singularly pragmatic, not in the least impressed by his station, his looks, or his reputation. Her opinions were offered freely and usually cast him in a dim light. Yet she was not unkind. Nothing she'd said of him was untrue or especially scathing. Perhaps that was why it stung so deeply. Had she been offering vitriol and recriminations, he could easily have ignored her as he did all others who spoke against him in such a way. But she was simply unfailingly honest and not at all swayed by his position or any of the charms that had worked so well on others. Not that he'd been overly generous in being charming to her. In fact, he'd rather been an ass. He found her prickly responses were far too satisfying not to be invoked frequently.

It had been a novelty at first, a woman who wasn't looking to cuckold her husband in a rogue's bed or, worse still, reform him through the venerable institution of marriage. Those thoughts led him deeper down that path. What would a woman like Willa expect in a marriage? Fidelity to be sure. She'd brook no nonsense on that front. She'd likely expect to marry for love. And romantic love, in his opinion, was hardly more than a tactic of seduction. It was simply a word that people uttered to make their dirty deeds seem less so. There was something, if not admirable, then at least understandable in succumbing to love. But succumbing solely to lust was simply a weakness of character, or so society would have everyone believe.

In short, their viewpoints would likely be diametrically opposed. Night and day. Black and white. Heaven and hell. There was little doubt in his mind that he'd make a miserable husband and, no doubt, any woman unfortunate enough to call herself his wife would be steeped in regret for the rest of her days. And yet, he couldn't stop thinking of their "betrothal". They'd not gone out in society. They'd not announced anything. If the truth were told, no one likely even realized who she was, what her role—real or fictional—was in his household, unless his servants had been gossiping. There was not a single reason to suspect that he would ever have to actually do the honorable thing by her, despite their earlier encounter.

But never in his life had he more fervently wished to have been caught in a damning situation. Had his aunt, who was clearly a terrible failure at being a chaperone, stumbled upon them in such a passionate embrace, there would have been nothing for it but to offer for her in truth. And yet his aunt had made herself scarce at his own insistence.

Turning over in his bed, Devil slammed his fist into the pillow. That small bit of temper actually made him feel better and so he did it again. But as he closed his eyes to will himself to sleep and forget the erstwhile and shockingly buttoned up temptress who was tormenting his every thought, a scream rent the darkness. It was Marina.

The nursery was not far from his own chambers. Though he suspected his presence would not comfort her, getting up to check on her appeased his own restlessness. Clad in breeches and only his shirt, Devil padded down the hall toward the child's room. When he arrived, the door was already open. He could hear Willa inside, murmuring softly to the little girl. After a moment, the child's cries subsided and he heard the soft, lilting notes of a lullaby. He stood there, listening to that sweet sound.

Such comfort and care was foreign to him. His own mother had died giving birth to Alice, and their home as children had been a cold place. Their father had never permitted such tenderness from their governesses toward them. In fact, their nurses and governesses had often been cruel and indifferent and had been hired for just that reason. Was it any wonder that Alice had been so vulnerable to West's advances? She'd lived her entire life without even a hint of love or affection and, false or not, the bastard had promised her that.

The singing from inside the nursery became softer and softer, the sound fading slowly into silence. A moment later, with Marina settled once more in her bed, Willa emerged from the girl's room wearing her nightrail and a velvet wrapper. When she saw him, she stopped immediately, her expression wary. It was an intimate thing, chance meetings in the hall while both were dressed for bed. Even as the thought occurred to him, she tugged her wrapper more tightly about her, but that only served to emphasize just how little covered her body beneath it.

"I've no intention of pouncing on you like a ravenous beast, Willa. You're safe enough in my presence," he said, and while his tone was soft, there was a bite to his words. He didn't like the notion of her fearing him. For perhaps the first time in his life, he wanted to be the hero rather than the wastrel villain.

"I'm not afraid of you," she answered. "I was simply startled by your presence."

Somewhat mollified by her answer, he commented, "I heard Marina crying out. Is she well?"

"It was only a dream. She has them frequently… I think they feature Mr. West though she has yet to tell me why. She is very afraid of him. She did say to me today, in the midst of all our other events this afternoon, that he is her father."

"I've believed him to be all along, though he hardly deserves the title."

Willa nodded. "I couldn't agree more. My own father is absent and unfeeling, but he certainly never went out of his way to be cruel. I suppose that is a point in his favor."

"No it isn't," Devil said. "Because he certainly never bestirred himself to halt anyone else's cruelty, did he?"

She glanced up then, her gaze locking on his for a moment. It left them both breathless, before she abruptly looked away. "No, I suppose he didn't. And you're right. It doesn't make him a better or worse man than West. They are just terrible in different ways. To that end, I think it isn't just Marina that West was cruel to. I think he was also very cruel to Alice, abusive even. And I'm very certain that Marina saw the worst of it."

Devil's jaw clenched. "I think it likely." And Alice would have tolerated it because their father had been just as vicious and cruel. How many times had he struck them? How many times had he locked them in their rooms? Alice, bless her, had continued trying to please the man up until West had come into her life. For himself, Devil had given up long before and had done everything he could to deserve the displeasure his father had heaped on him all along.

Willa nodded. "I believe that is the source of her fear and why she is so cautious with men. But until she begins to speak more, it's simply a guess."

"She needs you," he said. "I don't understand how or why your presence has made such a difference to her. But in only a short number of days, she's made more progress with you than in the entire time she was here before."

"We understand each other,' Willa answered softly.

Her head cocked to one side and her blonde braid slipped over her shoulder, drawing his eye to slender column of her throat.

"And why is that?" Devil asked. Despite the temptation she presented, or perhaps because of it, he was reluctant to see her go. He craved her presence. Not her body, not the pleasure they could find with one another, though heaven knew he wanted that as well. Perhaps it wasn't only Marina who needed her.

Her shoulders lifted in a small shrug as she shook her head thoughtfully. "We are alike in many ways, I suppose. Illegitimate. Fathers who are unfeeling at best, who viewed us as an inconvenience. She has seen the worst of mankind at a very early age."

"And you did as well?"

She paused for a moment as if considering whether or not to answer. Finally, after a moment, she met his gaze very directly. "Yes. I was living in a terrible place with my mother. She'd had an offer from a gentleman to become her protector, but not with me in tow. She deposited me on the doorstep to my father's bachelor abode and told him he could tend to me himself or sell me to an abbess. Then she walked away."

It was not what he'd expected her to say. She'd offered that explanation as a challenge, as if she were daring him to challenge his exalted position or her lowly one. "I'm sorry for that, sorry that those who should have cared for you failed to do so."

Her lips pursed in a frown, clearly not expecting his answer to have been so lacking in judgement of her. "It wasn't so terrible, not all the time, at any rate. My father put me in a school that was a terrible and cruel place. Lillian, my half-sister, was already there. That was where Effie found us. She couldn't abide the way we were treated. We were her first students... the very reason she founded her school. I was very happy there with her. Effie is the kindest person I know, but she is no one's fool. I don't think there is anyone whom I admire so much, and whom I aspire so much to be like."

"You inspire aspiration yourself, Willa. Far more so than you realize," he whispered.

They stood there in the corridor, silent for the longest time, watching one another. Both wary and painfully aware. The moment grew, stretching, becoming charged with the same tension that had exploded into passion between them earlier.

Finally, she spoke. "I should go. Goodnight, Lord Deveril."

Devil reached out, catching her wrist as she walked past. The idea that had been floating around the periphery of his mind since that heated exchange earlier in the evening reared its head again. It was a radical notion, something that he'd thought would never occur to him. And yet it had. In fact, the thought of it had been circling relentlessly. He could not let her pass without saying it. "I've watched you with Marina, Willa. You're not a woman who will be content to only love the children of others. Do you not want a family and home of your own?"

Her gaze was focused on his hand still clasped about her wrist. His hold was gentle, one she could easily break free of with the slightest of effort. Yet she did not. Instead, she stopped there, looking back at him over her shoulder. "I've never given it a thought. The unfortunate consequence of my education at the Darrow School is that I think of myself as a lady while I know, to my shame, that others will not. No gentleman would have the bastard daughter of a notorious rake, one who had worked as a governess no less, as his wife."

"There are gentlemen who would," Devil protested. Then he said something he would never have imagined uttering in a thousand years. "In fact, there is no reason why our sham of an engagement could not become a real one."

She laughed softly. "There is a reason, my lord. A man of your standing could not marry a woman like me!"

His hand slipped from her wrist to capture her hand, twining their fingers together in the darkness. "I have courted scandal all of my life, Willa. Why should my choice of bride be any different?"

Her head came up, chin jutting forward and fire dancing in her eyes. "And is that your reason for offering? That I might, once more, help you set society on its collective ear?"

"No, Willa," Devil said softly. "I offer because I desire you. Because you desire me. Because together, we could build a home for Marina where she would feel safe and cared for... where she would never again have to be afraid. And we could have children of our own, children who would never know the pain of cruel or indifferent parents such as we did."

"It's madness," she said. "And our earlier indiscretion is hardly a reason to court further scandal and ruin."

Devil stepped closer to her, close enough that he could smell the faint scent of lilies coming from the tightly braided waves of her hair. "That wasn't an indiscretion, Willa."

"If not that, then what would you call it?" she shot back at him.

"An inevitability. I thought, when you and I first met, that we could not have been more different. But in fact, I think we are far more alike than I could have ever imagined. I have made myself a reprobate in defiance of expectations of me, and you... you have remained upright and moral in defiance of expectation as well."

She didn't discount the notion. He could see that from the thoughtful expression that passed over her delicate features, her eyes flashing with curiosity and then resignation. At last, she replied softly, "I will not say you are wrong, but it is not a credit to either of us. My behavior with you earlier would certainly call my upright morality into question. I behaved terribly... lasciviously and with a recklessness that is counter to my nature. Perhaps that moment was inevitable, but I think it would behoove us both to avoid further opportunities for those sorts of things to happen again."

Devil stroked his thumb over the delicate skin at the inside of her wrist, feeling her pulse beat heavily at his touch. He stepped closer to her, pressing a soft kiss against her temple. "If you agreed to be my wife, there would be no sin or immorality in what occurred between us. There is much to be explored between us, Willa, to our mutual delight."

A SHIVER RACED through her at the sensual promise of his words. The memory of his hands on her, of the way he'd kissed her so passionately and so completely that she had forgotten all the many reasons she had to avoid such entanglements—those memories tormented her. They tempted and teased as surely as the low and impossibly seductive pitch of his velvet voice.

"It's madness. Complete foolishness," she said.

"Would you consider it? Truly? It is a good offer, Willa, and a genuine one," he said. "I think we could do well together."

"And your mistress? And your many lovers?" Willa asked. "How will they fare in this arrangement?"

He smiled. "Do you want me to promise you fidelity?"

"I've never given much thought to the idea of being a wife. But I know that I am not the sort who would be able to turn a blind eye to such flagrant indiscretions as you have committed in the past." The idea of being his wife and of having to share him with other women—Willa knew such a thing would breed only misery and resentment.

"I could tell you that I will be faithful, but you would not believe me because you do not think me capable of it," he said. "What I can say to you, Willa, is that I will be a good husband to you."

"By society's standards or by my own?" Willa asked.

"I will make you happy. I will endeavor to do so, Willa. Consider it. That is all I ask."

Willa met his gaze cautiously. He was too handsome, too tempting. Looking at him made her yearn for the very thing he offered her and that she so feared accepting. "I will consider it, but you know what my answer must be."

"That is not truly considering it then. Do not give the answer you must, Willa. Give the answer that you want," he urged.

Before she could say anything further, his hand slipped from hers and he strode off down the hall, leaving her alone outside Marina's door. Part of her wanted to beg him to come back, to feel his touch again. And she would consider his offer. In truth, she'd be able to think of nothing else. It warmed her heart and made her yearn for things that she should not. If she answered based solely on desire, it would be a resounding yes. But it would be unfair to him because while she was fully prepared to be a governess in a fine house, she was not prepared to be the mistress of one. Given that and her scandalous background, she'd do him no credit. And after years of courting his own scandal, if he hoped to turn his life around and give Marina the future she deserved, he'd need to court propriety with equal fervor.

With her heart heavy and her mind whirling, Willa made her way to her room. Her luxurious bed offered no comfort, and not even the softest of pillows or the smooth silk of the coverlet could ease her jangled nerves.

Chapter Nineteen

THE NOTE HAD been delivered by a child that was little better than an urchin. The butler's distaste was still evident when he brought the small, folded piece of parchment to her on a silver tray. The outside of it was streaked with dirt from the child's hand.

"Shall I have the boy await a reply?" he asked, his deep voice laced with disapproval.

"No, you shall not. If a reply is required I shall make my own arrangements," she replied smoothly, trying not to reveal how desperate she was to know the contents of that letter.

"Very well, Lady Carringden," he said, bowed in a manner that was infuriately slow, and then all but crawled from the room at a snail's pace.

When at least she was alone, Jeannette broke the seal and the read the first communication she'd had with Alaric since the debacle of his botched elopement with Alice.

My dearest J,

You've no idea how I've missed you, how I long for the comfort of your arms. I know that if I can bring Lord Deveril to heel, I will have the funds we need to begin a new life somewhere. Perhaps we could go to Spain. I long to bask in the warmth of a southern sun with you. But unless I can get the child out of his grasp, he'll never compensate me for the loss of her as he should. If you know of another way, or if you could bring yourself to help me reclaim her, then meet me in the park in one hour.

With love as always,

A.

Jeannette read it again, treasuring each of the words. He was lying. He always lied and she simply didn't care. All she wanted was to be with him. No man had ever excited her as he did. No man had ever given her such exquisite pleasure. Of course, she'd experienced his temper, his moods, and his volatile nature, but those things only excited her more.

Voices in the hall distracted her from her musings and fantasies. Rising, she crossed to the door of the morning room and peered into the hall while keeping herself concealed.

"Where are you off to, Miss Marina?" the cook asked in her jovial manner as Miss Marks and the child descended the stairs.

Miss Marks hesitated, leaving a space in the conversation for the child to reply if she was so inclined, but the brat remained silent. Finally, Miss Marks said, "I thought we'd go into the garden for a bit. Marina needs some sunshine, and it's nice for thinking."

Mrs. Farrelly nodded, and a sage expression crossed her florid, round face. "Aye, it is. And I'm thinking you've a great deal to consider, Miss Marks. His lordship is a good man, no matter what folks say."

Jeannette watched the younger woman's face, noting the blush that stained her cheeks and the way her eyes dropped to the ground. They were not truly betrothed, of that she was certain. She'd been suspicious from the moment Devil had written her asking her to act as chaperone. It was too sudden, especially for a man who had claimed he only ever intended to have other men's wives.

"I know that he is, Mrs. Farrelly, but you know the truth of my station," the young woman said. "That I am only a governess and not the affianced bride of a scandalous lord. And scandalous or not, he is still a lord and would need a wife far more suited to his position than I could ever be."

"It isn't his position that he needs a woman suited to, Miss Marks," Mrs. Farrelly said kindly. "It's himself. And you'll forgive me for saying, but I think the two of you suit quite well. And so does he."

Jeannette leaned closer to the door, hoping to hear better what the two women were saying. As she did so, her hip bumped against a small table and the vase on it teetered alarmingly. She caught it just in time before it crashed to the floor. Still, the two women on the stairs had heard it and clammed up. Knowing that to keep herself concealed would only increase suspicion, she pasted a bright smile on her face and stepped from the morning room. "Dear heavens, I am so graceless at times. I very nearly knocked over a vase on my way out!"

"You didn't injure yourself, I hope," Miss Marks said with concern.

"No! No! Not in the least, simply tripped over my own feet and nearly upset a table," Jeannette offered with a laugh. "Mrs. Farrelly, would you be so kind as to send my maid up for my shawl. I plan to take a walk this morning. I've been cooped up for far too long!"

"Certainly, my lady," the cook said, bobbing a curtsy and bustling off toward the kitchen.

Alone with the pseudo-bride, Jeannette smiled again. "Tell me, my dear, how did you and my nephew meet? Devil simply glossed over it the other night, and I'm dying to hear the tale of your whirlwind romance!"

Miss Marks' eyes narrowed, but her smile remained perfectly in place. "Your nephew is a far better storyteller than I. You must ask him when he returns from his errands. As it stands, I've promised Marina to spend the day in the garden with her so that she may play and get as dirty as she chooses."

Jeannette nodded. "Of course! Every child should get a bit grubby from time to time. I'm certain you did, didn't you, Miss Marks?"

The governess didn't nod or smile then. "I feel as if we are having two very different conversations, Lady Carringden, and that the best possible course of action for me is to simply excuse myself from it and see to Marina. Good afternoon, Madame."

Jeannette watched the governess sweep past her and toward the doors that led out to the small garden. She certainly had fine enough manners and haughty enough ways to be a fine lady, Jeannette thought, but she'd be certain that never happened.

Moments later, her maid descended the stairs carrying her shawl. Jeannette draped it about her shoulders and made her way to the park.

⤟⤟⤟⬞⬟⬟⬟

ALARIC SAW LADY Jeannette Carringden striding toward him and smiled. The middle-aged woman was holding up better than most. She still cut a striking figure. She was a lusty thing to be sure, and he'd enjoyed many an afternoon and evening in her bed. He wouldn't mind enjoying a few more, assuming they could come to an arrangement.

"Over here," he called out softly from the trees.

Instantly, she stopped, her head swiveling in his direction. She veered off the path, moving toward him in a less than discreet manner. Still, the park was not overly crowded at that hour so there were few enough to witness it. The moment she neared him, he reached out, grabbed her, and pulled her into the small copse of trees. He kissed her passionately, until she was breathless with it and falling against him.

"Oh, Alaric! I've missed you more than you know," she said, still panting.

"And I you, Jeannette. After the debacle with Alice… I tried to do right by her. I truly did. But she became so moody and reckless after her father cast her out. She was despondent and blamed me for her low status," he said.

"She was always a spoiled, ungrateful child," Jeannette huffed. "And Lord Deveril and that governess of his will make Marina precisely the same!"

"True, but I cannot take her from him. Alice and I married, but not legally. If we were to go before the courts, they would side with him because he has all the wealth, power, and privilege. But perhaps he will offer some small compensation for my cooperation," Alaric suggested.

"We both know better than that. He might despise his father, but when it comes to sheer stubbornness, there is little doubt that Devil is much like him. I think that your earlier attempt to liberate the girl by force is the only way... and you now have the perfect opportunity!"

"How so?" he asked, the very picture of innocent curiosity.

Jeannette leaned against him, pressing her body to his. "Miss Marks has taken the girl into the garden to play. I know Devil has hired guards and there is one posted at each end of the mews. If you get rid of them, you'd be able to slip into the garden and take the girl without even raising an alarm... though, I must tell you, you might have better luck ransoming the governess than the child."

"She's the governess, you said. Why would he care so much?"

Jeannette's eyes twinkled with a conspiratorial light. "There's something between them. He may not be in love with her, but he is certainly infatuated with her. And I daresay, you could sway her to be cooperative, at least. If you take the child, she'll scream until all of Mayfair is down on your head. Take the governess. He needs her to deal with the child, and his feelings for her are far more complicated than he can even begin to decipher. Trust me."

"The last time I trusted you, I wound up living in squalor in a rookery with Alice screaming at me that we had no bread to eat or coal for the fire," he reminded her.

She ducked her head. "And now I will make that up to you. Please, Alaric?"

"Very well," he said. "I've seen them together, and I do not think you are wrong. The governess will be our ace."

Chapter Twenty

"**M**UNRO."

That single word was uttered by Highcliff with what could only be described as glee as soon as Devil had entered the room. Having spent a sleepless night tormented by alternating lustful and indignant thoughts centered on one very maddening woman, Devil wasn't in the mood for guessing games. He'd said what he needed to in the hall. He'd made his declaration, and now it was very much in her court.

Devil raised his eyebrows. "Munro what?"

Lord Highcliff grinned, a wicked glint in his eyes. The man wasn't just a hunter, but a predator. There was nothing he loved better than ferreting out information unless it was ferreting out criminals. "It isn't Munro what, my friend, but Munro who. Alaric Munro. Fugitive. Smuggler. Kidnapper. Defrauder. And quite possibly… murderer. If it is counter to the laws of king and country, the bounder is guilty of it."

It was far worse than he'd thought, Devil realized. How on earth had Alice gotten involved with such a man? "How did you discover this?"

Highcliff settled back in his chair, propped his booted feet on his desk, and folded his hands together in a very satisfied manner. "You should know by now not to ask such things, my friend. Suffice it to say, Munro, or West if you prefer, had previously brought himself to the attention of some very influential people at Whitehall. His stepfather, a tradesman in the north, had several contracts with the war office. Producing munitions, as it were."

"Treason?" Devil asked. "West or Munro... whatever he bloody well calls himself, is involved in treason?"

"Indiscretion, at the very least. Munro talked too much, bragged too much, and lost entirely too much on the turn of a card. He shared information that he should not have with people who were linked to the wrong side, but likely without any real notion of what he was revealing. The result is the same, however. Lives were lost in India and on the Continent because he revealed information about shipments and those weapons were, in turn, delivered into the hands of enemies of the crown."

Devil seated himself in one of the upholstered chairs that faced Highcliff's desk. How many good men had he watched die in India? How many of them had bled their life's blood for Munro's greed? Even if he'd done so inadvertently, his actions had manifested terrible consequences. "And his association with my sister? How did that begin?"

"It's a bit more complicated there. He was at Oxford, gambling heavily, losing, bankrupting his very bourgeois stepfather, and he was cut off. When that occurred, he used all that he had at his disposal to support his lifestyle... primarily, his charm and his pretty face. He was rather brilliant about it. Those damned novels young women are reading now, with mysterious tragic heroes! He created a story about his terrible and overly dramatic past, and he began frequenting book shops where he could find wealthy young women who were eager for his fictions. Your dear sister was one of them."

"But not the only one?"

"No," Highcliff agreed. "Not the only one. Though I daresay she paid the highest price. He hedged his bets incorrectly once more it seemed. Of the women who'd fallen in with his scheme, Alice was the one with the wealthiest family and best connections. He severed ties with the others and focused solely on her, much to her delight and eventual doom. Your father's coldness to her left her uniquely vulnerable to a man like Munro, I think."

The weight of guilt settled on him like a familiar cloak. "As did my absence."

"Which can also be laid directly at your father's doorstep," Highcliff protested. "You did not leave her by choice. Your father didn't exile you for your behavior, Devil. Not really. He exiled you because he couldn't bear the sight of you. Never could."

"I thank you for your attempt, Highcliff, but you cannot absolve me of guilt in this instance," Devil replied. "I knew the risks of my behavior. My father had threatened it often enough. I was well aware of the exile I courted, but I was too young and too selfish to appreciate that the impact of it would harm anyone other than me."

"We are all able to identify our missteps when they are behind us."

There was a certain wisdom to Highcliff's words, but Devil wasn't quite ready to let go of his guilt and anger yet. They'd become familiar companions to him. "And do we have any idea where Munro is now?"

Highcliff reached for his quill and began scratching out the man's direction on a piece of fine parchment. "He was at an inn near the docks, The Cock and Crow Inn... I spoke with a woman who had been Alice's neighbor. He was there asking after Alice and was not overly troubled by news of her passing. Not to be indelicate, but are you entirely certain it was a fever that claimed your sister?"

Devil's eyes narrowed. "What do you suspect, Highcliff? Now is not the time to withhold information!"

"Mrs. Blye, Alice's neighbor, was given most of the things left in her rooms that you did not keep for the child... Mrs. Blye has been quite ill herself. She was using a box of tea that had been Alice's. Every time she made herself a cup of it, she became violently ill. When I examined it, I found that the very bottom of the box had been painted green. Paris green to be precise." Highcliff's tone was frank as he referenced the once popular pigment that had been discovered to have deadly consequences. "I can't say that it wasn't purchased that way, though most merchants know better by now. I do believe that Munro tampered with the inside of the box and then refilled it with tea that would absorb the poison from the paint and slowly kill Alice."

Devil couldn't speak past the lump in his throat. "She suffered terribly, and he knew. He did that to her and left her there to die from it." And Marina. She could have died from it as well.

"Yes," Highcliff agreed. "He did. He wanted rid of her so that he could find himself another wife, one whose family would not cast her off, penniless and ruined. I'm sorry, my friend."

"What else did you learn from this woman?" Devil asked.

Highcliff must have recognized his desperation for a change in subject, so he said, "Munro was keenly interested in the child and the fact you had collected her. Your suspicions on that front are correct. I think he means to abduct her and ransom her to you. And then there's your pretend fiancée."

Devil's brows rose at that. Lips firmed into a frown, he demanded, "How do you know we're pretending? Perhaps I've fallen desperately, tits over arse in love with her."

"She's pretty enough. I'd say you'd definitely fell tits over arse in lust with her, but we both know it isn't love. Not for you. What is she really?"

"Marina's governess. But posing as my betrothed, with a chaperone in the house, was the best way to maintain her reputation," Devil admitted. "Out of curiosity, why is the idea of me falling in love with a woman so ludicrous to you?"

Highcliff smiled. "Because you've often decried the state of marriage as something to be avoided at all costs. Haven't you? And a woman such as your Miss Marks could only be had through marriage. You are many things, my friend, but you are not a man who would despoil an innocent woman and lead her to ruin. We both know that."

It was true, and yet Devil found himself regretting the words he'd spoken in haste in the past, words that he might well have to eat. If their all too brief interlude in his bedchamber had shown him anything, it was that his ability to resist her was thin and weak. Devil rose to his feet, impatient to do something constructive about the threat that his sister's former love presented. "I'm off to find Munro. I mean to beard him in his den and put an end to this."

"And an end to your association with Miss Marks? Is that in sight, as well?"

Devil considered his answer carefully. "It was easy enough to dismiss the idea of marriage when, at the time, I'd never met a woman who tempted me that did not already have a husband."

"And are you tempted by her?"

Devil cocked his head. "You seem inordinately interested in my intentions toward Miss Marks. Why is that?"

Highcliff sighed. "For the sake of argument, let us say that I am indebted to Miss Euphemia Darrow. As such, I am bound by honor to see to the safety and welfare of her friend and pupil. If your intentions toward Miss Marks are honorable, I would not, hypothetically, have to intervene. But if they are not, then I must act."

"Hypothetically, of course," Devil replied.

"Naturally," Highcliff replied with smooth grace.

"At this moment, I have no intentions toward Miss Marks. Honorable or otherwise. If that should change, it would be in a manner that would require no action on your part," Devil said. *"Hypothetically speaking, of course."*

Highcliff nodded. "That is good to know, my friend. If you require more assistance with the matter of Munro, I will do what I can. I'm assuming you will want to handle this discreetly given that it could eventually impact your niece's reputation and future."

Good God. He hadn't even considered it. Marina was the bastard daughter of a traitor. Yes. Discretion would certainly be required. "You are quite right. For Marina's sake, her connection to him must never be known."

"Good luck, my friend. Munro is a coward, but that doesn't mean he isn't a danger to you."

Thinking of Alice and the slow, torturous manner in which it appeared the bastard had ended her life, Devil was quite certain of that.

⇛⬆⬅

WILLA SAT IN the garden. The air was crisp, but the sun was bright above her. The dawning of a new day had improved her outlook greatly, and while she was not fully recovered from all the events that had occurred the night before, she had calmed significantly. It had been a kiss and nothing more. Yes, she'd had a moment of weakness. Yes, she'd been foolish and perhaps reckless. But she was an intelligent, strong woman who knew her own mind and she both could not and would not falter again.

With that in mind, she turned her attention to Marina who played with her doll and the carved animals her uncle had given her. Watching the child, Willa noted the bright light in her eyes and the way she engaged with her toys. She was a bright child, and having someone who talked to her as if she were an intelligent being rather than staring at her like an oddity or cooing at her like an infant the way Mrs. Farrelly did was allowing that to come through. But Willa had no doubt that the trauma Marina had suffered, watching her mother die and being ripped from the only world she knew, would no doubt linger for the child for some time to come. And the threat of Mr. West and whatever schemes he was about would do nothing to abate that.

Mrs. Farrelly came bustling outside then, smiling happily at the little girl. "I've made the little lamb a bite to eat, Miss Marks. I thought the brisk air might stir her appetite. She hardly eats enough to keep a bird alive!"

Mrs. Farrelly would have happily had them all fatted like sacrificial lambs, but Willa nodded. Marina did need to eat, and it was a bit cool for the child to be out so long despite the bright sun above. "Run along inside with Mrs. Farrelly, Marina. I'll collect your things and bring them inside."

The little girl rose, the carved horse still clutched in her hand, and followed Mrs. Farrelly into the house. Taking the moment to breathe and enjoy the air, Willa turned her face up to sky. It cleared her mind and helped her to find the peace she so desperately needed.

But her sense of peace and tranquility did not last long. It might have been a sound, it might have simply been some instinctual awareness of danger, but Willa became aware after a moment that she was not alone. Lowering her head, she opened her eyes and found herself staring directly at Alaric West and two rather large men. They stood just inside the garden gate, the sound of their entrance likely camouflaged by the chattering of Mrs. Farrelly to Marina and the slamming of the door behind them.

"I'll scream," Willa warned.

"There's one maid and the cook in the kitchen," Mr. West said. "My compatriots can snap their necks and grab the child before they can even sound an alarm."

"What do you want?" Willa asked.

Mr. West opened the gate and gestured for her to go through it. "If Lord Deveril wants to keep me from my child, Ma'am, he will have to offer me some compensation. You are my collateral to see to it that he is willing to negotiate. You won't be harmed if you cooperate."

With more bravado than she certainly felt, Willa began, "There is a house full of servants—"

"No, there is not," he interrupted, cutting her off abruptly. While he did not raise his voice, it was still a tone that could only be described as warning. "It is Sunday morning, and half of the staff has taken their half-day to attend church. The few downstairs will be of no help, and by the time those in the upstairs chambers can reach this garden, we will be long gone from here! Lord Deveril himself has gone out, and the men he had guarding the front door saw nothing. The men who were patrolling the mews—well, they'll never see much of anything ever again. Do not try me, Ma'am. Come peacefully."

"And if I do not?" Willa demanded. She knew the answer, of course. But stalling seemed like the safest of tactics. The longer they stood there talking, the greater the chance of someone realizing something was amiss.

"I do not enjoy hurting women. But I will do so. And when I am done with you, I will go into that house and take the child," West said with complete sincerity. "There is naught you can to do to stop us... except come along in her stead."

It was highly likely that Lord Deveril would not pay for her return. Why should he, after all? But they did not know that. "I'm to assume then that ransom is your ultimate goal?"

"It is," he agreed.

"And do I have your word that if I cooperate I will not be harmed?"

He smirked. "And would my word be good enough for you?"

No. But it was the most she could ask for in that moment. She'd made a terrible error in judgement coming into the garden without actually bringing footmen with her. They'd offered to accompany her and she'd shooed them away, wanting to be alone with her thoughts save for Marina's too quiet company. Assuming that the guards stationed at the door and the entrance to the mews was enough had been foolhardy on her part. If she'd but waited for everyone to return from church services, they'd have been safe enough. "It will have to be, will it not?"

"Come along," he said. When he raised his hand to gesture toward the gate, it held a wicked looking blade. "I'll only use this if you force me to do so."

Willa shuddered but said nothing. Instead, she stepped forward, moving slowly but steadily toward the gate. Her shawl trailed behind her and, at the last moment, she let it flutter to the ground, trampled beneath the boots of the two large men who accompanied Mr. West. She hoped that if someone discovered it, they would recognize it as the cry for help she intended it to be.

Chapter Twenty-One

DEVIL RETURNED TO his home in Mayfair to find it in an uproar. His aunt, Lady Carringden, was in a full swoon that was clearly an affectation. Mrs. Farrelly was sobbing into her apron, and he could hear Marina wailing to beat the band. There was no sign of Miss Marks. Had she left? Had the events of the night before prompted her to flee? It was a terrifying thought for reasons that were not limited to his young niece's welfare.

"What pandemonium have I returned to?" Devil demanded. "What is going on here?"

"She's gone, my lord," the butler said. "From the garden."

"I need a complete explanation if you please. Who, what, when, and where!" Devil snapped.

The butler drew in a shuddering breath. "Miss Marks was in the garden with the child. Mrs. Farrelly fetched the little one to give her some luncheon and Miss Marks remained behind, stating she would collect the child's toys and follow shortly. But she did not. The toys remained in the garden along with Miss Marks' shawl, and the gate leading into the mews was open... and the men you stationed at the entrance to the mews—"

Devil frowned. "What about the men?"

"One has died, m'lord. His head bashed in with what I cannot presume to guess... the other one is not much longer for this world, I fear. He met the same cruel fate." The answer had come from Mrs. Farrelly, broken periodically by her sobs. "And now the poor, wee child is heartbroken for Miss Marks. We all are. What is to become of her?"

Devil's blood had chilled in his veins. He was furious but also utterly terrified. "She will return, Miss Farrelly. I will see to it. Take care of Marina, and I shall return as soon as I can." To the butler, Devil added, "Send a note round to Lord Highcliff. Alert him that things have taken a dark turn and I need him to meet me at The Cock and Crow Inn."

"Yes, my lord," the butler said with a nod. "I will see to it."

Devil turned and made for his study. From the drawer of his desk, he retrieved a brace of pistols and an assortment of blades. The pistols went into his coat pocket and the daggers he concealed in his boots and elsewhere on his person. He also collected a pouch of coins. Money was usually the most expedient method of encouraging cooperation. Determined to see Wilhelmina returned safely, he didn't care if it was by force or payment. When he felt sufficiently armed, he left the library. He wasn't allowing himself to think about what might be happening to Willa at that moment. Those thoughts would only distract him from what he needed to do to get her back.

Devil charged from his home, ignoring the chaos that still continued in the hall, and strode purposefully down the street. At the corner, he hailed a hack. It was a quicker option than having his own carriage readied or waiting for a horse to be saddled and brought round. Even then, it was a short journey. It was shocking, really, how little distance actually existed between the exalted halls of Mayfair and the desperate slums of St. Giles.

When the hack rolled to a stop, Devil got out, tossed a coin to the driver, and waved him on. He paused for a moment then to survey his surroundings before entering the small and none-too-clean inn known as The Cock and Crow Inn. A coin slipped to a busty and scantily-clad serving wench along with a whispered request had him shown up the stairs and to a small room under the eaves.

"This is where Alaric West lays his head?" Devil asked, surprised that the man hadn't managed to swindle his way into finer accommodations.

The wench smiled, revealing a gap between her front teeth. "Aye, my lord. Reckon it's where he lays a lot of things... including me. I could give you a tumble if you like."

"No, thank you," he replied, not even remotely tempted by her. Once upon a time, he might have been... just for the novelty. "My business is rather urgent today."

The girl opened the door and let him into the room. "Well, best get on with your urgent business then. I'll see if I can't find a different sort of urgency to fill my pockets below stairs," she said with a wicked grin and walked away.

Stepping inside, Devil surveyed the space critically. The bed was unmade. Dirty crockery and empty bottles littered the floor. Despite that, the room gave the air of being deserted. There were no articles of clothing or personal items left behind. In fact, he was fairly certain that the room, despite its untidy state, had not been slept in for some time.

"What are you doing in here?"

The gruff voice of the landlord behind him had Devil turning around. "I'm looking for the man who has let this room."

"Aye, I been looking for him, too. Owes me a week's rent he does!" the man groused.

"You'll get what you're owed... but only if I get satisfactory answers from you, sir," Devil replied, keeping his tone casual.

"What does he owe you then?" the landlord asked.

"He behaved dishonorably with my sister," Devil said. It wasn't the truth in its entirety, but it was enough of it that he didn't have to add lying to his conscience nor did he have to jeopardize Miss Marks' reputation by disclosing her abduction.

The landlord's expression soured even further. "I never liked the bounder. Winking and flirting with my girls downstairs in the taproom. I don't run that kind of establishment! Good girls working for me, I have. My own daughter and my niece!"

Devil said nothing to that. He'd seen those good girls when he came in and, even without being propositioned by one, they'd been displaying enough bosom that they would have looked less obscene if they'd been fully naked. He'd seen more modest gowns in bawdy houses. "Do you know where he went?"

"I don't. It's been two days since I've seen him, longer still since he spent a night under this roof, I think. Though he often slips in after dark to meet with folks in the taproom. I can tell you he's had two men coming and going with him of late. Big chaps, stout and looking a bit rough about the edges, even by standards here." The landlord paused, took a deep breath, and then added. "I heard him call them by name, and if you mean to make good on your promise to pay what's owed by him, I'll have the coin now and their names to you after."

Devil reached into the pocket of his waistcoat and produced the small leather pouch. He passed the man a sovereign from it. "I am assuming that will cover the lot."

"Aye, and then some. Called them by Jim and Joseph Colton. Brothers they are, and look enough alike that you can't miss it," the landlord said. "I'd seen 'em down at the docks before. Loading and unloading the ships for Jacobs and Stern Shipping. I reckon you could get more out of the man what works there. Big chaps, they are, one a might larger than the other. Bruisers, they be."

Fairly certain he'd made their acquaintance before, Devil nodded. "You've been very helpful. If he returns, send word to me in Mayfair… Lord Deveril by name."

The landlord raised his eyebrows in shock. "Well, don't you get around then? We've heard of you even down here, my lord."

"Gossip and rumors. Nothing more," Devil said, his expression shuttered and his tone firm. It was not the time for telling tales. "Keep it quiet that I was here, if you don't mind."

"Not at all, my lord. Quiet as the grave I'll be," the landlord vowed, holding up the coin he'd been given and flashing a wink.

Devil made his way to the taproom and ordered an ale. It was served up by the same wench who'd shown him to West's room. If possible, the bodice of her dress had been tugged even lower, and it appeared her ample bosom was ready to spill out of it at the slightest provocation. He turned away, ignoring her moue of disappointment, as he watched the door and waited for Highcliff's arrival. It was only a moment later that the bell tinkled and the door rushed inward on a heavy wind. Highcliff entered with it, but not dressed as the dandified gentleman most thought him to be. The man wore snug black breeches, boots of pitch black with not a hint of sheen to them. He wore a black shirt and coat as well, with no cravat. He looked like a house breaker.

Devil waited at the bar as Highcliff approached. "Are we to burgle someone then?"

"It pays to be discreet," Highcliff answered.

"And is that why you paused on the step like a deb with dampened petticoats waiting for everyone to get a look?" Devil queried. There was no denying that Highcliff had a flare for the dramatic. In another life, the man would have trod the boards at Drury Lane.

"And all they'll remember is a gent in black clothes. They'll not even know my face," Highcliff replied. "Now, to the business at hand. Has he been here?"

"Not for two days, likely. But we're going to head down to the docks and find a couple of chaps by the name of Jim and Joseph Colton. They'll be able to point us in in the right direction," Devil said. "Apparently they're very large."

"That's not always a problem," Highcliff said. "So long as they aren't overly smart."

Devil drained the tankard, tossed another coin on the bar, and headed for the door, Highcliff falling in step beside him.

THEY WERE IN a dirty shack at the back of a cemetery. There were broken bits of wood on the floor that likely were left behind from caskets set upon by grave robbers. They were on the outskirts of Lambeth. She knew that. She'd recognized the road they were on when she'd managed to get a glimpse of it through the slats of the small cart they'd used to transport her there. Covered with sacks that had once contained grain or flour, they had been none too clean and smelled of mold and heaven knew what else. Still, she was unscathed, thus far.

Aside from being cold, hungry, and frightened, she had not been mistreated, but there was no promise that such good fortune would continue. She also knew that West was counting on Devil to pay a ransom for her and, to that end, he was electing to keep her relatively unharmed. That could change at his whim, however, and she knew it.

"When do you mean to send your demands to Lord Deveril?" she asked. The shorter the time he planned to keep her with him, the more likely she'd emerge from the incident unharmed.

"That's no concern of yours," West replied sharply.

Willa arched one eyebrow at his dismissive response. "As the abducted person, I'd beg to differ. This room is filthy, cold, and dirty. I'm simply hoping to gauge how long I must remain in it."

West smiled, revealing slightly crooked teeth that were, so far as she could tell, the only physical flaw he possessed. And yet, she would never have called him handsome. Even that first day when she'd seen him in the park, her immediate response to him had been one of fear even when he'd done nothing that would engender such a response. And yet from the moment she'd first laid eyes upon Lord Deveril—

Douglas—her reaction to him had been entirely different. Both outwardly handsome men, both with completely different characters and they both sparked within her intense but opposite reactions. Handsome as he was, Alaric West only made her feel fear, disgust and anger. Why?

Because he reminded her of her father, she thought. Because he was utterly callous and had no feeling for anyone other than himself. Everything he did was selfish and self-serving. He was a man who would go to any lengths and hurt anyone in his path so long as it meant he could ultimately have his own way. And Lord Deveril was not that at all. He was a man who had done wrong, certainly. He'd indulged in countless vices and done so in a very public manner. Yet, it was never his intent to bring harm to anyone. In fact, he'd gone out of his way to soothe his sister in her final hours and was devoting himself to seeing that Marina could recover from the loss of her mother and live a good and happy life with him. All of society might revile him, but having had the opportunity to compare his character to the gossip that circulated about him, Willa had the uncomfortable revelation that she, along with many others, had misjudged the man. Just as Alice had misjudged West. She'd been misled by his too-handsome face and fallen prey to his empty promises.

"Miss Marks, as I said before, I won't enjoy hurting you, but that will not keep me from doing so if it means keeping you quiet. I'm not overly fond of loud females."

"I'll keep her quiet," one of the other large men present offered with a leer. He'd been watching her in a way that had left her distinctly uncomfortable from the very moment they'd entered the small, derelict building.

"Now, now, Jim. We can't be sending her back... spoiled," West said with a grin. "Though if she doesn't cooperate, I suppose there are certain ways to take your pleasure with her that would leave her virginity intact, assuming that it is. Is it, Miss Marks? Or is the Devil

Lord as skilled with the ladies as they say?"

Willa didn't answer. He was goading her, but she would not be baited. She simply turned her face away and refused to look at the lot of them. The sound of their coarse laughter and their ribald comments made her stomach churn. Fear coiled in her belly, hot and tight. Nausea threatened, but she'd not do anything else to draw their ire or their attention. She could only hope that when they sent their demands to Devil, he would pay them. Of course, she was also depending on them to honor their end of the bargain. It was a thought that brought no comfort.

Chapter Twenty-Two

THE LARGE WAREHOUSE of Jacobs and Stern Shipping was located midway between the London Docks and those of the West India Company. As the city went, it was certainly one of the lesser populated regions, and growing late as it was, it would not be long before darkness descended in force. Still, as Devil made his way into the ramshackle and likely unsound building, Highcliff was at his side.

There was a small office at the top of a set of rickety stairs with a dim glow emanating from it. "I'm going up," Devil said.

"If he expects to be paid for the information—"

Devil cut a warning glance at his friend. "I am well aware that such intelligence will come at a cost. I'm willing to pay whatever it takes. This is my fault, after all."

"It's Munro's fault," Highcliff corrected. "No one else's."

Devil said nothing in response to that. He appreciated the other man's effort, but he was not so easily absolved. Climbing the stairs, he stopped in the open doorway and found a squat man in rough clothes, sorting through a handful of manifests. "I need to speak with you about two of your dock workers."

The man eyed him cautiously, his eyes lighting as he took in Devil's obviously expensive and finely-tailored clothing. "I reckon I could spare a minute... for a price."

"Of course," Devil agreed, keeping his tone neutral. "Jim and Joseph Colton. Brothers, I believe."

"Aye, twins they are. Big as houses and only one brain betwixt 'em and I'd say it's a few eggs shy of a dozen. What you want to know about them?"

"I need to find them... they've taken work with a man by the name of Alaric Munro. He may also be calling himself Alaric West."

"I know him well enough," the man said with a sneer. "Owes me for a case of brandy. If he thinks to stiff Jim or his brother, he'll regret it. They're big and they're mean with it. They'll cut his throat and dig his grave with their own bare hands. Big as spades anyway, they are." The man held up his own hand for the purpose of illustration.

What had been said had not set Devil's mind at ease. "Do you know where they stay?"

"Don't stay in one place too much, Guv. Move about a bit. They take rooms in St. Giles when they can afford 'em. Sometimes they sleep under the bridge, yon. I've caught 'em in here a time or two, but I don't tolerate that. Last thing I need is this place to go up in flames from them smoking and drinking... or fighting as they do and knocking over a lantern. But I reckon there's an old shack out near Norwood where they hole up from time to time. If they're doing aught they shouldn't, I'm betting that's where they'd go."

"Norwood? The cemetery?" Devil said.

"Aye. I reckon they might be doing a bit of resurrection work on the side. No business of mine so long as they show up here to work and don't reek of the grave. I'll be having that shilling now, Guv'nor."

Devil's eyes narrowed. "A shilling, was it? We agreed upon that?"

"I reckon they could smash my head like a rotten apple. I figure it's worth at least that," the man replied with a nervous laugh.

It was an argument he could not refute. Devil slipped a coin from his pocket and tossed it to the man. "This shack... what's the actual direction of it?"

"Backside of the boneyard. I'll say no more," the man said and pocketed the coin. "And you'll not tell 'em it was me what told you. I don't need the trouble."

"Silent as a grave they have yet to desecrate," Devil agreed and turned to leave.

"What is it you want with 'em?" the man asked. "Do they owe you money as well?"

"They've abducted the woman I mean to marry."

The man shook his head. "Then you best find her quick. Jim's got a fierce appetite for women... and the less they like him, the better he enjoys it. Banned by every cathouse nearby and the street girls won't have nothing to do with him either. Stout as an ox. And mean with it like I said."

"I'll keep that in mind," Devil said and tossed the man another coin for his trouble. Heading back down the stairs, he found Highcliff waiting for him.

"Well?"

"An abandoned shack near Norwood Cemetery is the most likely place... and we need to hurry. Time is of the essence," Devil said. "I pray we are not already too late."

"You think they'll kill her?"

Devil shook his head. "I don't think that's their purpose. They mean to ransom her back to me, I've no doubt. But apparently one of the men West hired has a history of being very violent with women."

Highcliff nodded. "Right. I'll get a hack. They can let us out at the cemetery gates and we'll approach on foot. Should we get reinforcements?"

"No. Apparently the Colton brothers are virtually beasts of men, but I think the element of surprise is in our favor. A large group and we'll lose that," Devil said. "And I can't risk taking the time to secure them."

Highcliff nodded and then hailed a passing hack as they stepped out of the building. For Devil, he'd never felt such urgency. He'd underestimated West or Munro or whatever the bloody hell he wanted to call himself. The stakes were getting higher by the minute.

WILLA WAS KEEPING quiet and being as unobtrusive as possible. Not that it mattered. The larger of the two men, slight as that difference was, in West's employ had kept his eyes on her the entire time. It was as if his gaze left a trail of fetid muck in its wake. He was not the first man of such an ilk that she had encountered, but it was the first time she'd ever been in such a powerless position with one.

No sooner had that thought crossed her mind than West rose to his feet. "Joseph, come with me... it's time to deliver our demands to Lord Deveril. And as for you, Jim, you can't tup her while we're gone."

The big man looked at him with a grin. "Can I do anything else with her?"

"You cannot leave me here with him," Willa protested. "Take him with you and leave the other man behind. Please! I beg of you."

West approached her then. He dropped to his haunches in front of her. He reached out one hand and captured her chin, turning her face up to the light. His grip was bruising and painful, just as he intended.

Willa moved to smack his hand away, but he caught her wrist and gave it a sharp and painful twist.

"Jim, would you agree to sacrificing a quarter of your agreed upon pay for the opportunity I've presented you?" West asked, still studying her face intently.

The man considered it for a moment. "I reckon I would. I've paid more than that for some whores. Less for others. Though she ain't a whore, is she? I suspect I'm gettin' a bargain!"

West smiled coldly at her as he replied to his compatriot, "Indeed you are, Jim. Women such as Miss Marks here, virginal and trained in all the ladylike arts, they auction them off at some houses for hundreds of pounds. I saw one sold for a thousand once. Pretty little thing she was, though certainly much younger than our Miss Marks here. Why, I believe you might be considered a spinster, my dear. Aren't you?"

Willa ignored his question and said, with far more bravado than she actually felt, "If I am harmed, Lord Deveril—"

"Lord Deveril will what? I asked who you were... his betrothed, according to rumor, but I have inside information to the contrary. If that's the truth, I'll bare my ass and wade right into the frigid Thames. No, Miss Marks, you're a hireling. He might be calling you his betrothed in order to spare your reputation, but a chit like you? Hardly, Miss Marks. If you were an opera dancer, or an actress, or even a known demirep, then perhaps I could see it. But you're none of those things. I was reared under well enough circumstances to know a governess when I see one, no matter how fine her gown may be. By the way, don't get too attached to that one. I'll be taking it with me. There's a shop that will pay a pretty penny for it. Street girls pay to rent them. Dress lodgers they call them."

Willa gaped at him. "I cannot give you my gown! What on earth would I wear in its stead?"

"I neither know nor care," he said. "There are rags enough around here that you may cover yourself with... assuming Jim gives you the opportunity to do so."

"You are a vile, wretched man," Willa murmured softly. "And you will pay for all that you do here!"

"This is hardly the worst I've done, Miss Marks," West said softly. "Mind your tongue or it will not be Jim who puts you in your place... and if I'm forced to do so, know that I will endeavor to make it both as painful and as humiliating as possible for you. Is that understood?"

Whether it was cowardice or wisdom, Willa kept her mouth closed firmly in the face of his threat. When he grabbed her wrist again and hauled her up, twisting it even more cruelly in the process, she couldn't bite back the yelp of pain.

"Remove your gown or I will do it for you," he warned softly.

He'd lied, Willa realized. He did enjoy hurting women, or perhaps he simply enjoyed hurting anyone he deemed weaker than himself. Anger, shame, terror—so many emotions warred within her. But Willa knew that what she needed more than anything was time. Her hands trembled as she reached for the small buttons that held closed the bib front of her gown. When the fabric parted, she loosened the tapes and let it fall to the floor where she stepped out of it. West scooped it up, his gaze traveling over her insolently.

"Perhaps there's more than being a governess to you, after all. What a pity your gowns hide so much, Miss Marks."

Hope that Lord Deveril would rescue her, somehow, was all that she had. With her gown in his hands, standing before him in only her shift, stays, and petticoats, it was a state of undress that no man, not even Lord Deveril, had seen her in. Willa reached for a dirty blanket that was hanging over what was left of a broken chair. She quickly draped it over her shoulders, hiding as much of herself from him as possible. It was hardly modest, but it was the best she could do under the circumstances.

"You have the gown, Mr. West. Now leave me be."

He laughed. "How eager you are to be rid of me... you may change your mind, Miss Marks. The boots as well, if you please. They'll fetch a pretty penny also."

"You're a blackguard!"

"Yes. I am. Right now, Jim might fondle you a bit. Have a bit of fun with you, but he'll not take the virginity you cherish so proudly... unless I give him leave to do so. Your boots, Miss Marks. Now."

Willa shivered at the implied threat and stooped to remove her boots. When the task was done, she tossed the footwear at West's feet. He laughed softly as he picked them up, before he turned and walked away. He called out for Joseph to accompany him, and they both left the small shack. She spared a glance in the direction of the man called Jim and immediately regretted it. A dozen blankets could have been draped over her and it would not have been enough to offer her any real sense of modesty in his presence. Her skin prickled with unease as West and the other man exited their makeshift shelter.

The rickety door hadn't even closed behind them before Jim was up on his feet and approaching her.

"Stay away from me," Willa said, hating the way her voice trembled. It wasn't in her nature to be fearful, but he was a large man and there were naught but silent graves around them. Even if she screamed, there'd be no one to come to her aid.

"It's just a bit of fun, girlie," he said, a wicked and terrifying grin spreading across his craggy face to reveal stained, dirty teeth.

"I'd hardly call it fun," she snapped. "Leave me be!"

His twisted smile widened as he stepped toward her. The expression chilled her to the bone. She realized that he was enjoying her fear. It only increased his pleasure in what would undoubtedly be her inevitable fate at his hands. Willa stepped back, retreating from him as he continued to approach. Her foot struck a loose board and, instinctively, she reached down and grasped it up, wielding it like a club. "Stay back," she warned.

His smile gave way and a menacing growl escaped him. "I'll not be threatened by a woman! Someone needs to teach you your place, you uppity quim!"

Willa gripped the board more tightly. She had no illusions about her ability to defend herself against him, but she refused to simply give in without a fight. Backed into a corner, she faced a man twice her size with nothing more than a rotting remnant of board. He surged toward her and, without hesitation, Willa swung her impromptu weapon at him. Had she inspected it more closely, she would have known it was a more effective weapon than she had realized. A lone nail remained in the wood. It struck him, raking over his forehead, and blood welled in its wake.

He yelled out in pain, covering his damaged face with his hand. "Hateful bitch!"

"Stay back!" she warned, holding the board aloft once more.

He lunged again, and this time he was ready for her attack. When she swung, he caught the board and ripped it from her hands. It was tossed aside, and then he grabbed her, shoving her roughly against the wall. Willa let out a startled scream as her head connected painfully with the rough timbers of the wall. The sound was cut off abruptly as his hands closed about her throat. He was so large it seemed his hands wrapped nearly double about her neck, his own clumsy fingers in his way as he tried to choke the life out of her. She struggled in vain to pry his fingers free, but his grip held firm. The room began to dim, growing blacker with each passing second, and then the loud report of a pistol echoed throughout the shack. There was no time to even wonder where it had come from or who might have discharged the shot. The threatening blackness claimed her and Willa slipped into unconsciousness.

Chapter Twenty-Three

H IGHCLIFF HELD THE still smoking pistol aloft as Devil rushed past him. He didn't even pause to check the assailant. There was little doubt the man was dead as Highcliff's aim had been quite true. The pistol ball had struck the man in the head, and he'd been felled like a tree. It was Wilhelmina who held his attention. She lay on the floor much like one of Marina's often discarded dolls, her body limp. Dark bruises were already forming about her throat. But as he checked for a pulse, he found it beating steadily and with a strength that prompted a great sigh of relief from him.

"She lives. But we must get her far from here," Devil said and lifted her easily into his arms. She was as light as a feather, delicate in ways that her often fierce personality belied. Seeing her thus would haunt him for all of his days, mostly because she was only in such a predicament due to her involvement with him.

"I'll summon a carriage. It would be best to carry her beyond the church. If you're caught carting her through the cemetery in such a state, they'll think you are a resurrection man," Highcliff warned.

Devil followed his friend from the dirty hovel and past the church toward the street. It was not a highly trafficked area, especially at night. But they were in luck and a hack was passing them as it headed back into the city. Giving their direction only as Mayfair, Devil guessed that Highcliff was hoping for a bit of anonymity. Both their addresses were well known, after all.

As the vehicle lurched forward, Willa stirred. Her lashes fluttered for a moment and then her eyes slowly opened. Recognition was instant. "You came for me," she said, half in wonderment. Her voice was hoarse and thick from the abuse she'd so recently suffered.

"Always, darling girl. Now rest. We'll be home soon," he said softly. Her eyes closed again, and she relaxed in his arms. Unable to help himself, he pulled her closer still, the firmness of his hold on her far more for his own peace of mind than for hers.

"My God! You really do love her," Highcliff said. "I never thought I'd see the day!"

A quick denial sprang to his lips, but Devil didn't utter it. Perhaps for the first time in his life, he was not quite so eager to completely disavow the notion. For his part, he wasn't certain it was love. But then he'd never known love and would be unlikely to recognize it, Devil thought. But he cared deeply for her, more so than for himself, and he supposed that was the start of it. "Are you shocked at my ability to have such depth of feeling or scandalized by the recipient of those feelings?"

"A bit of both, actually," Highcliff said. "You know she will never be accepted in society. Are you prepared for that?"

Yes, he was. He'd found himself in such trouble prior to his exile to India because he'd been bored. His disenchantment with London and its entertainments had led him to take stupid risks for stupid reasons. Wenching, gaming, fighting, dueling. He'd been struggling to feel something, anything. And within a matter of days of entering his life, it was as if Wilhelmina Marks had brought him to life. "I think I'd rather like rusticating in the country for some time. I think I might even prefer it."

Highcliff shook his head. "I would never have thought this day would come."

"What day is that?"

"The day that you give up your wild, wicked bachelorhood for a mere slip of a girl... but I daresay if she is anything like Euphemia Darrow, she would be worth it."

There was something in Highcliff's tone that alerted him. He might have fallen entirely under Willa's spell, but it was clear that Highcliff was just as enamored of her benefactress and mentor. "What precisely is the nature of your acquaintance with Miss Euphemia Darrow?"

"I admire her greatly," Highcliff said. "And she tolerates me... well, tolerably. We are both in a fine kettle, my friend, enamored of women too fine in character and too low in station for either of us."

Devil looked down at her once more. "Does any of that really matter? Station and legitimacy?"

"Not to me, no. But they matter to Miss Darrow... just as I imagine they matter greatly to Miss Marks. You and I, Devil, have the benefit of being born with a kind social currency that protects us from censure, even when we deserve it. Had any other man engaged in the wild escapades you had, they'd have been disowned, imprisoned, or swinging at Tyburn. You were spared by virtue of your birth and your name!"

He knew all of that, Devil thought somewhat bitterly. His father had made it a point to remind him of it almost daily until the cold-hearted bastard had finally shuffled off the mortal coil. "I'm well aware."

"You must also be aware that without such social currency, women such as Miss Marks and Miss Darrow must walk a very narrow path or face utter ruin. Whatever their stations may be, they have a far firmer grasp of propriety than either of us ever shall," Highcliff noted. "But at least in the case of Miss Marks, I imagine you may sway her to your way of thinking. She seemed to be exceedingly glad of your presence. I can only presume that her feelings for you might be a strong inducement to ignore any perceived obstacles in regards to your social standing."

"Let us hope that is the case," Devil agreed. He hadn't any notion of what he would do otherwise. The very thought of her continued refusal made him feel reckless and unsettled in ways that he had not for many, many years.

"I would caution you, my friend, to have a care what promises you make," Highcliff said. "She's a beautiful woman, and no doubt very different from anyone you have ever known. Be certain that you love her for who she is and not the novelty she presents. Because novelty fades. And she deserves far better than that. You both do."

AS THE HIRED hackney rolled to a rather abrupt stop before the Mayfair townhouse that she'd come to think of as her home in only a short while, Willa had finally managed to attain some degree of wakefulness. The events of the day were repeating themselves again and again in her mind, and yet with each repetition, the outcome was different and wholly disastrous. Lord Deveril and Lord Highcliff had not arrived in time. They had not arrived at all. They'd arrived and then simply abandoned her to her fate. A dozen scenarios played out for her, each one horrifying and each one playing on a different aspect of her fears. But she was safe, warm, and cared for within the confines of that hired conveyance, if only she could make herself believe it.

At some point, someone had draped a heavy cloak over her, shielding the fact that she wore only her underthings. As Lord Deveril disembarked from the carriage, he reached back for her and lifted her out easily.

"I'm awake. I can walk," she protested.

"You're shaking like a leaf, Wilhelmina. Do not let pride send you tumbling into the street," he said softly. "Besides, you haven't any shoes."

Any protest would have been simply that—her pride. She was trembling from head to toe, and it felt as if she hadn't drawn a full breath in ages. Panic and fear had seized her lungs, leaving her breathless and her heart pounding in her chest like a battlefield drum. Unable to formulate a response, Willa simply granted a jerky nod.

Seemingly effortlessly, he lifted her out and carried her up the wide steps to the front door. It was opened by the butler long before they reached it, and she could hear Mrs. Farrelly wailing inside.

"Oh, heavens, she's dead! She's dead! I knew it."

"She is not dead, Mrs. Farrelly," Lord Deveril said with a snap as he entered the foyer, his voice echoing in the space. "However, if you do not cease your caterwauling, her head may ache so that she would wish for it!"

The cook immediately dropped her head, chastened. "Aye, my lord. I'm just ever so glad to see her back. Poor wee thing upstairs would be heartbroken without her."

"I'm quite all right, Mrs. Farrelly, just a bit unsteady on my feet at the moment," Willa offered as she leveled a halting glance at the man who still held her cradled in his arms. "And Lord Deveril did not mean to be short with you. Did you?"

He cocked one eyebrow at her and asked softly, "Am I apologize to my own servants then?"

"If an apology is warranted, the station of the recipient should make no difference," she replied. "She was worried. With good reason."

He sighed in response. "Pardon my sharpness, Mrs. Farrelly. It has been a trying day for us all."

"Aye, my lord, aye it has!" the cook replied, beaming at him beatifically.

"Let's get you upstairs," he said to Willa.

"It would be better if I walked," she protested.

"I'm going to remind you that you have no shoes upon your feet, and this cloak, held as you are, camouflages the fact that you wear only your underclothes beneath it," he reminded her, whispering against her ear. "Let me carry you."

Relenting in the wake of such compelling arguments, Willa submitted. It was difficult being so close to him, not because it was an unpleasant sensation, but because it reminded her too greatly of the events that had passed between them in his chamber. And because, if she were to be honest, it offered her such comfort that she feared it. Needing him, craving his touch, his company, the sound of his voice— it would be her downfall.

Willa sighed. She wasn't oblivious to the fact that the traumas of her day had left her vulnerable, that his heroic rescue of her had only complicated her already tangled feelings for him. As they neared her room, the maid that had been assigned to her during her stay rushed past them to open the door. He swept them inside and carried her directly to the bed, depositing her upon it.

"Have a bath prepared for her... steaming, if you please, and a pot of tea with brandy," he said.

"You're drinking?" she asked.

"The brandy is for you... under the circumstances, a bit of bracing of the nerves will be a requirement I think," he replied.

Willa didn't deny it. Truthfully, she'd have preferred just the brandy to the laced tea, but she could hardly tell him so when she'd made such a fuss about his consumption of spirits. When the maid left to do his bidding, she uttered the lie, "I'm quite all right. I'm fine, really."

"I'm not," he said and settled onto a chair near the fire. "Not in the least. I'm horrified that you were taken from my home, where you should have been safe and protected."

"It was the garden. And it was foolish of me to be out there alone. I took an unnecessary risk."

"It was foolish of me to assume that two guards would be enough to keep West away... Munro, actually. His real name is Alaric Munro.

He's a traitor, by the way, and if I can manage to see him apprehended, he will be hanged."

"A traitor?" Willa asked. "How?"

"His stepfather supplied munitions to the army... and Alaric supplied information about those shipments of guns and ammunitions to our enemies. Likely over a card table or to cover his gaming debts," Devil explained. "But I don't want to talk about him anymore today. I want to talk about you, and more specifically, I want to talk about us."

"There is no us," Willa denied quickly. "Not really."

"There can be. There should be," he insisted. "And to that end, I have a proposition for you, Miss Wilhelmina Marks."

Willa's heart sank. She knew what was coming. He'd spoken of marriage, but surely he'd seen the error of such a plan. He was likely on the cusp of making an indecent offer to her, and while it pained her, it thrilled her as well. "And what is that?"

"Half *the ton* thinks Marina is my child... a bastard I sired before my exile to India. And given who her actual father is, I'm reaching the conclusion that it might be best for her if all of society views her as such. But only if I were to marry the woman whom they would believe to be her mother."

It was not at all what she'd expected. "You can't be suggesting that I take on that role," she protested.

"I am suggesting it. Marry me, Wilhelmina. Not some sham we've concocted to cover your presence here... I want you to be my wife in truth. And Marina's mother. She is so young, I am not even certain she will hold any memory of Alice as she grows up. And while it pains me to say it, I'm not even certain she should, given what I learned today."

"What did you learn?"

Lord Deveril looked up, his gaze haunted and impossibly sad. She'd never seen such grief before. "He killed Alice. Not just with neglect and poverty, as I had initially suspected. He slowly poisoned her to death, and only by the grace of God did Marina not succumb to the same fate."

"I don't understand. How? Unless I am mistaken, he was an absentee father at best!"

Devil rose and crossed to the window, looking out onto the streets below. "It was a tin of tea, the inside of it painted Paris Green and then refilled so that until it was empty, no one would ever know. Every cup she savored was slowly killing her."

"Marina hates tea. She prefers milk or lemonade," Willa said softly, horrified at the notion. It would have taken so little of the lethal substance to end the life of such a small child. "But I doubt he knew that. He wouldn't have cared enough to know. It was his intent for the both of them to die at his hand."

"I need for her, and you, to be out of his reach. And marriage is the most expedient way to ensure that is the case," he said. "Will you consent to such a bargain, Wilhelmina Marks?"

There was a part of her that wanted to say yes. But it was for all the wrong reasons. Her feelings for him were growing more complex by the day, and yet she had no indication of his feelings for her. Oh, certainly he desired her, but in that regard, their sexes could not be more different. Her desire for him was only spurred by her feelings, and the reverse was rarely true. Men, especially those such as Lord Deveril who had indulged his vices so freely, did not require any involvement of the heart to spark such urges. Even then, desire wasn't enough. There had to be some deeper and finer feeling involved.

"I've never given thought to marriage," she said, after being silent for a very long while. "It's something that, well, given my station, seemed out of reach for me. But if I were to marry, it wouldn't be because a child needed a mother and I was an acceptable substitute. My selflessness has limits, Lord Deveril, and giving up the rest of my life to a man who will never love me is testing that limit. If I marry, Lord Deveril, I deserve to be married for myself, for who and what I am. I thank you for your offer, but I must decline."

Chapter Twenty-Four

DEVERIL LISTENED TO her pretty little speech and then said something so autocratic that it stunned even himself. "My dear, it wasn't an offer or even a request. We will be married and that is the end of it."

Her head shot up, brows arched with her chin jutting forward stubbornly. "I beg your pardon?"

"Wilhelmina, we will be married. As for your ridiculous assumption that I am only wedding you for Marina's sake, I need only remind you of what happened in my chamber just yesterday to combat that idiotic notion."

"Idiotic?" she snapped. "If your hope is to obtain my acquiescence, insulting me is hardly a manner I would recommend!"

"I want you for my wife, Willa," he said boldly and without any hesitation.

"And your mistress? How will she... or should I say they? How will the bevy of women at your beck and call respond to such news?" Every word was bitten off in staccato manner, indicating just how far her temper had escalated.

"I have no mistress. I have not had a mistress since Marina came into my life. The last one, if you must know, presumed that Marina was actually my child and pitched a tantrum equal to one of Marina's before storming out of this very house. And I've had other things on my mind in the interim!"

"Oh, so you simply haven't had an opportunity to replace her yet? I see!"

"No, you bloody well do not!" he snapped. It was the bark of his tone, the fact that he was almost yelling at her after what had been an impossible day for them both that brought him back to reason. Devil sighed and scrubbed a hand over his face. In a softer and more conciliatory tone, he said, "I cannot change my past, Willa. But I can dictate my future actions. I vow that I will be a good husband to you."

"And a faithful one?" she queried, her doubt evident in her tone.

"So long as that is your desire, yes." It was a far easier promise to make than he would have thought. In truth, no other woman had ever held him in sway to the degree that she did. It had been boredom or convenience that had driven him to the arms of most of his former lovers. Only with Willa did he feel compelled to be there, to be solely with her. From the moment he'd first met her, it was as if all other women had ceased to exist. Of course, it was one of the first times in his adult life that he'd been sober enough to actually examine his feelings instead of simply moving from one vice to another to fill the emptiness of his life. It had taken that moment of clarity to understand what it was that was missing. "I have done many things in my life that I am not proud of, Willa, but I am a man of my word, and that is what I give you now. Marrying you is what I want. That it benefits Marina is simply a fortuitous turn of events… I cannot pretend that your relationship with my niece is not part of this. Had it not been for her presence here and my need of your assistance in reaching her, in helping her, you would have not entered my life, Willa, and I would not have seen what was missing from it. Can you understand that?"

"You do not love me," she said. "We barely know one another."

"I do not believe in love. Not in that way," he said softly. "I believe in caring for a person. I believe in attraction and taking pleasure in a person's company as well as in a more intimate fashion," he said evenly, trying to highlight his very rational viewpoint on a matter that only ever seemed to bring irrationality even to the most staid of persons. "I also believe in honoring ones promises to them... but romantic love is little more than a myth or a fairy story for children. It's fine for little girls to dream upon. But in this very ugly world, it's simply a thing used by those who have no appreciation of the truth so they might manipulate others and get what they want from them. You have only to look at my poor sister to see that."

Her answering gaze was a mixture of disbelief and pity. "I cannot marry you, Lord Deveril. Perhaps I will regret that choice one day but, for now, I cannot accept that the world is utterly devoid of love. I may never find it, but I do desperately want to believe, foolish as it may be, that it exists."

He stared at her for a long moment, his gaze caught somewhere between amusement and pity. Then it hardened, became serious and rather stern. "You're forgetting one very important fact, Willa. Your future employability as a governess is dependent upon your retaining your sterling reputation... today's events will tarnish it beyond repair."

"No one knows," she protested.

"Servants know. And no matter the house, the rank, or the repercussion, they gossip. Our neighbors know. And their neighbors will soon know if they do not already. You are already an object of curiosity to them because of my reputation. The fact that I was seen carrying you back into this house after your ordeal will not have gone unnoticed," he stated firmly.

He could see the desire to protest written plainly upon her all too expressive face. No doubt she wanted to rail at the unfairness of it all, but Miss Marks was nothing if not a realist. It was likely that half of Mayfair had heard Mrs. Farrelly's wailing and all of them would have been on alert following the incidents with his guards in the mews. He knew the instant that she recognized the inevitability of her fate. It was not a joyous moment for him because he could see that it troubled her no small amount.

"Oh, no," she murmured. "Oh, I hadn't thought of it. I must warn Effie. I cannot let the fallout from my situation taint the Darrow School—"

"Miss Darrow will be fine. It will all be fine, Willa, if you only consent to marry me in earnest," he implored. "It will make all of our problems go away and could be a very pleasant experience for us both."

Her eyebrows shot up, and she sent him a scathing, withering glance. "Do you mean the marriage or the marriage bed?"

"Both, I daresay," he answered levelly.

The glaring truth of it all but smacked her face. What choice did she have?

She took a deep, steadying breath and met his gaze directly and dispassionately. "I give my consent, Lord Deveril. I will be your wife."

He didn't crow. The urge was there. Hearing her acquiescence, regardless of the reluctance with which it was uttered, was akin to victory in battle. "I'll obtain a special license, the sooner the better, given recent events. When we are wed, the stakes for Munro will be much higher. He might have no qualms about harming a governess, or even my betrothed. But when you are Lady Deveril, he would be a fool to court such ruin."

"We are fools courting ruin in one way or another. He's made it quite clear that he thinks himself beyond the reach of consequences," she replied. "I'll continue to be cautious. And more guards should be employed. I won't risk having Marina leave this house without them… not again."

"On that point, we are in agreement. When this is done, when Munro is apprehended and punished for what he did today, things will be different. Perhaps we can host a ball if you wish, or simply go about in society as you desire."

"I do not desire. Society has no allure for me," she replied. "I've no wish to be whispered about and stared at while half the world calls me a social climbing fortune hunter and the other half calls me a fool for marrying you."

He didn't bother to offer up a token protest, for that was all it could be. She spoke the truth. He'd been the third wheel in many a marriage, and sometimes the fourth or fifth wheel. While he had never lured a wife to stray and had contented himself with sampling the charms of women who had already veered far from the straight and narrow path, his exploits, both true and false, were bandied about freely. Gossip marked him a despoiler of innocents, a threat to the holy institution of matrimony and, in general, a menace to good women and boorish husbands the world over. "Then we shall retire to the country... or travel somewhere if you prefer."

"Let's not pretend, Lord Deveril. I'm marrying you because I've been left with no other choice. You're marrying me because you desire me and because it is the most expedient way to have what you want." Her words were spoken softly, but the bitterness in them echoed through the room and pierced him like a blade. "If I had other options, beyond ruin and disgrace, I would take them."

Devil rose to his feet, eager to end the evisceration he was under-going from her wicked tongue. "You've made that abundantly clear, Miss Marks. Have you considered that the information you have about me might very well be false?"

Her lips curved in a mocking smile. "So you're not a rogue? A rake? A man who has made free with the wives of other men while drinking, gaming, and dueling your way through England?"

"I am all of those things, but I am not a man who breaks his word. And I am not a man who offers promises that I have neither the intent nor the will to keep. I've offered you my fidelity. I've offered to be your husband in good faith... I would hope you might accept the proposal in the same fashion. It isn't a punishment, Miss Marks, unless you choose to make it one for the both of us. I will not be home for dinner. You may have it served in the dining room if you like or I can instruct the servants to bring up a tray."

"I'll take care of it myself, thank you," she said.

Devil said nothing further, just nodded and walked away.

⫸⫷

ALARIC MUNRO RETURNED to the small shack that butted up to the cemetery. He knew instantly the she was gone, but finding one of his hirelings dead was a bit of a surprise. It was also a complication he could ill afford. His other minion might well wash his hands of the entire mess or become enraged at the demise of his brother. Enraged meant unpredictable, and unpredictable meant dangerous to his cause.

"Damn it!" he hissed out. Joseph was approaching the shack even then. Hurrying back outside, Alaric cut him off. "They've gone. Your bastard brother has absconded with my abductee." It was the first and most reasonable lie that came to mind.

"He wouldn't have done that!" Joseph protested. "Not without orders!"

"Unless he killed her by accident. He could even be disposing of her body. You need to go and look for him! Go to any places where he might have taken off to if things went wrong," Alaric said.

Joseph frowned at him. "And what will you be doing?"

"Going to Mayfair to watch that blasted house and see if, perhaps, she managed to escape and returned to the safety of her pseudo-betrothed!" Munro lied. He was going back to Mayfair, but not for that reason. "Go, Colton. Find him and find what has happened to Miss Marks!"

Alaric watched the larger man lumber off and breathed a sigh of relief. He had little doubt that the governess was safely ensconced in Lord Deveril's posh home. He needed to corner Jeannette and find a way inside, and he needed to get Marina or he'd never see a single tuppence from Deveril, not after the man had put a pistol ball in the brain of one of his men. It was clear to Alaric that he'd underestimated Alice's brother. He wasn't the same weak, mewling sort that his sister has been. Ridding himself of Alice had been the best decision he'd ever made. Completing the task at a distance, using the gift of a simple tin of tea that Alice had responded to as if he'd given her jewels, had been a stroke of genius. But he hadn't known at the time that Marina would not drink it. But that was fate serving him up an opportunity for recompense, a chance to get what was his due. But first, he'd need to dispose of Jim Colton's corpse and pray his brother never found the truth.

Chapter Twenty-Five

A FTER A LONG and sleepless night, beleaguered by dreams of the lovely and far too prickly Miss Marks, Devil had left the house early and obtained a special license. It had not been easy. He was known to the archbishop, after all, just as he was known to everyone else in London society, as a man of low morals and extravagant vices. He'd had to offer assurance upon assurance that the woman he was to marry was both willing and worthy of marriage, rather than some tavern-side doxy that he would use to thumb his nose at society matrons. In all, he'd been in chambers for over an hour pleading his case. Finally, the man had relented.

Now, official document in hand, Devil was climbing the steps to his home when a dirty urchin suddenly rushed past him, raised the knocker, dropped a slip of paper, and then rushed off again. Both amused and somewhat befuddled by the experience, Devil stooped and retrieved the missive himself. It was addressed to Lady Carringden. Finding it odd that any such disreputable creature would be currying messages to his aunt from any of her society friends, Devil frowned.

The door opened and his butler looked askance at not having been there to open the door prior. "Relax, I didn't knock. It was some filthy, bedraggled boy... I think it was a boy. It was hard to tell. He delivered a note for my aunt. Has he been here before, Carlton?"

"Yes, my lord. Yesterday morning."

Tension and a sense of *knowing* filled him. It was not a coincidence. "Some filthy child shows up and delivers a note to my aunt on the very day that Miss Marks was abducted and you didn't think it important?"

The butler's already pale face blanched. "I do beg your pardon, my lord. I simply forgot. With everything else that happened... but upon reflection, I can certainly see how the two events occurring in such close proximity would be a significant detail that I should not have overlooked!"

"Do not castigate yourself too much, Carlton. I don't have time to replace you," Devil replied dryly.

Rather than wait for his aunt to explain the situation, Devil did something he would not normally. He opened the letter and scanned the contents.

J,

The plan failed. Deveril rescued the girl and we are back to nothing. I won't get another chance at her. My only hope now is the child. You must bring her to me in the park. This afternoon. If we cannot get the money from Deveril, there is no hope for us, my love. It is the only way we could ever be together.

A.

Devil read it a second time, his gut clenching with fury and betrayal. He'd brought her into his home on the premise of protecting Willa from social ruin and, in turn, had exposed her to even greater dangers. He had, unintentionally, placed her in harm's way.

"Not a word to Lady Carringden, Carlton," Devil said. "She is not to know this was delivered. Is that clear?"

The butler nodded gravely. "I will be as silent as the grave, my lord. It is not my place to speak against a member of the family, but I find such treachery deplorable."

"So do I, Carlton. So do I."

With that matter settled, Devil climbed the stairs and went directly to Willa's chambers. He knocked lightly on the door but did not wait for an answer before turning the handle and stepping inside. She was seated at her dressing table, placing the last pin in her simple coiffure. He could see the dark bruises on her neck and felt renewed rage at the sight of it.

"I wish I'd been the one to shoot the bounder," he said.

"I'm just glad someone shot him," Willa answered. "I'm assuming that some pressing matter has brought you to my chamber this morning?"

"I have the license. And I think we should go immediately to be married," he said.

She blinked at him in confusion. "Now?"

"Yes. We need to be back here by two o'clock so that we can finally put an end to Alaric's plans."

"What is happening at two o'clock?"

Devil sat down on the small bench at the foot of her bed. "I think Lady Carringden is involved with Alaric Munro... and I think that she may have had a hand in helping him to carry off your abduction."

Willa shook her head, her expression conveying just how stunned she was by the revelation. "I have no idea how to respond to that. Her lack of regard for me has certainly been obvious, but I would not have thought that she was capable of such a vile thing. Are you absolutely certain?"

Devil retrieved the missive from his pocket and passed it to her. "That was dropped on the doorstep this morning by some beggar child that Alaric pressed into service. The same child, according to Carlton, who delivered another such note yesterday morning. I can't attest to the contents of it, but based on what I read there, it's damning enough, I daresay."

"I cannot believe this. She's your family," Willa said, scanning the note. "Why?"

"I've always wondered how it was that Alice came to his attention to begin with," Devil admitted. "Now, I have to examine the possibility that it was Lady Carringden all along who placed Alice in his path and who ultimately brought about her ruin and downfall."

⋙⋘

THE PAIN AT such betrayal, his love and his grief for his sister, his determination to keep her safe and to do what Marina needed to be able to grow and thrive—it wasn't any one of those things that cracked the hardened shell of her heart. It was all of them together and the fact that, time and again, he showed her that he was not the man society had painted him to be. It was an uncomfortable moment for her to admit that she'd never judged him fairly. She'd entered that house certain of his character, and while he'd played to that on numerous occasions, it was easy to see why. He'd become so accustomed to people having so little faith in him that he'd stopped trying to convince anyone that he was anything more than a thoroughly debauched rogue and wastrel.

"I owe you an apology, Lord Deveril—Douglas," she corrected. "I've misjudged you terribly. You're a better man than the world knows and a better man, I think, than you give yourself credit for being."

His eyebrows lifted in surprise. "I am all that has been said of me, Willa."

"Yes, but that is not the totality of you. And I feel rather fortunate to have had the opportunity to realize that... I am not certain that marriage is the best option for us, but I know it is our only option at this time. To that end, I think we should just go and see it done."

His lips quirked in a rueful smile. "It's hardly the excitement one hopes for in a bride but, at this point, I suppose I should take what I can get. I'll see you downstairs."

Willa took a moment to dash off a note to Effie letting her know what they were about. There was a moment where she considered if perhaps Effie had not seen this coming and engineered it all to some degree. It would not be the first time that Effie had taken it upon herself to clandestinely manage her grown pupils' lives. When it was done, she donned her pelisse, as the day was chilly and gray, and then made her way downstairs. She entrusted the note to Carlton, the butler. "Please have that delivered to the Darrow School."

"I'll see to it, miss," he said. Devil emerged from the library then, and the butler bowed. "The carriage is waiting, my lord."

Willa's heart began to beat faster as Devil walked toward her and held out his arm.

"Shall we go?" he asked.

"Yes," she whispered softly. "We should be on our way."

Willa let him lead her from the house and to the waiting carriage. She caught sight of the hired guards outside; one was riding with the coachman, another was perched on the back of the carriage. The others remained where they were, surrounding the entrance to the house. Devil paused to whisper instructions to them. Most likely, Willa thought, regarding Lady Carringden and what should be done if she tried to leave.

Afterward, Devil stepped toward the carriage, opened the door, and helped her inside. He climbed in after her, the door closed, and the vehicle lurched forward, carrying Willa toward a fate she could only pray would not be filled with heartbreak and regret.

Chapter Twenty-Six

A S WEDDINGS WENT, it was a subdued affair. Two strangers had been pressed into duty as witnesses at St. James Piccadilly Church. The vicar appeared scandalized by their request for a hasty marriage, but when presented with the special license, he relented quickly enough.

In all, the service took only minutes. Then they were once more bundled back into a carriage and heading back the house on Park Lane. It didn't seem real to Devil, and he imagined that it was much the same for Willa. *Lady Deveril.*

"We will become accustomed to our changed status," he offered.

"I'm certain we shall, though I cannot imagine it will be soon," she said. "What will we do now?"

"We will return to the house. You will closet yourself in the nursery with Marina and Mrs. Farrelly and a guard or three outside the door. And I will secret myself in Hyde Park, watching the Brook Gate which seems to be Munro's preferred point of entry and the most likely meeting point with Lady Carringden. And at a quarter till two, Carlton will deliver to her the recently discovered note that some urchin had carelessly left for her on the steps. I and the remaining guards will confront them together," Devil said, outlining his plan. It was loose at best and fraught with the potential for disaster.

"It sounds remarkably dangerous and not well thought out at all," she said.

"It certainly lacks finesse, but it has come together very quickly. If it is any consolation, I plan to enlist the aid of Lord Highcliff. He's a master of such exploits."

"Lord Highcliff? I know he is a master of elegantly tied neckcloths and perfectly-tailored coats," Willa protested. His aid the day before had surely been some sort of fluke. "Surely there is someone more capable!"

"There is no one more capable. The fact that he served on the Peninsula and again in India, and all you know of him is his sense of fashion, is a testament to his discretion. The man is a master of many things, Willa. Do not be so quick to dismiss him simply because he cuts a dashing figure and keeps the Bond Street merchants in gales of rather mercenary ecstasy."

"I defer to your judgement. He is a friend of Effie's," Willa said. "And I think, perhaps, more than a friend at times."

"I think that you are correct. He holds her in very high regard," Devil replied. "But I do not wish to discuss Highcliff and Miss Euphemia Darrow at the moment."

"What would you care to discuss then?"

Devil surveyed her delicate face, noting the pale green eyes and the small dusting of freckles upon her nose. But it wasn't the arc of her cheekbones or the arch of her perfect brows that captured his gaze. It was the cupid's bow of her lips and the desire to taste them once more. "I would have us stop talking altogether, Willa, and put our lips to better use. What better way to begin a journey as man and wife than with a kiss?"

"In the carriage?" she asked, clearly scandalized.

"It is possible, my dear wife, to do far more than kiss in a carriage. I will show you one day but, for now, a kiss it is," he said, and without warning reached for her. Grasping her hand, he tugged her forward from her seat until she had sprawled across his lap. They were nose to nose and only a scant inch separated their mouths.

"Lord Deveril—"

"Douglas," he corrected her, but did not give her the opportunity to speak his name. Instead, he placed his hand at the back of her head and tugged her down so that their lips met.

As always, it was instant heat. He felt the need cut through him like an arrow. His blood rushed in his veins, his pulse pounding in his ears. He hardened instantly, eager for her, craving far more than their present opportunity would permit. So he focused on the kiss itself, plying her lips with his, stroking his tongue into the honeyed recesses of her mouth. It was a carnal kiss, a blatant imitation of other things he longed to do with her. She melted against him, her breasts pressed against his chest, her thighs parting over his so that he was pressed intimately against her. With his arms locked about her and her hands tangling in his dark hair as the kiss continued, it was the most natural thing in the world to thrust against her, to let her feel precisely what she did to him. And when her hips rocked with him in that ageless rhythm, he let out a tortured groan.

Breaking from the kiss for just a moment, he whispered, "Christ, you will be the death of me!"

"That's blasphemy," she pointed out.

"It's a heartfelt prayer for mercy," he replied. "I cannot think for wanting you, for needing you."

Her brows furrowed with a slight frown. "And when you've had me? When I'm no longer a novelty to you and boredom has set in?"

"That is not what will happen, Willa," he said with a slight smile. "Some things are too perfect and too precious to ever be deemed boring, no matter how familiar they become. And after tonight, you will understand why."

In the distance, a clock chimed. It was nearly noon. "We're running out of time, aren't we? You need to get to the park ahead of Munro." Willa uttered the words quietly. They were not a question.

"That is correct."

She looked up then, worry etching her face. "You will be careful. Promise me that?"

"Do you fear for me, Willa? Or do you fear what will become of you and Marina if I were to die?" She had every right to fear the latter. He'd had no time to make any preparations for her future, to ensure that she would have the finances to live as she chose. No guardian had been specified for Marina. They were gross oversights on his part. But a selfish part of him wanted to believe that her concern was prompted more by her feelings for him.

"Both," she answered honestly. "But the latter hadn't crossed my mind until just now. He's shown just how ruthless he can be, Douglas, and I am afraid for you."

"I will take every precaution, Willa," he vowed. "I will do everything in my power to keep all of us safe from him."

⇛⇚

ALARIC MOVED INTO position in the park. Near the Brook Gate, concealed by a stand of trees, he waited for Jeannette to make her appearance. Joseph was still on his fool's errand of looking for his brother in his usual haunts. It was the best way to get him out of the way for now. Jim was buried in a shallow grave in the churchyard, atop the recently deceased wife of a merchant.

It took only a few moments before the door of the Park Lane home opened and Jeannette emerged. She did not have the child in tow and that did not bode well. He watched her cross the street, glancing furtively over her shoulder the entire way. She could not have been more obvious had she been screaming his name as she did so. When at last she breeched the gate and came to stand only feet away from him, she was breathless and trembling.

"I only just received your missive," she explained. "That worthless boy you hired to deliver it simply dropped it outside the door and fled. The butler only just found it!"

"And where is my daughter?" he demanded.

"She's tucked up in the nursery with the cook and Miss Marks. There is a guard outside the door. It would have been impossible to reach her. But tonight, when the entire house is asleep, if you come to the kitchen door, I will get you inside. I promise, Alaric! Please don't be angry with me! I couldn't bear it," she said, whining at the end of her statement like a petulant child.

"It must be tonight," he said sharply. "Your nephew killed one of my men. I've concealed the body for now. If his brother discovers the truth of it, he will be out for blood!"

"Well, let him kill Devil then! What do we care for his fate?" Jeannette demanded.

"Your idiocy is boundless at times! Think, woman! I cannot have him getting in the way or raising the alarm while trying to get to Deveril if I'm to take Marina unnoticed. Further, Devil can hardly pay the ransom if he's dead!" Alaric snapped.

"Devil's not going to pay the ransom anyway."

The droll voice was soft spoken but menacing for it. Turning in the direction of the speaker, Alaric saw that Lord Deveril himself had graced them with his presence. The man had emerged from a copse of trees, pistol drawn. Two other men flanked him, each one moving forward from the surrounding foliage as if they were part of it. All of them were heavily-armed.

Alaric snarled at him, "I see you've gotten it all figured out, don't you? Protect the precious brat at every turn if you must!"

"I shall," Lord Deveril responded. "I only wish I had not failed to protect my sister. And you will be tried for her murder. If it is the last thing I do, I will see to it."

"It will be," Alaric said, as the other two men moved toward him to take him into custody. Bow Street Runners, he thought bitterly.

"I've left a note for Joseph Colton. It might take a day or two to reach him, might take a day or two for him to find someone to read it for him, but he'll know that you killed his brother in due time, and then he'll come for you."

"He's welcome to try," Deveril replied easily enough.

"What about her, my lord?" one of the runners asked, gesturing toward Jeannette.

"The satisfaction of seeing her carted off to prison would not be worth the cost of the scandal it would create," Lord Deveril said thoughtfully.

"There are asylums, my lord. Women are put in for a lot less," the other man offered generously.

Deveril shook his head. "No. I think my aunt may go back to her little cottage in the country, via the public coach, and she may remain there for the rest of her days, without a single pence from me. Poverty will not suit her I think."

Jeannette began weeping. "Devil, you must not abandon me! You need me! If you do not have a chaperone for Miss Marks—"

"Miss Marks is no longer Miss Marks, Aunt. She is now Lady Deveril, and I do not think she would welcome you into our home any more than I would," he said coldly. "Do not beg. It is beneath us both."

Alaric saw the raw fury on Jeannette's face. It was all the warning he had that she was about to do something disastrous. She shoved her hand into her reticule and produced a tiny and ridiculous-looking pair of muff pistols. Small as they were, he knew they would be deadly. "Jeannette, don't be foolish," he warned. "If you kill him, you will hang!" He was not overly concerned for her, but she was his best hope of affording a decent solicitor. She might still have some jewels she could sell off.

"It isn't for him," she said. "I won't be separated from you again, and I won't live like a beggar. I'd rather die!"

Alaric heard the discharge, the loud report of the small gun, long before he felt the burn in his chest. She'd shot him, he thought. If it hadn't been so bloody painful, he would have laughed. As it was, he could do nothing but sink to the ground. His shirt was wet through with blood already. He could smell it, the coppery scent overwhelming.

One of the runners lowered him to the ground while the other went after Jeannette. She still had one pistol primed and readied. Turning his head, Alaric saw her retreat deeper into the trees. But the fence was at her back. With only a few feet between her and the runner, Jeannette did something that he'd never imagined. She placed the pistol against her temple and pulled the trigger. He watched her sink to the ground, screaming. It had misfired. Instead of death, she had a deep and ugly gouge along her temple and burn marks from the barrel, but she was very much alive. It was his last thought as the air whistled slowly from his perforated lung and his eyes fluttered closed.

Chapter Twenty-Seven

THE ENTIRE HOUSE was in an uproar and for good reason. A doctor was seeing to Jeannette, repairing the damage she'd done as best he could. It seemed, Devil thought, she would wind up in an asylum after all. Whether it was guilt at having murdered her lover or whether the misfire of the pistol at such close proximity had addled her brain permanently, he could not guess. Suffice it to say, she'd been doing little more than muttering nonsense and gibberish since the incident in the park. Of course, Devil also wouldn't put it past her to be exaggerating her symptoms in order to avoid the consequences of her actions. It was a terrible thing to be so suspicious, but given the events of the past few days, it wasn't unwarranted.

Striding the length of the corridor, he found himself outside Willa's chamber. He knocked softly, but there was no response. Concerned, he opened the door and found her room empty. The bottles and brushes that had adorned her dressing table were gone. Other than the faint, lingering scent of her perfume, there was no trace of her. Stepping out into the hall once more, he caught a passing maid. "Where is Miss—where is Lady Deveril?"

"Mr. Carlton had us move her things to the chamber that adjoins yours, my lord," the maid replied with a blush. "Should we not have done so?"

He shook his head. "No, that's quite all right. I didn't anticipate such efficiency."

With that, he turned and made for his own chamber. Entering the room, he crossed to the connecting door and knocked lightly upon it. He heard a soft voice bid him enter. Opening the door, he stepped inside and found her seated at a small table before the fire. There was a veritable feast spread upon it along with a bottle of champagne.

"What is all this?" he asked.

She glanced at the table with a blush staining her cheeks. "This would be Mrs. Farrelly's idea of a romantic interlude. I'm afraid your servants have certain ideas about our marriage that we do not have the luxury of disabusing them of."

He crossed the distance to the table and picked up the bottle. "It's an excellent vintage. A shame to waste it," he said, and then poured the bubbling liquid into the waiting glasses. "What sort of ideas about our marriage should they have?"

"That it's real? That we're a couple blinded by love," she said dryly. "I understand that there is a necessity in fooling the rest of the world, Douglas, but I think it would be remarkably unwise if we were to lie to ourselves about it. Don't you?"

He took the seat opposite her and began examining the numerous covered dishes filled with delicacies that the very thoughtful cook had provided. "The only thing I can think about at the moment is that I am not paying my cook nearly enough. She has rather outdone herself."

"Will you be serious for a moment, please?" The words escaped her on an exasperated sigh. "We need to have some parameters and rules about how we are to proceed!"

He smirked at that. "I thought we covered those this morning. Love, honor, obey... forsaking all others. I realize it's been a rather trying day, but surely you haven't forgotten already?"

"I've forgotten nothing," she said sharply. "And this isn't a jest or a game, Douglas."

"No," he said, suddenly serious. "It most certainly is not. And I find it not at all humorous. I made a vow to you this morning, Willa, and for whatever it may be worth, I mean to keep it. We are not pretending here, there is no illusion to maintain. You are my wife and I am your husband. Till death do us part, or so we said."

"If you're implying that I do not mean to keep my vows—"

He raised his hands in mock supplication. "I'm not implying anything of the sort, Willa. I'm only asking that you stop assuming I am not able to keep them myself or that I am somehow less determined to or less capable of doing so. This is as real as we wish to make it." He paused then, his gaze settling on her very intently. "And I want it to be very, very real. In every way."

SHE WAS DOING it again. Judging him. To be fair, it wasn't only him. She was actually judging all men by the very poor example her father had set. Her father had gone through two wives already, countless mistresses, and each one had been left heartbroken, dead, or in the case of his most recent bride, locked away in an asylum. She was likely not mad at all, but unmanageable, and that was something he could not abide. He wanted to come and go as he pleased, with whom he pleased, and he liked for his wives to stay home and rusticate in the country, far from any gossip that might reach them about his extravagant behavior. It wasn't a need to spare their feelings, but a need to spare himself lectures and arguments.

Looking at Lord Deveril, she knew that he was cut from a very different cloth. He might have indulged some of the same vices, but he lacked the general coldness that her father possessed.

"I'm sorry. I shouldn't make such assumptions... and you are right. This marriage is as real as we wish to make it and I—" Willa broke off abruptly, not quite able to make herself utter the words.

"And you what, Willa?"

His tone was gentle. It was that more than anything else that prompted her to meet his gaze once more. It offered her courage. "Kiss me, Douglas, like you did before."

It was not a request she had to make twice. No sooner had the words escaped her than he'd risen from his chair and hauled her up before him. They were standing together, their bodies touching. One of his arms was about her waist, holding her close, leaving his other hand free to roam. His roughened fingers settled on her face, cupping it gently, his thumb stroking the delicate skin at her temple as he tilted her face up to his.

It was a delicate thing, that kiss. His lips settled on hers lightly, moving against them in a gentle, persuasive manner. Willa pressed closer, urging him for more, and yet he did not. As he drew the fullness of her lower lip gently between his, Willa was struggling, chaffing at his newfound restraint.

"Devil," she said, uttering the word against his mouth, "Kiss me! Really kiss me!"

He smiled. She could feel the curving of his lips against hers. "You mean scandalously? I thought you wanted a respectable husband?"

"I want you as my husband—respectable or not." The moment she said it, the truth of that struck her. She could have refused. While his reasons for their marriage were sound and valid, there were other options. But she hadn't wanted them. She'd allowed herself to be steered into marrying him because it was precisely what she'd wanted in her most secret heart all along. Whatever doubts she might have, whatever she might fear of their final outcome, for the moment, she was precisely where she wanted to be.

As if her words had stoked an answering passion in him, his arm tightened about her waist, his hand sliding down to cup the fullness of her behind as he pulled her closer. She could feel the hard press of his arousal against the softness of her belly. Her blood heated in response, the thrum of her pulse heavy and fast. She was nervous, but eager to know what lay beyond fevered kisses.

He lifted her in his arms easily and carried her to the waiting bed. Depositing her on it, he immediately reached for the buttons that closed the front of her gown. Within seconds, he had managed to extricate her from the garment. Lying there in her shift and petticoats, her stays came next. He loosened the laces and whisked it away. It seemed, within seconds, he'd divested her of everything but her shift, an item of clothing so transparent it did nothing to conceal her form beneath.

He stepped back then, his gaze sweeping over her boldly. "I've pictured you just like this. A dozen different variations on the same theme and not one image produced by my feeble imagination has done you justice."

"Flattery—"

"Truth," he said, and his voice was gruff, deeper than normal, with a slight growl to it that made her shiver in response. He removed his coat and waistcoat along with his cravat. Still wearing his shirt and breeches, he climbed onto the bed with her and gathered her in his arms. "You've haunted my dreams from the moment I first saw you."

"I feel very underdressed," she said.

"I'll join you soon enough," he vowed. "Let us not tax my already tenuous control any further, shall we?"

Willa had no idea what that truly meant. But as he kissed her, questions were forgotten. Instead, she gave herself up to the glorious sensations of the weight of him against her, of the warmth of his body as it pressed against hers. This kiss was much different from the teasing kiss they'd only just shared. This was wicked and carnal. It was all the things she'd come to associate with him, all the things she craved from him.

She pressed closer to him, her body seeking his without any conscious thought. And he gave her what she asked for. His hands roamed over her, from her shoulders to her ribs, down to her hips, over the gentle curves of her bottom and then back up until he could cup her breasts in his hands. As he stroked the taut buds of her nipples with the pads of his thumbs, the sensation jolted through her, eliciting a tension inside her that she'd never experienced before. It was as if every muscle in her body had contracted in anticipation of what was to come next.

He did not disappoint. His mouth left hers, coasting along her jaw, then down the column of her throat. Then his lips drifted lower, over the arc of her collar bone and to the upper swells of her breasts. She craved his touch there, the heat of his mouth upon her. The tip of his tongue touched that taut bud of her nipple through the thin fabric of her chemise. A startled gasp erupted from her as his mouth closed over her. The heat and pull of it amplified the tension inside her. There was heat pooling low in her belly, spreading outward to that forbidden place between her thighs.

It seemed as if he'd read her thoughts. With his knee, he parted her thighs and his hand slipped beneath her chemise, his fingertips trailing over her skin in a way that raised gooseflesh in their wake. When he touched her intimately, his fingers brushing the hair that shielded her sex, she gasped. Then he was sliding one finger inside her, touching her in a place she had not known existed. She closed her eyes at the intensity of the sensations, at the sweep of pleasure as it coursed through her. His touch became more insistent, the pleasure climbing higher with each stroke of his skilled fingers.

"Douglas," she breathed. "What are you doing to me?"

"I told you I would introduce you to pleasure, Wilhelmina, and I mean to do so... you must simply give yourself up to it," he whispered hotly against her ear.

She could do nothing else. Her body seemed to no longer be her own. Her hips arched upward against his hand, seeking, demanding. And he gave, answering her desperate cries.

It happened suddenly. The tension inside her broke, waves of it spiraling through her as she shuddered against him.

DEVIL WAS ENRAPTURED by her. There was nothing so beautiful as a woman in the throes of passion, but to see Wilhelmina in the full flower of pleasure was something else entirely. Every breathless cry, every shudder of her delicate body, the slick heat of her sex as he stroked her tender flesh—his own desires were beyond his control. He needed to claim her, to possess her, and to know that she was his in every way.

With his knee, he pressed her thighs further apart and moved between them. Desperate to feel the heat of her closing around him, he fumbled with the buttons of his breeches, finally managing to free them. Aligning his aching member with entrance, he pressed in slowly, easing his way until he felt the fragile barrier of her innocence. It was an easy enough thing to stop then. The idea of causing her pain, even at the expense of his own pleasure, was enough to halt him.

"You won't like this part, I'm afraid," he said softly.

"Will I like what comes after?" she asked, still breathless.

"I certainly hope so... there's always a bit of pain for women their first time. But it's quick, I'm told."

She cocked one eyebrow. "You've never been with a woman who was a virgin?"

"I've never been with a woman who wasn't one apoplectic fit from widowhood," he reminded her. "Old, fat husbands were the favorite accessory of my past paramours."

She laughed softly, and that movement quickly erased all humor from the situation. He was gritting his teeth, fighting the urge to simply drive into her.

"If something is unpleasant," she said, "It's best to get it done quickly."

With that, Devil withdrew from her almost entirely, only to surge forward again, breeching the barrier of her innocence. It robbed him of breath. The pleasure of being buried inside her, the silken heat of her sheath gripping him so intimately, was more than he could withstand. He gripped her hips, urging her to be still, striving for some semblance of the control and finesse he'd always prided himself on. Somehow, he managed to lay claim to a shred of it. When she'd ceased squirming, he asked, "Does it still hurt?"

"No," she replied. "But you may be wrong about me liking this part of things."

"Defer judgement, darling girl, defer judgement," he whispered encouragingly. Determined to bring her pleasure, to erase even the slightest memory of pain, he began to move within her. Slowly at first, building a gentle, steady rhythm that very soon she began to match. As her hips moved against him, meeting his thrusts, he increased the speed and intensity. He knew the moment she gave herself up to it. Her knees lifted higher, and she locked her ankles just above his buttocks, holding him more tightly to her. Broken whimpers and sobs escaped her parted lips, and they were like a symphony to his ears.

He didn't stop and, despite the cost, he refused to succumb to his own need for release until he felt the first shuddering contraction within her. Only then did he let go and push deep one last time, spilling his essence deep within her.

Chapter Twenty-Eight

J OSEPH COLTON ENTERED The Cock and Crow Inn. His mood was black and foul, and he was spoiling for a fight. There was no sign of Jim, and he was quickly beginning to realize that Alaric West had pulled the wool over his eyes.

"Joseph," the serving girl said. "There's a letter for you."

"Can't read, now can I?" he sneered.

"If you'd toss me a coin, I'd read it to you. If you'd toss me two coins, I'd read it to you while I was naked," she replied saucily.

Since he strongly suspected that West was long gone and the money owed him was gone with him, Joseph was in no mood for her teasing and flirting. Reaching out, he grasped her wrist and pulled her close to him. "Read me the damned letter and save your games for those've got the coin to spare!"

The girl swallowed convulsively, clearly intimidated by his display of temper. Normally, it was Jim who set the ladies running in fright, but in his current mood, he simply didn't care. He let go of her arm abruptly and she stumbled back. Still, she clutched the slip of paper in her hand like it was a lifeline. After a moment, and a deep breath, she broke the seal and read the note.

"It's from Mr. West," she said. "It's about your brother."

"What's it say?" he demanded gruffly.

She shook her head and began to cry. "I don't want to say! You'll hit me!"

"I will if you don't answer my questions! Tell me what it says!"

She glanced back at the note. "It says that it was Lord Deveril who killed your brother... says that Jim were dead when you got back there to the boneyard, and he kept you from going inside and seeing what become of him."

"That bastard... I'll see him dead."

"Mr. West?"

"Aye, him. Him and Lord Deveril... and his governess. She's as much a party to it as the lot of them," Joseph murmured. Without a backward glance, he left the shabby and disreputable inn. He made one stop, at a shop near the corner where he'd pawned an item he now required. With the weapon retrieved, he cut through back alleys and side streets until he once more found himself emerging onto the paved and artfully maintained streets of Mayfair. And then he set about doing what he was good at and so often paid for—he watched and waited.

WILLA WALKED DOWN to the breakfast room with Marina holding on to her hand. When she'd risen, Lord Deveril—Douglas—had already been gone. Somewhat disappointed by that, she'd pasted on a smile nonetheless and tolerated the maid's fussing and numerous blushes as they'd gone through her morning toilette. Afterward, she'd fetched Marina from the nursery. It was as much for her benefit as for the child's. She needed something to occupy her thoughts that was not her husband and the fact that she'd behaved like a wanton hussy with him the night before. *And the morning after.*

She could feel a blush heating her cheeks as she entered the breakfast room. Immediately, she halted. Devil was seated at the table perusing the news sheets with a plate piled high with food before him.

"Good morning," he said with a sly and knowing smile.

"I thought you'd gone," Willa said by way of response as she walked to the sideboard and began filling plates for herself and Marina. The child had reluctantly disengaged her hand from Willa's own, but she remained close by her side.

"I had an early meeting with my solicitor to take care of some things," he answered. "But I found myself in rather a hurry to return. I find that there is no place I'd rather be than here in my home with the two of you."

Willa felt a smile tugging at the corners of her lips. "And what business had you out so early this morning that it could not have waited until a more reasonable hour?"

"You mean after I was up so very late last night?" he asked, the picture of innocence.

She graced him with an arch look as she placed the plates on the table and then helped Marina onto a chair. "Behave."

"I shall, but the manner in which I do may set you to blush, my pretty wife," he said with a wicked grin. "But in answer to your question, I had to see my solicitor to make arrangements for you. It dawned on me yesterday, when things could have gone so terribly wrong in the park, that I had not made the proper preparations for you or for Marina, that if I were to meet an untimely end, you could well be destitute."

"Don't speak of such things!"

"My untimely end or your being destitute?" he teased.

"Either," she snapped. "And I wouldn't be destitute. I'm more than capable of providing for myself."

"Well, now it's a moot point. A generous settlement has been provided for the both of you in the event that I should, heaven forbid, meet an untimely demise," he replied. "And since we have most of the ugliness behind us and no longer need to live like prisoners here, I thought that you might wish to pay a call on Miss Darrow today. After breakfast?"

Willa's heart thumped painfully at the thought of it. Would Effie be terribly disappointed in her? She didn't know. The agreement that they'd reached before, of a fake engagement with a chaperone, had been sorely tested almost from the outset. There would have been no way of predicting what Alaric West would do or that he would place her in such a compromising position that marriage was the only possible outcome. "I suppose we should."

"I hardly think it something dreadful," he chided. "I daresay, your friend will offer you felicitations, and if she has any recriminations at all, it will be that she did not get to attend the service."

"I do hope so," Willa replied. "I'd hate to think I have disappointed Effie in any way."

"By marrying me?" he asked with a frown.

"No. By getting into such compromising situations that marriage was the only option... Effie is very egalitarian in her thinking, Douglas, and not the judgmental sort at all. That's why so many gentlemen are willing to place their daughters in her school, because no one tries to guilt, shame, or extort them!"

"Then we shall face her together and any censure she may have to offer, regardless of which one of us it may be heaped upon."

Breakfast continued in the same vein. The talked and laughed, teased. Marina even smiled shyly at her uncle a time or two. As they finished their meal, Willa felt Marina tugging at her hand. Leaning down, until her ear was level with Marina's cupped hand she listened to the little girl's loudly whispered secret. "He didn't give you a ring. You always get a ring when you get married. Mama said."

"Did your Mama have a ring, Marina?" Devil asked.

The little girl looked back over her shoulder at him and nodded.

"Do you have the ring?"

Marina lifted the small doll that had been placed on the chair beside her. Lifting the hem of the doll's dress, the ring was tied about the dolls waist with a bit of twine.

"You should keep your Mama's ring," Devil said. "I know she'd want you to have it. That way you'll always remember her."

Willa heard the pain in his voice, the grief. Her heart broke for him. Whatever his many faults, he'd loved his sister, and the loss of her would haunt him always.

"Are you finished eating, Marina?"

The little girl nodded in response.

Willa smiled at her. "Will you be very brave and let one of the maids take you back to the nursery?"

The nod was slower and less enthusiastic, but still present.

Devil rang the small bell that was on the table, and a maid entered. Marina rose from her chair and walked over to the shocked serving girl and placed her hand in the maid's.

"Would you escort Marina back to the nursery?"

The maid bobbed a curtsy. "Yes, my lady."

When the little girl and the maid were gone, Devil spoke softly. "She's right, of course. I didn't give you a ring yesterday, and I should have. But I didn't want to give you my mother's ring because there is too much misery attached to it. Marriage was a curse to her, and I would not have it be that for you."

"I don't need a ring. I have your promise, and that is enough."

He smiled. "You may not need the ring, but I need to give it to you. While you were sleeping so soundly after our exertions, I took care of more than one errand this morning in an effort to rectify my oversight."

Willa was stunned when he pulled a small leather box from the pocket of his waistcoat and placed it near her hand. She picked it up with trembling fingers and gently opened the clasp. Nestled inside on a satin bed was a gold band etched with a delicate filigree pattern and set with diamonds and pearls. "It's beautiful." It was. Delicate, feminine, and not at all ostentatious, it suited her perfectly. She could not have chosen a ring more suited to her had she done so herself.

Devil removed the ring from the box and lifted her hand, sliding the ring onto her finger in a moment that seemed almost reverent. "There. Now all is as it should be."

"It's too much. I shouldn't accept it."

"But you will?" he said.

She looked at the ring glittering on her hand. "I will. I couldn't give it up now if I tried. It's perfect."

"As are you... let's go for a walk in the park, shall we? And allow the nasty, pinch-faced society matrons to get a gander at us in all of our connubial bliss."

"You're just looking to stir gossip!" Willa protested.

Devil picked up the news sheet he'd been reading and turned it over, placing it in front of her. "Unfortunately, it's stirred already."

Willa glanced at the article and gasped.

The devilish Lord D has finally done it. Married, ladies! Though given his history, it will likely not slow his amorous pursuits at all. Still, what female of questionable sense and morals would be unwise enough to become Lady D? It appears she's a governess from the famed Darrow School and has a scandalous connection to another rogue of some renown, a younger son of Lord H (hint, it rhymes with Featherton). Considering that Lord D had a rather notorious affair with Lady H and dueled with Lord H for her honor, this is something of a quandary to be sure. Family gatherings are bound to be interesting.

"Do you wish to call on them and make some attempt to set things right? I hadn't the awkwardness of it all, all things considered," he explained.

"No. Because I cannot abide him and he cannot abide me. Did you know that he never paid Effie for my schooling? She never asked him to. When I said she took me from my other school, I mean that she rescued me. We were being horribly mistreated there, Lillian and I. I think it was at his request. He wanted us to run away, I think. Though the outcome of some of their abuses could have been much worse. They locked us in attic rooms with no heat and no blankets, without food and water. I managed to sneak a letter to him once, begging for his help. He came, and we were beaten for our impertinence in front of him. We were dressed in rags, thin and half-starved. He didn't care. He isn't my father. He's a man I despise. That is all."

"My past relationship with your stepmother is certainly a bit awkward," he admitted.

"Your past relationships with half the married women of the *ton* are a bit awkward," she pointed out. "And I hardly expect that we will see either of them."

"Not half. That's a bit much even for me," he protested. "Get your pelisse. We need to face them before it gets worse."

"How can it possibly?" she demanded. "I've been publicly outed as the bastard daughter of one of the most hated men in society, whom you shot several years ago after having an affair with his wife. How on earth did this get out?"

"Obtaining a special license is a difficult process, but it isn't a private one. I'm certain the moment it was issued, someone was already writing this drivel," he said. "There's nothing left but to face them and their viperous scorn."

"Must we?" Willa asked, dreading the very notion of it.

"At some point, yes. Eventually, Marina will need to enter society. We will have children who will also need to enter society. For that to happen, we cannot simply sever ties. We may even need to consider inviting your father and stepmother to dinner... with other guests as well, of course. Enough of them that we will all feel compelled to be on our best behavior. Not immediately, mind you, but perhaps in the future."

"Fine," she agreed. "I'll get my pelisse and meet you in the foyer."

She started to walk away, but he clasped her hand, brought it to his lips, and kissed it where his ring now rested. "It won't be so bad. I promise."

Chapter Twenty-Nine

I T WAS WORSE than she'd expected. For a person who'd lived her life very circumspectly, being whispered about, stared at, or blatantly cut by everyone they passed was an exercise in torment.

"I detest this," she whispered.

"Detest it all you want to, love," he replied. "Just keep smiling."

"I cannot believe, of the two of us, you are giving advice about appropriate behavior," Willa replied. "And the guards, are they really necessary?"

"Perhaps, perhaps not. But my dealings of the last few days with Alaric Munro have made me cautious. I think it best to err on the side of caution. It's a novel approach for me."

That did elicit a genuine smile from her. "So it is. But at least we're nearing the end… aren't we?"

"Just around that bend is the Brook Gate. We're done with the lot of them," he said. "I think we've seen and been seen quite enough for one day."

Willa turned to look in the direction he'd pointed. A movement from the trees drew her eye, and she started to speak. But then she saw the flash and there was no time. She whirled, placing herself before him. There was a loud bang, and then she felt a burning pain spread through her shoulder and down her arm. It felt as if even her fingertips were on fire. She looked up, seeing the shock and fear on his face, but she couldn't speak. Darkness was seeping in, claiming her, and she felt herself sinking into it, as if pulled down by heavy weights.

Death, she thought. She was surely dying. Her last thought was that one day with him had not been enough. Perhaps it was greed, but she wanted more.

⤷⤷⤷⬸⬸⬸

DEVIL CAUGHT HER before she fell to the ground, lifting her easily and cradling her against his chest. The guards had rushed off in the direction of the shot. At that very moment, they had tackled the man responsible, subduing him on the ground. He didn't care; he could only think of the woman in his arms. Blood spread outward from the wound at her shoulder, on both the front and back of her gown. The ball had gone straight through, but if they didn't clean the wound thoroughly and stop the bleeding, it wouldn't matter.

Devil began to move, one foot in front of the other. By the time he reached the Brook Gate, he was running. Dodging carriages and other pedestrians, he reached the house, climbing the steps two at a time. Carlton opened the door and a footman went rushing past him.

"I'm sending him for the doctor, my lord. I'll have clean water and bandages sent up," the butler said, all but wringing his hands.

Devil didn't stop to reply, nor did he waste the breath. He climbed the stairs to their chambers and placed Willa's limp form on the bed. A maid appeared with a pair of shears, and he began quickly cutting away her clothes to reveal the wound. Her skin was pale and slicked with bright red blood. At the sight of it, he simply stopped. It robbed him of breath and thought.

"Let me tend her, my lord, while you sit," the maid said. "I'll get her cleaned up before the doctor arrives."

Devil, unable to do anything else, just backed away. He watched as they cleaned the blood from her skin, as they placed a thick pad beneath her shoulder to absorb the blood and pressed another one atop it. They covered her with a sheet to preserve her modesty, something he himself had not given a thought to. They had just finished covering her when there was a knock upon the door and another maid came in bringing the doctor.

He was an older man, round in the middle and bald on top. He'd treated Devil in the past for injuries he'd sustained in various duels and brawls. The weight of the man's disapproval was stifling as he walked in. "What have you gotten in to this time, Deveril? Diddle the wrong man's wife, did you?" the physician demanded.

"Someone shot my wife," he said. "And if she dies because you wasted time haranguing me, you'll regret it."

"Your wife?" the physician scoffed. "Didn't think you'd ever be foolish enough to get one of those yourself! Let's take a look at her."

Devil stood back, observing. The physician crossed the room to the bed where Willa rested, painfully still.

"So they did. Shot her clean through. There's not much to be done for it, I'm afraid. She'll heal or she won't. I can't do anything for her."

Devil stepped forward and the grasped the man up by his waist-coat. "You'll help her. You'll do whatever it takes, or so help me, if she dies, you'll die with her."

The physician sighed, his expression sympathetic. "My boy, not even you can defy death. Your bride is young, healthy, and it's far better for the ball to have gone through than for me to have to dig it out. I can't help her other than to offer my prayers… and those you shall both have. I am sorry."

Devil let the man go abruptly and snapped at the maid. "Send for Whittinger. Perhaps my valet can do what you cannot!" As the girl scurried to do his bidding, he moved past the useless doctor and seated himself on the edge of the bed next to Willa. She never stirred. Reaching out, Devil touched her face gently, stroking the soft curve of her cheek.

"You genuinely care for her, don't you?" the doctor asked, clearly shocked.

"Is that so difficult to believe?"

The doctor made a harrumphing sound. "It is, indeed. For the longest time, I had thought you cut from the same cloth as your father. It seems I was wrong. I wish there was more I could do."

Devil was beyond hearing him. The doctor left the room as Whittinger entered. The valet had brought his supplies and began applying the foul smelling unguent that he had always applied to Devil's wounds.

"It is not typically used on wounds so severe, my lord," the man explained. "I do hope that it will ease her pain and protect her from any fevers."

"Then join the doctor in his prayers, Whittinger, for that is all any of us can do now." To the remaining maids who had gathered in the doorway, he added, "All of you are dismissed for now. I'll call if there are changes or if any of you are needed."

There was a great deal of sniffing and sobbing along with a few muttered "yes, my lords," and then Devil was alone with Willa and alone with his guilt. He'd put her in danger because he'd been focused on trying to remedy his tattered reputation. In an effort to assuage the gossipmongers, he'd placed her at risk.

Was this love? Was this anguished hell he found himself in what all of the poets spoke of? It must be, for surely nothing else could cause such pain.

"I am so sorry, Willa. I did this to you… with pride and shortsightedness. If you perish, it will be because of my impulsiveness, just as Alice did."

Taking her hand in his, he held it gently, savoring the warmth of her skin and the life that still flowed with in her. "Please, don't leave me," he said. "Whatever you do, however hard you must fight to survive, I beg of you, do not leave me."

Chapter Thirty

WILLA AWOKE SLOWLY. Her shoulder ached. In fact, her entire body ached. Blinking against the bright morning light, she found herself staring at the dark, rumpled waves of her husband's hair. His head was laid next to hers on the pillow.

"Devil?"

He murmured and then sat up slowly, blinking at her. "You're awake."

"Why wouldn't I be?" she asked.

"Because you've been unconscious and raging with fever for the last three days," he said. "I had prepared myself for the worst. I believed you on the verge of death."

"Three days?"

"You were shot while we were in the park by the man who had worked for Alaric Munro. He was determined to avenge himself upon me for his brother's death," Devil confessed softly. "I failed you."

"You saved me, Douglas. The only person responsible for this is the man who shot me. And I don't need to remind you that his brother would have done unspeakable things to me," she said. "You put yourself at great risk to keep Marina safe from him, and from Alaric Munro. It may defy your very skewed vision of yourself but, in this instance, you are the hero. You are not responsible for any of this!"

"I should have known, should have suspected—"

"And you did, and that is why we still had guards with us in the park. Did they capture him?"

"He's already been hanged."

"For shooting me?" Willa asked.

"No. That got him arrested. He was hanged for his many other crimes. He and his brother had done horrible things, Willa. Truly terrible."

"I see," she said. "This man was a hardened criminal, one who had blackened his soul possibly beyond redemption, and you're angry at yourself because you could not predict every action he would take?"

"I had not thought he would be a danger to you, Willa. I had assumed that if he was a threat to anyone, it would be me," Devil said.

Willa reached for him, placing her hand on his cheek and feeling the rough growth of beard that had accumulated there while he maintained his vigil over her. "He was trying to hurt you, Devil. I saw him... I saw that he meant to shoot you, and I made a choice to put myself in front of you. The injury is the fault of the one who dealt it, and if you like, mine as well for putting myself in its path. But you are blameless in this instance."

"Hardly that," he said. "And if you ever place yourself in harm's way again in an effort to protect my worthless hide—"

"You'll what?" she demanded. "You're a wreck because I was hurt at all. I hardly think you'll take it upon yourself to beat me!"

"I may well turn you over me knee," he warned. "Willa, in the three days I've sat here at your side, not knowing whether or not I would have the opportunity to keep the vows and promises I made to you, I—"

He'd broken off so abruptly, his voice thick with emotion. Willa stroked his face tenderly, savoring the heat of his skin and the prickly sensation of his unshaven jaw. "What is it? I'm well. Perhaps not overly energetic at the moment, but I will heal!"

"I love you, Wilhelmina. I love you when I didn't know such a thing was possible. I thought love such as this was a myth, a thing for poets, authors, and painters. I didn't think it was for me. I think the truth is that I was broken inside until you."

Her heart thumped in her chest at his proclamation. It wasn't something she'd dared dream of, though in her heart, it was the thing she'd longed for most. "And I love you. Do you honestly think I would have consented to marry you otherwise?"

"I had very persuasive arguments," he pointed out with a crooked smile.

Willa laughed, but it ended on a pained wince.

"The doctor left laudanum. You should have some," he insisted.

"Later. For now, I'd rather speak with you. Do you really think you forced my hand?" she asked.

"Didn't I?"

"No. You did not. While your arguments were keen, we both know that I am more stubborn than you are persuasive. I married you because I wanted to. Your arguments simply allowed me to do so without sacrificing too much of my pride by admitting how much I wanted just that... because I love you, Douglas Ashton, Lord Deveril, against all reason and judgement. And possibly to the betterment of us both."

He cupped her face tenderly, his thumb stroking along the underside of her jaw. "We are a pair of fools... besotted and bedeviled."

"But happy. Or at least we will be," she said. "Let's leave London, Devil. Let's go to the country where we can breathe, where can be ourselves far from gossiping, spiteful people."

He nodded. "When you are well, we will do just that. But for now, I think there is someone who may need to see you awake and talking even more than I did. I'll return shortly."

Willa closed her eyes as he rose and walked away. Relief swept through her that her secret feelings for him were secret no more. That her feelings were returned was a wonder she could never have expected but rejoiced in nonetheless.

It took only moments for him to return. Marina walked beside him, her tiny hand dwarfed in his. Her eyes were wide and her lower lip trembled, but it was clear the little girl was trying to be brave.

As they neared the bed, he lifted Marina up and placed her on the bed so that she could crawl over next to Willa. "I'll be back in a moment," Devil said. "I think it would be good for you to have a moment alone."

Willa nodded. "Yes, it would. Thank you."

When he had gone, Willa reached up and stroked Marina's hair. "I'm quite all right, you know? Hale and hearty as ever."

The little girl stared at her wide-eyed for a moment. Then her gaze tracked down to the bandage that peeked out from the neckline of Willa's nightrail. "He hurt you. The bad man."

"A bad man, but not him... not the one who hurt your mother," she explained. "There are lots of bad people in the world, unfortunately. But you'll never have to worry about that. Your uncle and I will keep you safe, Marina. No matter what."

"You won't go away?"

Willa smiled at her. "I'll never leave you. I'm your aunt now. I'll stay with you always."

"Mama went away," Marina said softly, her lip trembling a bit harder now.

It broke Willa's heart. The little girl was so terrified of losing those she cared for. It was as if Marina feared to trust that any of them would remain with her. "It wasn't because she wanted to. Your mama was alone then. Your uncle hadn't found her yet to be able to protect her from those bad people. I promise you, Marina, we will both be here for you for a very, very long time."

The little girl laid down and pressed her face against Willa's side. She shed a few tears, hiccupped a few broken sobs, and then simply slept. The whole while, Willa stroked her hair and rubbed her back.

She loved that child with her whole heart, she realized, and would fight tooth, nail, and claw to protect her from anyone that might mean her harm.

"That's a rather fierce expression you are wearing, Wife. Should I be alarmed?"

Willa looked up to see Devil standing in the doorway.

"Only if you mean her harm," she said.

A smile curved his lips. "Never... because I love her, and also because I am wise enough to fear the warrior's heart that surely beats within your breast." He stepped deeper into the room, pausing at the side of the bed as he stared down at the pair of them.

"What is it?" Willa asked.

"Things I have never known until now," he said. "Happiness. Contentment. Hope. What you've given me is beyond riches, and I shall spend the remainder of my days trying to show you just how grateful I am to have you here with me."

Willa reached for his hand and tugged until he sat down beside her. "How is it possible that we have given one another the same gifts, my lord? I never imagined when I entered this house on that first day that this is where it would lead... fate has gifted us both."

He leaned forward and pressed a kiss to her lips. "Fate it is. If I give you the credit, you'll be intolerable."

Willa grinned. "I'm sure intolerability is something you're very familiar with."

He stretched out on her right side, Marina still sleeping soundly on her left. "How is it that the littlest one of us takes up the most room?"

"It's a question we will have many, many years to ponder," she replied.

Epilogue

Three Months Later

THE CARRIAGE ROLLED along the country lane at a sedate pace. So sedate that Marina was jumping up and down on the seat in anticipation. Willa gave her a quelling look, and the girl stilled, but her lips were split into a wide and mischievous grin.

"I do not understand, Husband, why we have traveled in pace with the mail coach until we are less than a mile from Goringham Abbey and you've decided to slow the conveyance to a point that I could walk faster than this carriage now," Willa commented.

"Because I don't want you to miss the view. There is a vista as you near the abbey that is well worth the delay," he said. "And Marina should get the best vantage point of her new home."

The little girl bounced again then remembered she was not supposed to and settled more comfortably on her seat. Willa suppressed a smile. While Marina was not entirely out of her shell, she had made leaps and strides in the last few months. She'd also learned very quickly that for nothing more than a pretty smile or a batted eye, she could get whatever she wanted from her uncle. That had thawed her mercenary little heart greatly. It was the way of children though, and Willa was happy to see her behaving as other children would, no matter the situation.

"There," Devil said and tapped upon the roof of the carriage. The driver slowed the horses even further until, eventually, the vehicle halted altogether. Devil alighted quickly. He reached back inside for Marina who went eagerly, more than ready to be outside in the fresh air.

He reached into the carriage once more, and Willa placed her hand in his. Her pulse quickened at even that innocent touch. Traveling to reach Goringham, with Marina always tucked between them in their beds at the inns where they had stopped, it felt as if their journey had taken months rather than days. She craved his touch more than ever, and she craved those perfect moments of intimacy when his body was joined to hers. Certainly the pleasure was not to be dismissed, but it was that closeness she desired above all. More so in the last few weeks.

Stepping down from the carriage, she walked with him, Marina holding on to his hand and his other arm about her waist, toward a break in the trees. Beyond it was a rocky and craggy ravine. Water trickled over those stones creating a kind of music that could only be found in nature. On the opposite side, atop a gentle rise with sea and sky meeting behind it, was Goringham Abbey. Spires, towers, and crenelated battlements were juxtaposed to buttresses and intricate stained glass. It was half-church and half-fortress.

"So many styles and periods of architecture and yet it all works together beautifully," she mused. "It is magical."

"It is home," he said. "For us and for Marina."

"And for our children," she said.

"When we are blessed to have them," he agreed.

"That may well be sooner than you think, my devilish lord," she offered with a grin. She had thought to keep her news and guard it close to her heart until she was certain naught would go wrong. But in that place, looking at the majestic house where they would build their life together, it seemed only right to share.

"Willa, are you..." He stopped, unable to form the words, but looking at her with wonder in his eyes.

"I am with child. We shall soon welcome our very own son or

daughter. A cousin for Marina," Willa said.

"What's a cousin?" Marina asked.

"It's like a brother or sister, but better," Devil said. "And much more fun."

"Oh," Marina said and quickly lost interest in the adult conversation.

"Be careful of those rocks, Marina," Willa warned.

Devil smiled and pulled her close. "I didn't think it was possible to be happier, but I am. I love you, Wilhelmina."

"When you preface my atrocious name with those words, I find I don't mind it so much," she said with a laugh. "And I love you, too, Douglas. My very own devil."

He leaned in and kissed her. As he drew back, he looked at her with wicked promise gleaming in his eyes. "And tonight, when we do not have a child with six arms, twelve legs, and a snore that could wake the dead lying between us," he whispered, "I shall entice you to sin in ways you've never imagined."

"Then you should convince your niece to climb back into the carriage so we may make our way home and do all that you have said," she replied. "My love. My husband."

"Marina, if you get back into the carriage, I will have cook give you sweets as soon as we get to the house!" he shouted.

The little girl went scampering back to the carriage obediently, well bribed for her cooperation.

"You're spoiling her," Willa pointed out.

"As I mean to spoil you and all of our children," he said. "Now, what do I have to do to bribe you to get into that carriage?"

"A kiss should suffice," Willa teased.

So he kissed her and kissed her well. She was breathless with it when he simply hoisted her into his arms and packed her to their carriage, eager to reach their home.

The End

About the Author

Chasity Bowlin lives in central Kentucky with her husband and their menagerie of animals. She loves writing, loves traveling and enjoys incorporating tidbits of her actual vacations into her books. She is an avid Anglophile, loving all things British, but specifically all things Regency.

Growing up in Tennessee, spending as much time as possible with her doting grandparents, soap operas were a part of her daily existence, followed by back to back episodes of Scooby Doo. Her path to becoming a romance novelist was set when, rather than simply have her Barbie dolls cruise around in a pink convertible, they time traveled, hosted lavish dinner parties and one even had an evil twin locked in the attic.

If you'd like to know more, please sign up for Chasity's newsletter at the link below:
eepurl.com/b9B7lL

Website:
www.chasitybowlin.com

Made in the USA
Monee, IL
03 February 2020